The Empire

Constantinoplis Under Siege

George Mavro

The Empire Series™ Book 1

TotalRecall Publications, Inc..
1103 Middlecreek
Friendswood, Texas 77546
281-992-3131 281-482-5390 Fax
www.totalrecallpress.com

All rights reserved. Except as permitted under the United States Copyright Act of 1976, No part of this publication may be reproduced, stored in a retrieval system, or transmitted in any form or by any means electronic or mechanical or by photocopying, recording, or otherwise without prior permission of the publisher. Exclusive worldwide content publication / distribution by TotalRecall Publications, Inc..

Copyright © 2017 by: George Mavro
Edited by: Tammy Mavro
All rights reserved

ISBN: 978-1-59095-489-8
UPC: 6-43977-2890-7

Printed in the United States of America with simultaneous printings in Australia, Canada, and United Kingdom.

FIRST EDITION
1 2 3 4 5 6 7 8 9 10

This is a work of fiction. The characters, names, events, views, and subject matter of this book are either the author's imagination or are used fictitiously. Any similarity or resemblance to any real people, real situations or actual events is purely coincidental and not intended to portray any person, place, or event in a false, disparaging or negative light.

The scanning, uploading and distribution of this book via the Internet or via any other means without the permission of the publisher is illegal and punishable by law. Please purchase only authorized electronic editions, and do not participate in or encourage electronic piracy of copyrighted materials. Your support of the author's rights is appreciated.

I want to dedicate this book to the men and women risking their lives to protect this nation from International terrorism

About the Author

George Mavro is a 24 year Air Force, Security Force veteran. He was stationed over 22 years in Europe, eight of those in Greece. He holds advanced degrees in Government and International Relations. He presently lives in Florida with his wife.

About the Book

While escorting a supply convoy to an off base communications site north of Bagram Airbase Afghanistan, Master Sergeant George Mavrakis and his team are ambushed by the Taliban. Running for their lives with the few survivors of the ambush they manage to flee to an underground mine, but are trapped inside when a Taliban suicide bomber blows himself up in the entrance, sealing them inside. Traveling deeper into the mine they discover an underground base left there by the Soviets. While exploring the base they find a control room filled with computers and equipment which activated after generator power was restored and a countdown is automatically started.

The arrival of George and his troops from the future have drastically altered the timeline. The Ottoman Sultan Mehmet II will soon put the city of Constantinople under siege, with over 80,000 troops and 60 huge guns that can tear down the city's walls. In the American's past time line, the Ottomans do capture the city and the emperor is killed in battle. It will be race against time to assist the Byzantines in building up their technical and military capabilities with the skills and knowledge, they brought back from the future, to stop the Ottomans. If they are unsuccessful the future is very bleak for George and his team, whom are lost in time.

List of Characters:

George Mavrakis: Main protagonist of novel. Commander of the American air force security and General and security advisor to the Byzantine Emperor.

Emperor Constantine XI: last Byzantine emperor and commander of Christian forces during the Ottoman siege.

Sultan Mehmet: Main antagonist. Sultan of the Ottoman Turks and commander of Moslem forces during the siege of Constantinople.

Zaganos Pasha: Grand Vizier advisor to the sultan.

Gustianni Longo: Mercenary commander of the 700 Genovese Italian soldiers who fought for the Byzantines.

Captain Anna Marone: USAF doctor that marries George Mavrakis.

Airman Roger Green: is part of George's security detail. He is an experienced sailor and a student of the age of sail. Helps build the Byzantine navy.

Technical Sergeant: Mat Jenkins is an air force small arms trainer and weapons smith. Will help design fire arms and cannon for the Byzantines.

Staff Sergeant Jay Burns: air force civil engineer has experience with engines designs first steam engine.

Foreword

This is an alternate history novel of what if 15 soldiers with today's technology and equipment traveled back in time to 1453 Constantinoplis just prior to the siege? Will they be able to significantly influence the events and outcome and save the city?

The Empire was written purely for enjoyment but is steeped in the rich history and culture of the period.

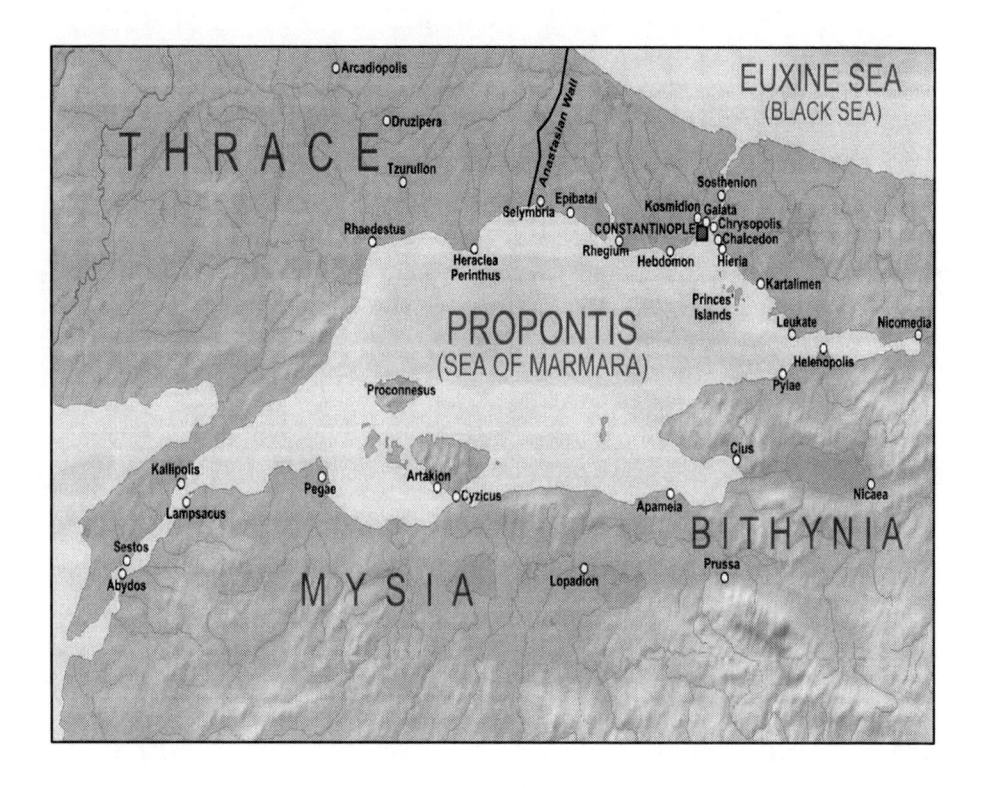

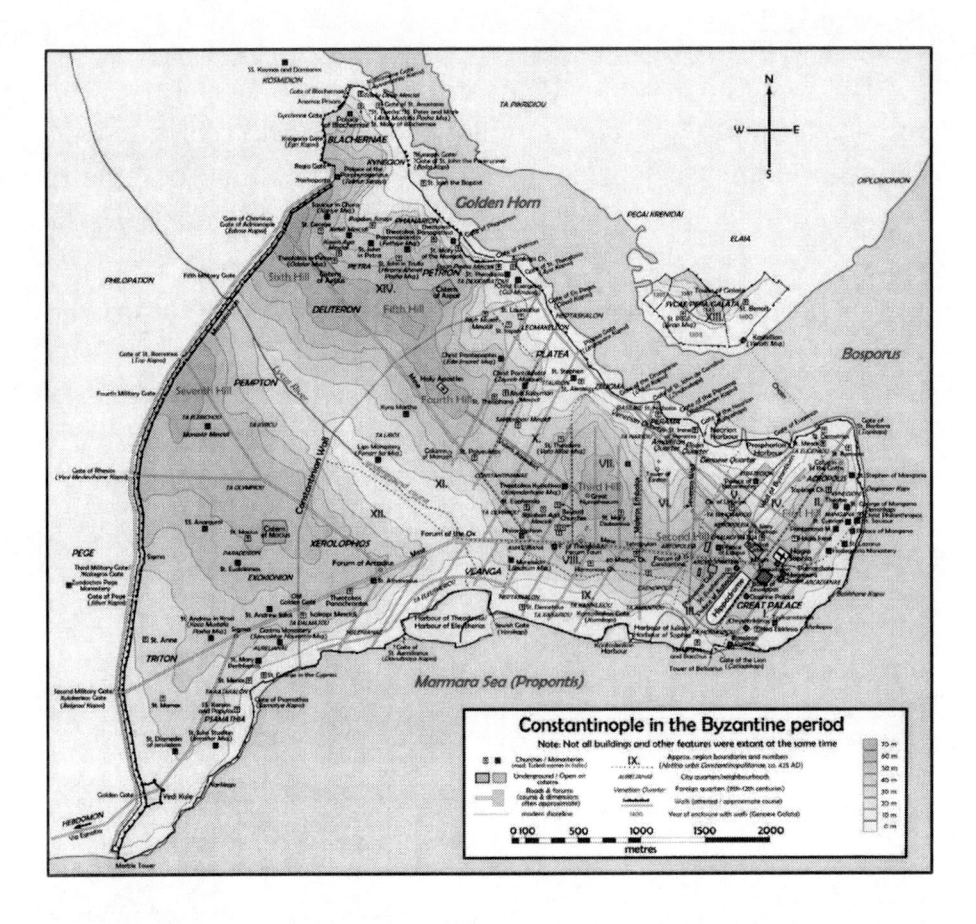

Topographical map of **Constantinople** during the Byzantine period. Main map source: R. Janin, *Constantinople Byzantine. Developpement urbain et repertoire topographique*. Road network and some other details based on Dumbarton Oaks Papers 54; data on many churches, especially unidentified ones, taken from the University of New York's The Byzantine Churches of Istanbul project. Other published maps and accounts of the **city** have been used for corroboration.

--by Donald L. Wasson

www.ancient.eu/Constantinople/

Chapter 1

Afghanistan
09 January 2014

Master Sergeant George Mavrakis stood atop the machine gun cupola of the armored Humvee and scanned the terrain with his binoculars, looking for anything out of place, that could indicate a Taliban ambush or an improvised explosive device (IED). His Humvee was the lead vehicle, escorting four supply trucks to a small communications outpost, located 50 kilometers north of Bagram airbase, Afghanistan. He had been assigned to the 455th Defense Squadron for almost a year and was due to rotate back to the states next month. So far his tour had been relatively uneventful. Except for a couple of rocket attacks on the base by the Taliban, he had never fired his weapon in anger. He was hoping it would remain that way. Unfortunately fate had other things in store for him and his squad.

"Another twenty minutes and we'll be there, sarge," said Staff Sergeant John Smith, a tall blond haired youth from Arkansas. Smith had worked in a machine shop, but after 9/11 he enlisted in the US Air Force.

George had sat down back down in the passenger seat and had given the M240B machine gun back to the gunner, Airman Leroy Davis, a skinny black kid from south Chicago, who joined the air force to get away from the gangs.

"I'll be glad to get off this road, John."

"Me too, sarge."

The convoy was beginning to climb up the mountain which would take them to the communications site. Neither George, nor his driver saw the slight depression on the road they had driven over. It contained a buried IED, an ex-Soviet 150mm shell.

A loud explosion rocked the convoy, as the lead and the last duce and a half including their passengers was blown to pieces. Gunfire erupted almost immediately from the side of the tree lined road. "Step on it Smith and get this vehicle turned around." Davis opened fire towards the vicinity of the ambush, keeping the Taliban's heads down.

Jones gunned the Humvee, as the roof mounted M240B machine gun began spitting out 7.62mm rounds at over 800 per minute. George called out to the rear Humvee Zulu two, to find out their status. It had taken up position to defend the surviving vehicles shooting at the Taliban, trying to save what was left of the convoy. By now Smith had turned the vehicle around and headed towards the others. George watched as an RPG round took out another one of the Trucks. Fortunately the crew had abandoned the vehicle and was running towards Zulu two.

"Sarge, look over there. I see three Taliban technicals heading this way. Looks like they got pretty large guns mounted on them. They're probably 14mm heavy machine guns."

"Those will rip us to shreds. We got to get the hell out of here. Head towards Jenkins' Humvee."

"Zulu one, this is Zulu 2. It looks like we also have company coming from the rear, two more techincals. We have the two survivors from the second vehicle on board."

"We're screwed." George was about to give the order for everyone to dismount and make a last stand.

"Sarge, see that small road thirty yards to the left? I say we take it. We stand a better chance running, than staying here."

"Go for it, Smith. They'll be on us in less than a minute. Zulu 2, follow us and tell the surviving duce and a half to do the same."

Smith gunned the vehicle and headed down the small bumpy road he had discovered, followed by Zulu two and the surviving truck. "If this is a dead end sarge, we've bought it."

"Keep driving, just don't wreck us."

After driving for several miles, they saw a rusted sign with red Cyrillic letters. "It looks like it was left by the Russians when they were here. I wonder what it says."

"I don't know Smith, just keep driving.

After about another mile of driving the road ended in a large clearing at the side of the mountain. They could go no further.

"Shit, it's a dead end. Looks like there is a large mine shaft up ahead, sarge."

"We're all going to die here," Airman First Class Janie Harris, an attractive blond haired twenty two year old, shouted out in terror.

"Don't worry, we'll get out of this," George said trying to reassure the rest of his squad.

"Pull the vehicles into the mine. Zulu two, follow us inside. We'll fight from in there if we have to."

The two Humvees and the duce and a half pulled into the mine shaft. The vehicle headlights shined into the tunnel, illuminating a small road that went deeper into the mountain. Once the vehicles had gone about fifty yards into the mine shaft, George had everyone dismount and take up fighting positions at the entrance of the mine.

"Here they come, stand by to fire. Airman Green, aim for the lead vehicle."

"Got it Serge."

"Fire!"

The mineshaft echoed with the noise of rifle fire. The lead Taliban pickup disintegrated, when it was hit by a 40mm HE grenade fired by Green's M203 grenade launcher. The other Taliban quickly moved to a safer location and began returning fire.

"We're trapped here," Technical Sergeant Jenkins, a fifteen year a security force specialist with two previous tours in both Iraq and Afghanistan said.

"Kinda looks that way."

"I was unable to get out a radio call to Bagram, nor reach the communications site, due to the signal being blocked by the surrounding hills. I don't know if anyone heard us."

"The com site should have picked us up."

"Not if the Taliban took it out."

Commander Hamid, a gray bearded older man, blessed the prophet for his successful ambush against the infidel. His men had attacked the American communications site and destroyed it before the infidel could call for help. The attack on the site had been quick and brutal, helped by two of the Mujahedeen who had been posing as Afghan army guards. One of them had blown himself up in the radio room and the other had opened the gates before detonating his explosive vest in the machine gun bunker, taking many of the infidel defenders with him. Before killing all the surviving Americans he had taken his pleasures with one of the female soldiers. She had told him that a supply convoy was enroute to the site during the short but brutal interrogation.

"Commander Hamid. Blessed is the prophet. We need to either quickly kill the infidel or leave. Sooner or later the Americans will send out one of their deadly gunships to check on the convoy and the communication site," his second in command said.

"You are right Hassan. The infidel can probably hold out in the mineshaft until help arrives."

"That mine is cursed my brother. There are demons in there. Some say the shaft leads straight down to hell."

"I have an idea Hassan, which will send the infidel to hell. Fill one of the trucks with the remainder of our explosives and chose a volunteer to drive it into the mine."

"I will see to it at once, my brother."

The rate of fire had tapered off in the last few minutes. George was wondering if the Taliban were leaving, fearing an American rescue mission.

"Sarge why do you think they pulled up that lone vehicle?" Technical Sergeant Jenkins. His second in command asked.

George knew right away, as the vehicle began to move forward. "Shit they're going to ram the tunnel entrance with explosives. Everyone fall back! That truck is going to blow. Run!"

George began running backwards as he and others shot towards the speeding vehicle. George dove for cover, just as a bullet struck the driver causing the detonation of the 200lbs of explosives, as it entered the mouth of the tunnel. The blast went upwards, causing the roof at the entrance to collapse, sending hundreds of tons of rock down blocking the opening and effectively sealing everyone inside.

"Allah be praised! Yes, my brother. Jamal is now in heaven," Sayed said.

"They may have survived the explosion."

"Then I hope Allah will be merciful to them. Let's leave."

George woke up with a ringing in his ears. A flashlight belonging to Jenkins was shining in his face and most of his squad had gathered around him. "Are you okay sarge? We were worried for a moment; you were pretty close to the blast."

"Except for ringing in my ears I think I am fine. How is everyone else?"

"The driver of the shot up truck may have a broken arm but except for some minor cuts and bruises, we're okay."

"Well we aren't getting out the front entrance. Hopefully there is a rear one. You would think the Russians would have a rear exit. Let's get to the vehicles and drive inside as far as we can. This part of the tunnel is pretty unstable and may further collapse."

They had not driven more than 50 yards when the tunnel ceiling weakened from the explosion began collapsing behind them. It would now be impossible to dig them out without bulldozers and explosives. Ten minutes later, they entered a large cavern filled with equipment and boxes.

"Well look at that!"

"That is rather strange, Smith. Let's check it out." They stopped the vehicle and got out. The vehicle headlights shined on the cavern wall over 100 yards away making eerie shadows.

"This place gives me the creeps, "said Sergeant Thompson one of George's squad leaders.

"Yeah, me too. Let's look around, maybe we'll find something useful. It's strange that the locals and Taliban have not looted this place."

George spotted a metal door; he opened it and went inside. The room was full of what looked to old main frame computers and monitors. It appeared to be some type of control room. Papers were strewn all over the floor. "Hey Sergeant Mavrakis, I found a pretty large generator and there is plenty of fuel available to run it," Sergeant Thompson said.

"Can you start it, Ken?"

"Possibly, if I grab the jumper cables and use the truck battery. Electronics is my hobby."

"Okay, then, give it a try."

Fifteen minutes later, after several attempts the generator which had been sitting idle for almost 25 years came sputtering to life. "You did it Thompson."

"Let's see what happens when I throw the switch."

"Do it."

"Here goes nothing." Thompson threw the switch and the cavern lights came on. "We got juice! Wow look at those cables and electrodes running into the ceiling. I wonder what that is all about?"

George walked in to the computer filled room followed by Jenkins. One of the main frames was coming back to life. "I can't believe these computers are still working. The Russians left Afghanistan over 25 years ago."

"The cavern air is pretty dry; there is no humidity to cause them to corrode. It also looks like the Russians left this place in a hurry."

"This is strange," George said as he watched data streaming on the monitors. "I think the Russians were doing some type of research and experiments in here."

"I believe you're right." Jenkins pulled out his compass and showed it to George. "Ever since we entered this place my compass is going crazy. The needle is spinning in circles."

George pulled out his compass and saw that it was doing the same thing. "This mountain must be some type of giant electromagnet."

"I also found what looks to be a barracks. It has running water and beds."

George heard footsteps and saw a very attractive dark haired woman, most likely in her late 20s, approaching him. She was wearing Captain's rank. He also noticed that she had on medical corps insignia. "Hello mam, I believe we have not met?"

"I am Doctor Anna Marone. I was a passenger on the surviving truck. I was scheduled to replace the doctor on the communications site."

"I am Master Sergeant George Mavrakis, commander of this motley crew of sky cops and this is my second in charge, Technical Sergeant Matt Jenkins."

"Pleased to meet you and thanks for saving our lives."

"Don't thank me yet doc, seems were stuck in here for the time being."

"I set Sergeant Ross's arm. He'll be fine in a couple of weeks. What is this place anyway?"

"Looks like the Russians were doing some kind of experiments here."

"Wow! That was over 25 years ago."

"Sergeant Mavrakis, come here."

"Excuse me, doc."

George walked over to where Airman first class Thomas Capone, a dark haired pimply faced teen from New York was standing. He was holding what looked to be the sniper version of the Mosin Nagant 91/30 bolt action rifle. "Look in these crates, sarge. They're full of Ak-47s and other types of weapons along with tens of thousands of rounds to go with them. George looked in another crate and it contained RPGs.

"Don't screw with the RPGs they may be unstable. Bring the Nagant and a case of ammo."

"Don't worry, I won't mess with them, sarge."

"George turned around hearing footsteps. It was Sergeant Thompson. "Sarge something is weird here. I followed the wires into another room and found hundreds of batteries in array linked together. They are building a charge."

"I wonder what for?"

"I don't know, but they could send one hell of a charge into this mountain."

George thought about what Jenkins had said earlier about the compass. "This mountain probably becomes a giant electromagnet once the juice starts flowing. The Russians were probably conducting some type of military experiment here."

"You're probably right sarge."

"How long before those batteries are charged?"

"Probably a couple of hours with all the juice that generator is putting out."

"Let's have some food and then see what we can do with that juice. Maybe if we charge up the mountain, Bagram may detect something and send a rescue party."

After having a meal of MRE rations, George and the rest of the squad began exploring the abandoned Russian facility. They discovered several rooms that had been workshops and machine shops and several more store rooms containing military supplies storing scores of barrels of diesel fuel for the generator. An hour later they all met in the control room to discuss their options.

"Okay everyone, I don't know what this place is, but from what I can tell the Russians were conducting some type of experiments with electricity. This entire mountain is a giant electrical conductor. I am proposing that when those batteries are fully charged up, we send a charge through the mountain. It may cause enough of an electromagnetic disturbance that it could be picked up by Bagram. If someone is looking for us, they may just find the tunnel entrance and dig us out."

"That will take days."

"Yes it will, Airman Harris but we don't have any other choices other than try to find a back way out through the tunnels. We have food, running water and the Russian ventilation system is working, so we don't have to worry about the air running out. If anyone has a better suggestion I am all ears."

"What if the mountain blows up?"

"I don't think that is possible Airman Davis. There is nothing explosive in the rock."

"How are they batteries, Thompson?"

"This gauge is showing 100% charged."

"How do we start the show?"

"I don't know. Press enter on the keyboard maybe?" Thompson hit the enter key. "Well that didn't do anything. Wait a minute this thing has started a countdown. Ten seconds, 5, 4, 3, 2, 1, 0." The lights flickered but nothing happened.

"Nothing," said George. "Wait I hear something. Sounds like high pitched shrieks." The noises started getting louder and louder, causing an intense pain in their heads. Everyone collapsed to the ground holding their ears. All of a sudden the lights flickered out. The pain kept getting worse. George could see strange brightly lit objects hovering above them. They looked like ghosts or demons. The last thing he remembered before passing out was one of those ghosts passing right through him.

George opened his eyes. The lights had come back on and he had a hellacious headache. He glanced at his watch. It was almost 5 AM. They had been passed out for several hours. Several of the others also began to stir.

"Is everyone okay?"

"Oh my head," Jenkins said.

"What happened? Did anyone else see those horrible things that were floating in the air above us?"

"I don't know what happened doc and yes I saw them too." Everybody else said the same thing. Let's try and get the hell out of here. This place gives me the creeps. Jenkins, load up the vehicles. Take those RPGS we may need them and the guns. We don't want to leave them for the Taliban."

"Okay, sarge."

"The Humvees may also need fuel by the time we get out of here. Top them off and load a few barrels on to the truck. Once we load up, turn off that generator. We don't need any more surprises. This one was bad enough."

An hour later the duce and a half had been loaded up with additional weapons and ammunition. "Okay everybody, mount up let's get out of here. Thompson shut off that generator."

With a turn of the switch the generator went dead and the cavern was again bathed in darkness except for the light generated by the three vehicles. Zulu1 led the way thru the tunnels. After about fifteen minutes they reached a dead end. The way forward was blocked by a rockslide. "We can't go any further sarge we're trapped, "said Airmen Green his driver.

George did not reply he just looked at the blocked tunnel. For a moment he though he saw something out of place. "Zulu 2 shut off your lights. "You too, Green."

"What, sarge."

"Green, shut off the vehicle headlights!" George got out of the Humvee and walked towards the rockslide. He did not imagine it, a slight rays of light was penetrating trough.

"We can get out. I can see light shining through. Bring one of the RPGS."

"Sarge, it might bring the entire tunnel down."

"I don't think it will cause an additional cave in. Bring the RPG.

"Wait a minute, there is a better way to clear the rubble. There's C4 in the duce and a half. We were delivering it to the site to clear out a ruble strewn rocky area, to build another antenna. I am an explosives expert," said Staff Sergeant Larry Williams.

"Okay Williams, have at it."

Thirty minutes later, Williams had set the charge and was ready to blow it. The vehicles had been backed up to a safer location. "Fire in the hole!"

Williams pressed the detonator. A loud explosion rocked the tunnel sending up large clouds of dust. As the dust settled, they could see sun light. The way through was open, but the road still needed clearing of debris before a vehicle could be driven out. George decided to see what was on the other side. He took a fire team along, just in case there were Taliban in the area that that had heard the explosion. They walked outside weapons at the ready.

"What the hell?" They had come out on the side of a large hill. Below them they could all see olive trees and what looked like a large body of water several miles in the distance.

"Sarge, that looks like the sea. How the hell is that possible? We should be hundreds of miles from any large body of water."

George scanned the area with his binoculars. "I don't know Smith. I see several structures, probably a village, just a couple of miles from here. It's surrounded by plowed fields. I am going back to the cave for a few minutes. We need to find out what's going on here. I want to go and check out that village. You and Jones stay here and keep watch till I return. If you see anything, hustle back."

"Okay, sarge."

George returned to the cave and told everyone what he had seen. No one believed him, they had to go outside and see it for themselves. When they all saw the water, no one said a thing for over a minute, as they all took in the scene.

"Sergeant Mavrakis, how is this possible?" Asked Dr.

Marone.

"Your guess is as good as mine."

"Jenkins, I'm taking a fire team to go and check out what looks like a village a couple of miles from here. I see smoke rising, looks like there is a fire burning there. In the meantime clear the rocks so we can get the vehicles out. There is no nearby road, but we should be able to off road it till we hit the coast and find a one."

"Okay, just be careful."

"I'm coming with you, sergeant. There may be injured people there."

"Doctor, it may be very dangerous."

"We have not heard any shooting coming from that direction. I'm also still the ranking person and furthermore I insist."

"Let's get one thing straight, doc. You may be an officer but I am in charge of security and safeguarding your life. So I can over-rule you. But you may have a point that there may be injured civilians. So grab your kit bag and let's get moving."

"Jenkins, once you get the vehicles out, I want you to cut some branches and camouflage the entrance. There is a lot of stuff at the Russian base we may need in the future. I have a bad feeling we may be stuck here a very long time."

Chapter 2

Eastern Thrace
10 January 1452

Thirty minutes later, they were hiding behind a clump of trees several hundred yards from the village. From their vantage point, they could see several horsemen wearing funny clothes and carrying what looked to be lances and scimitar swords, riding around the village. A couple of the stone houses seemed to be on fire. They also heard women's screams. George wondered if they were putting on a show or filming a movie.

"This is very strange, sarge".

"Let's go crash the show and find out where the hell we are."

As they neared the village they were spotted by one of the horseman who immediately yelled out to his companions and then he charged towards the Americans. "Sarge this guy is not slowing down and he is pointing that lance towards us."

"Maybe it's part of the show."

"I don't think this is a show." George brought up his M4 carbine to the ready position; the rest waved their arms for the horseman to stop. He would be upon them in seconds. Figuring that the horseman would not stop, George brought the carbine up and fired. The 5.56mm high velocity round hit the man in the chest dropping him from his saddle. The three other riders heard the shot, turned and charged towards the Americans with their lances thrust forward.

"I got this." George aimed at the lead horse and fired. The

bullet struck the animal in the chest throwing the rider. The two other riders seeing what happened to their fellow cavalry man immediately turned and galloped away.

"Jesus, what the hell was that?"

"I wish I knew, Airman Green."

Doctor Marone ran over to the two men and checked them out. The first rider George had shot was dead, the other one was suffering from a broken leg. George went over to the injured rider who was dressed in a very colorful costume and had what looked like eagle wings on his back. The man was in obvious pain and was speaking in a Turkic language, it was definitely not Pashtun.

"Smith, Green, take his weapons away and make sure he does not try anything funny."

"Will do Sarge," Smith said.

"Looks like we have more company, sarge. Check out the way these guys are dressed and look what they're carrying, swords and spears," Airman Green added."

Several of the villagers had come out of their homes and began to fight the fires. A few others armed with swords and spears walked cautiously toward the Americans. When they saw the injured horseman, they became visibly agitated. The one that seemed to be their leader walked up and pointed to the horseman. "Akinici, Tourkos."

"What?"

The man pointed at the rider. "Ottoman, Tourkos!"

"That's what I thought I heard." George pointed at the rider. "Tourkos?"

"Nai Tourkos," (Yes, Turkish) the man replied."

"Holy shit. If that's what I think he just said this is totally crazy."

"What's that, sergeant?"

"Just a minute, doc. I need to clarify a few more things."

"Are you Greek?" George asked the man in Greek.

"Yes I am." the man replied. "We are all Greeks here."

"What is your name?"

"Yiannis Papagou. I am the elder in charge of the village.'"

"Yiannis, who is this man?" Asked George pointing to the rider.

"He is a Turkish raider," the man replied. "Who are you?"

This was getting weirder by the moment. "My name is George Mavrakis and we are friends and allies. Where are we exactly?"

"You are in eastern Thrace, a half day's ride west of the city."

"Which city?"

"Constantinopolis."

George's face went white. "What is it sergeant?"

"Well doc, this man just said he was a Greek and the rider is a Turkish Ottoman raider."

"What?"

"Oh, it gets even better, doc. I asked where are we and he said half a day's ride from a city, which is called Constantinopolis in Greek and Istanbul in Turkish."

"That's insane. Istanbul is thousands of miles away."

"Let me ask him another question. "

"What is the date?"

"January 10, the year of our lord 1452."

"Please repeat the date, Yiannis."

The man replied the same date. George was floored. It had to be a joke.

"What did he say sergeant."

"He said we are in eastern Thrace, less than a half day's ride to Constantinopolis, in the year 1452."

"That's impossible!"

"Is it? Look where we are and what just occurred. Maybe that Russian experiment did something? Maybe we opened some type of time portal or gateway through another dimension?"

"That's crazy."

"Is it doc? Look at the body in front of us? They are armed with medieval weaponry. This guy is Greek. They are dressed in clothing of the period and no one is carrying a fire arm."

"Yiannis, can you tell me who the current emperor in Constantinopolis is?"

"What's left of the empire is being ruled by Emperor Constantine XI."

"Well doc, he just answered the question correctly on who is emperor in Constantinopolis."

"Sarge, we have more company," Green said."

George looked at the direction Green was pointing at. About a dozen riders wearing armor were quickly approaching. George peered through the binoculars, the riders were definitely military cavalry and they were carrying a yellow flag with a double headed eagle on a pole. It definitely was the flag of Byzantium. "Well Doc, these guys are Byzantine cavalry."

"Oh, my god! Tell me I am having a dream."

The cavalry men approached the group and pointed their weapons at the Americans. George did not want to have to shoot any of the Byzantines. They would need friends in this new world. Yiannis raised his arms to stop the riders and told the leader of the group what happened. The tension quickly subsided. The officer in charge got off his horse and walked up to George. "I'm, Decarchos (commander of ten) Petros Tomas. Who are you? You are dressed in very strange garb."

"My name is George Mavrakis, officer in charge of this unit.

We are here from a land very far away. We are here to help the emperor defend the City which will soon be attacked by the Ottomans. "

"How do you know this? Where are your weapons?"

"What is he saying, sergeant."

"Don't say another word doc? In this period women stayed home, cooked, kept house and raised lots of children."

"I think you are Frankish spies. Arrest them!" The officer brought up his sword, but George quickly butt stroked the man knocking him down. Before the other soldiers could react, George brought up his M4 and fired a burst of automatic fire in front of the horses, causing several of the mounts to panic and throw their riders. George put the barrel of his weapon up to the officer's head. The other soldiers had all dropped terrified to their knees and began praying.

"You are a fool, Petros. I could have killed all of you by myself. I told you I am a friend and ally."

"I apologize. Please forgive me. I heard you speak Frankish."

"It is not Frankish, it is English. I told you we are from a land that is very far away."

"Decarchos, they must be angels. No mortal can make thunder like that," one of the soldiers said.

George helped the Byzantine officer up. "We must take you to the emperor immediately," the man said.

"Yes, we will come with you. I have several other soldiers besides these here."

"Who is this woman that speaks out to an officer disrespectfully, she should be flogged. We will flog her to teach her a lesson. "

"Thank you, but that is not necessary. She is a physician. She is also a medical officer."

"As you wish. Is this Turk your prisoner?"

"Yes, I killed the other one."

"We will take him with us to the city. Maybe we can ransom him back to the Turks, for some of their Christian slaves."

"You can have him."

The officer motioned to his men to secure the prisoner. Doctor Marone who had set the prisoner's leg was about to say something, George motioned to her to not say a word, but she refused to listen.

"Sergeant this prisoner has rights and you are being very disrespectful to an officer. I will report you."

George began to laugh. Captain, there are no rights or rules of war in the 15th century. If you a have the misfortune to be captured by the Turks, they will gang rape you, then sell you as a slave. Furthermore, you are nothing here, but another woman to these men. You are forgetting where we are. These men wanted to strip you, tie you to a tree and flog you for being disrespectful to me. Get used to it, this is the 1400s. It will be another 500 years before women even get the right to speak out. So please show me respect in front of these men."

"Tell her sarge," said Smith as the rest of the fire team began to laugh."

"Can it Smith. She's the only modern doctor we have. If you catch the clap in this era your dick will fall off."

That got everyone laughing again, even doctor Marone.

The decarchos had the Turkish prisoner tied to one of the horses. "We are ready to go back to Constantinopolis. Where are the rest of your men?"

"They're about a 30 minute walk from here."

"We can have you ride on our horses and get there faster. You can use the horse that belonged to the dead Turk."

"Okay, everyone climb aboard. Doctor you will ride with me."

"But I never rode on a horse before."

"Well get used to it. This is the only mode of land transportation in this era for the next 400 years. Oh and it's been over 20 years since I rode one as a teen during a summer in Greece."

George helped her up on the saddle, strapped the M4 behind him and then he got on the horse. "Now hold on tight."

George made a motion for everyone to follow him and he struck the horse's ass with the reins and took off in a slow gallop.

Twenty minutes later, they had reached the area of the cave entrance which was now pretty well camouflaged. George spotted the Humvees and the duce and a half. His men had taken up fighting positions just in case they were attacked by what they thought would be Taliban. Jenkins was manning one of the machine guns.

"Hey, Sergeant Mavrakis, when did you join the cavalry? We were starting to get worried about you after we heard some shooting." Jenkins shouted out.

"Get used to it. You will be seeing lots of horses, Jenkins."

"Who are these guys in medieval suits and gear anyway? Are they making a movie?"

The Byzantine soldiers did not say a word. They just stayed on their mounts and stared at the Americans in fear and awe. They were in total shock after they saw the vehicles. George dismounted the horse and helped the doctor down. "Thank you, sergeant."

"Please call me, George."

"You can call me Anna, when we are in private."

"I will do that."

"Do you speak any Italian, Anna?"

"Yes I do."

"Excellent, it will come in very handy in this period."

"Well sarge, tell us what's going on?" Jenkins asked.

"Okay everybody gather around here. Don't worry about these soldiers. They are our friends. A minute later everyone had gathered around George and the returning fire team.

"What I have to say may sound totally unbelievable and it may sound right out of a B rated Sci. Fi movie, but I do believe it is true. It seems that the Russians were experimenting with time travel. When we activated the generators and the computers something happened. We went back in time."

"Wait a minute, that's insane," Airman Harris said.

"Just wait till I finish, then you can all ask questions. We have gone back in time to 1452," George heard everyone gasp.

"We are in the area in what would be modern Turkey, about half a day's ride from the city of Constantinopolis, the seat of the Byzantine Empire. Look down there, that's the Sea of Marmara. How do you explain that? If you don't believe me look at these soldiers. They are wearing armor and carrying swords and lances. They are Byzantine cavalry. Look at their prisoner, he is Turkish. By this time all that is left of the once great Christian empire is the capital city and some surrounding lands that are constantly attacked by Turkish raiders. I had to kill one. Those were some of the shots you heard. These men will escort us to Constantinoplis and we will meet their emperor. I told them we came from a very far place and we are here to help them. Now does anyone have any questions?"

"Shit, where do I start?" Jenkins said. "We can go back inside and turn on the Russian equipment again and go home?"

"We can, but it may send us further back in time, maybe to the stone-age. Or it can kill us. The Russians sure left there in a very big hurry. Don't forget that we are also buried inside a mine, under thousands of tons of rock. Do you want to take the chance?"

No one said a word. "That option is always open if we ever want to try it."

"Sarge, I just took an online medieval history course and if I remember correctly the city falls to the Turks after a great siege. I still have the book on my IPAD."

"That's Very good, Airman Capone. That book may prove very useful."

"Yes, you are correct. The City well be attacked on 6 April 1453, by the twenty one year old Sultan Mehmet II, with approximately 80,000 troops and some very large cannon. The city will fall on May 29th 1453 and three days of rape, pillage and looting will take place."

"You want us to go there?" Jenkins said.

"The surrounding area is mostly under loose Ottoman control. We have limited ammo, fuel and food. Where else can we go? The only hope we got is to ally ourselves with the Byzantines and help them defeat the Turks."

"There are only sixteen of us and 80,000 of them."

We have modern weapons and fire power so multiply us 10 to 20 fold," Jenkins. Plus, I hope to help the Byzantines develop more weapons with our help."

"Doesn't seem that we have much of a choice at this point anyway," Doctor Marone added.

"Okay, we will go to Constantinopolis."

George walked over to where Petros and his men were waiting. "Take us to the City. Is there a road we can use to travel on? Our machines work better if they have roads. How far is the City?"

"The road to the city begins about three Milia (Miles) from here. The city is about 30 Milia from here. But there may be Turkish raiders on the roads.

"Don't worry, we can handle them."

"What are those machines?"

"The two smaller machines are used for war. They are like your horses, they are used for transport, but we can also fight from them. The larger machine carries cargo. Now lead the way, Petros. You can go as fast as you want." The vehicles started their engines causing the horses to get very agitated, but the riders were able to control their mounts. Several of the horsemen were even contemplating running away in fear but they all remained in their formation.

Fifteen minutes later they reached a stone paved road heading east. The road must have been from Justinian's time. It was not being up kept and was full of potholes. George figured at their present speed they would arrive at the City sometime in the afternoon. An hour later, he spotted a column of about 20 riders 500 meters ahead of them blocking the road.

"Davis, hold up."

The column came to a halt and Petros galloped over to find out why. "Why are we stopping?"

George handed him the binoculars. "Put them up to your eyes and look up ahead towards that clump of trees."

Petros put them up to his eyes and almost dropped them.

"What sorcery is this?"

"It's not sorcery; they are two pieces of glass that magnify things. Now who are those soldiers?"

Petros grudgingly put the glasses back up to his eyes. "They are Sipahi, Turkish heavy cavalry. We are in trouble. But we will fight them."

"No Petros, they are in trouble if they attack us."

"We are not officially at war with the Ottomans, but they don't care, they know we can't do much against them other than protest."

"Do you think they will attack us?"

"Yes, they outnumber us and believe we are easy prey. They have heavy bows that can shoot far."

"Let them come closer. I can shoot much farther." George had his M4 that at the ready and waited to see what the Sipahi would do. He hoped that since the Byzantines were not officially at war with the Ottomans they would be left alone, but that was not to be the case. At 300 meters the Sipahi charged. George brought up the M4 and fired dropping the officer that was leading the charge and fired two more times taking down two more of the riders. The Sipahi were now in bow range and launched their arrows. Before they could shoot again Staff Sergeant Smith manning the Humvee's M240B mounted machine gun, fired a short burst that broke the charge. With over half of their number killed or wounded, the remaining survivors turned and ran.

George looked around to see if there were any casualties, he noticed an arrow protruding from the ground only a couple of feet in front of him. He saw several arrows protruding from the duce and a half and some were stuck in the Byzantine's shields. One of Petros men had taken an arrow in the arm and was being treated by doctor Marone

"How is he, doc?"

"Just a flesh wound, the arrow head went through the fleshy part."

"Will we see them again, Petros?"

"After that drubbing, I doubt it. That was amazing. I have seen some fire arms before, but nothing like this. The weapon on your iron horse just mowed them down."

"I told you we have special weapons to destroy our enemies and those of the emperor."

"Then it is a miracle that you have arrived."

"They're killing the wounded!" Doctor Marone shouted as

she watched Petros' men kill some of the wounded Sipahi.

"Welcome to the 15th century doc. There is no mercy shown to the loser."

"That's murder."

"Don't worry about it, doc. The Turks would do the same. Let's move on."

After traveling through desolate areas that had once been farmlands and villages, but now lay in waste after having been pillaged by marauding Ottomans, they finally could see the huge battlements and walls built by the Emperor Theodosius, for the once great capital of the Byzantine Empire. The traffic on the road had picked up as merchants flocked toward the city to sell their wares. People stopped and looked on, some doing the sign of cross as the vehicles escorted by the Byzantine cavalry passed by. Petros sent two of his men ahead to brief the Imperial Guard and the emperor on the mysterious soldiers they had found.

A mile from the city gates, they were met by a large contingent of Imperial Guard troops that served as the emperor's personal body guards. The officer in charge said that he would escort them to the Imperial Palace. George agreed and followed them into the city. As they drove through the huge city gates, George was awestruck by the history of this once great city that had ruled a huge empire. He was now saddened to see that the city was only a shell of its former glory. They passed old crumbling buildings and walled off neighborhoods inside the main walls. The population which had once been over 500,000 now had dwindled to only 50,000 inhabitants, decimated by wars and disease. Nothing short of a miracle, could save the city from the ravages of the Ottomans, who would arrive in a little less than a year. Maybe they were the miracle, George thought?

Twenty minutes later, they reached the Blachernai Palace courtyard, which was in the far northwest corner of the city. In the middle of the courtyard was another group of heavily armed infantry soldiers in formation. Standing beside them was a bearded middle aged man, dressed in armor and wearing a cape. It had to be only one man, Constantine Paleologos XI, the last Byzantine emperor. George had the vehicles pull up next to the formation and shut off their engines. "Zulu 2, fall out and get into formation when you see us exiting my vehicle. Everyone else stay put in the vehicles, until I tell you to get out," George said into the radio.

"Okay guys, here is where we make history and possibly reshape the future of the world. I want you all to get out and fall in. We will march up to the emperor and present arms. This man is a warrior in all sense of the word."

George exited the vehicle with his team and quickly fell into formation. They were quickly joined by Zulu 2. The Byzantines did not make a move, they just watched dumfounded. The Americans marched up to the emperor and presented arms.

"Your majesty we salute you. I am George Mavrakis commander of this unit. We have come from a very faraway place. We are here now as allies and will help you save the city from the Moslem hordes that will soon be at your walls."

The Byzantine emperor was almost at a loss for words. "You are a Greek? Your dialect is very strange."

"I will explain more to you later your majesty, but you are correct I am Greek. My comrades do not speak, Greek. Our physician also speaks Italian, everyone speaks English."

"I am versed in the Romantic languages, but not English. Please have your soldiers relax."

"Thank you, your majesty." George turned around and put his troops at ease.

"My two soldiers that announced your arrival, said you are angels come to save us with magic weapons that kill men at great distances. Are you the miracle we have all been praying for?"

"We are not angels but we might be that miracle. Some power sent us here, either man made or divine."

"You have iron chariots and magical weapons, how is this possible?"

"Is there anywhere we can talk in private, your majesty?"

"Why of course, forgive me for my lack of hospitality. Please, all of you follow me into my palace for food and refreshments."

"We will your majesty but we must guard these iron chariots with our lives. That large one over there is called a truck and it is carrying weapons and other supplies that can help save this city."

"Don't worry; I will have my Imperial Guard watch them."

"That is most welcome, your majesty."

"May I see your machines?

"Why of course, sir. Everything and everyone, is at your service."

"Thank you."

"Please, follow me, your majesty." The emperor turned and told his body guards to stay put. George took him first to the Humvees and explained their function to him and then to duce and a half and introduced him to doctor Marone and her driver.

"Your majesty, this is our Physician, Doctor Anna Marone."

"What a surprise, a woman physician and a very beautiful one at that. I am Constantine Paleologos, emperor of what is left of this once great empire," he said in perfect Italian of the period. He took her hand and kissed it.

"I am honored your majesty," she replied and bowed.

"We maybe in need of your services very soon my dear."

"I will do my best to serve you, sir."

"Thank you. Now would you please join us in the palace?"

Several minutes later they were all inside the palace. Everyone was amazed as to the beauty and décor. Byzantine frescoes and colorful tiles adorned the walls and floors and servants hustled back and forth bringing food and drink.

"Please, everyone grab some food and drink," the emperor said.

"Listen up gentlemen, we are guests, stay sober and be at your best behavior. If anyone screws up I will have them thrown into the darkest dungeon. Captain you and Jenkins are in charge."

"We got it, sarge," Airman Green said as he devoured a chicken leg.

George turned to the emperor, "sir is there anywhere we can talk in private?"

"Yes, please follow me."

George followed the emperor through several doors ending up in an ornately decorated room containing a large table with chairs. "This is where I normally eat. Please sit down."

Both men sat down and a servant poured them each some wine into two silver goblets that were adorned with the Byzantine eagles. The emperor picked up the cup and offered a toast, "to our savior Jesus Christ who brought you here in our time of need."

"To our lord Jesus Christ," said George. "Good wine."

"It's from the Peloponnese. We don't have much land available to grow grapes. What we have is needed to feed the City."

"Hopefully we can remedy that. What I will tell you sir will sound totally unbelievable, but it is god's truth. I am sure you are very curious as to who we are."

"To say the least," the emperor replied.

"Here are the facts your majesty. On 6 April 1453, Sultan Mehmet will put this city under siege with 80,000 men and over 60 heavy guns. On the 29th of May the City will fall to the Turks who will proceed to rape and pillage it for three day. You will die in battle and Byzantium will come to an end. The Ottoman Empire will conquer all the Balkans and the Middle-East. It will survive for almost 500 years before it collapses for almost the same reasons as Byzantium's demise."

George looked at the emperor who had turned white. "How do you know all this? You must be angels from heaven."

"No your majesty, we are mortals, just like you. I told you we came from a very faraway place. We came from another land, another time. We came from the future, from the year 2015. Our country will be located on a continent across the Atlantic Ocean which will be called America. An Italian will discover it in 1492, searching for a passage to India to avoid passing through lands controlled by the Turks. We are called Americans. There are great riches on the continent we came from."

"But how is this possible?"

George explained the war in Afghanistan, the fight with the Taliban, being trapped in the cave and their experiences there.

"So you are soldiers who are lost in the sands of time and have arrived here to help us fight our war against the Turk and Islam."

"That is basically it your majesty, we have absolutely no time to lose if we are to save this city from the ravages of the Turk. We will help you develop weapons and improve the city's defenses with the weapons we brought along and the supplies still in the cave. We ask that our origins remain secret for now.

If the Ottoman Turks find out they will pay assassins to have us murdered or invade before we are fully prepared."

"You are correct in that point. We must keep this as low key as possible. I will assign you some body guards."

"Can I have the officer and the men that found us?"

"Of course, consider it done."

"Thank you, your majesty."

"Pardon me for a moment." The emperor stepped outside the room and came back in less than a minute. "You said the Turks will have many large cannons. Who will build these guns for the Ottomans?"

"A young Hungarian will build them."

"Was his name, Urban?"

"I believe it was."

"He had very recently offered his services to us, unfortunately the treasury is empty. But you and your soldiers are very powerful you can defeat the Turk?"

"Not on our own, sir. We have a finite amount of ammunition for our weapons. Once it is all used we are just like you. They will come with 80,000 soldiers. We can strongly influence events and even do some pre-emptive damage to the Ottomans to push their plans back. We will teach you to manufacture much better gun powder weapons then you have now."

"Why don't you make more ammunition?"

"Even if we had the material ready available, the technology does not yet exist to reload the cartridges we use."

"Cartridges? "

"George unholstered his Beretta M19 pistol and ejected a round "These are called cartridges or commonly known as bullets. The powder, spark and bullet are all in one. This copper ball is shot out of the pistol I am holding, at very high velocity."

"I see what you mean. How many bullets are in that pistol? "

"Fifteen bullets and I have two more magazines holding 15 bullets each; I can change them very fast."

"So you can kill 45 men in minutes?"

"Theoretically, yes. Our larger rifles have 30 round magazines, and we carry usually six each.

"My god, killing has become more efficient in your time."

"If we had one hundred of those weapons we could stop the Turks."

"Remember your majesty, once we run out of a bullet that's it. We are done. We can't reload these cartridges. We don't have the technology yet to do it. Even the powder you use is of very poor quality. We can improve that immediately. Fire arms are in their infancy in your era. The Turks will demonstrate to the world what these new gunpowder weapons can do, when their guns knock down the walls of this city."

"Then we must use your knowledge and quickly build better weapons for war and stop them."

"In the future, 500 years from now man will go to war in flying machines that can carry weapons that can destroy entire cities. In my time, mankind has reached the point where he can destroy all life on this world."

"So it seems that god has put man's fate, in their own hands."

"Yes, your majesty. There were a couple of times we came close to annihilating ourselves. We fought great wars causing the deaths of tens of millions. But we survived. Mankind has even gone to the moon."

"The moon?"

"It is a bleak and inhospitable place. Nothing can live there. But with all out scientific advances we are still having our religious wars, nothing has really changed other than the ability to kill and destroy more efficiently."

"You have told me many things of the future, but how will you save this city? We have very little money."

"Each one of the people that are here with me, have different skills they brought with them before they joined the military. Some even brought books containing vital information we can use. We will have to pool all our minds and begin planning and immediately designing new technology and improving what is in existence. First my people will need to quickly learn Greek and yours English, which is close to Latin."

"That will be arranged immediately. You will have the best tutors assigned to you."

"We have brought several cases of Russian weapons we found in the cave, enough to arm maybe 30-40 of your best men. There are more weapons and supplies there. We must secure that cave and keep its existence secret at all costs. It is 30 miles from here. We will also need more soldiers to defend the city. You will announce a levy for all males 18-50 to serve the state. They will undergo a training period to be determined by your officers then released and be ready for call up."

"They will complain and not like it. There are only 50,000 inhabitants in the city."

"It is the duty off all citizens to serve the state. We can create a parliament to serve the people and have elections once the threat of the Turk is over. You will be the head of state. Also your majesty, we must contact Trebizond and request a meeting. We will also ask the Venetians and other Italian City states for help."

"I have already done that."

"During the battle in my timeline the Genovese had provided 700 soldiers that fought bravely. Perhaps we can offer the Europeans and maybe the northern Europeans something in return, such as the knowledge of a new world across the sea. We have maps of the entire world with us. The French and English though are locked in a dynastic war that will last for years but we shall see. First off all we must convince your generals. We need their buy in. Any sort of disloyalty or rebellion cannot be tolerated, we can't afford it. Internal dissent destroyed Byzantium."

"You are right my friend. I will do my best to convince everyone. I will make you a Strategos (General) and my Imperial military advisor. That also carries the title of duke. You will live in the palace and teach me of your time and ways. My head is still spinning from everything you just told me. Let's go back to everyone and enjoy some food and drink. We have much work starting tomorrow."

"Of course, your majesty. I am truly honored. I would have offered my assistance as a common soldier."

George and the emperor went back to where they had left everyone. His troops had been joined by Petros and his men, despite the language barrier everyone seemed to be getting along. The emperor took a seat at the head of the table with George next him. By now everyone had loosened up with the food and drink that had been provided. But as a whole everyone was behaving accordingly. George motioned for doctor Marone to set by him. "I hope you are having a goodtime Anna?" The emperor asked.

"Yes your majesty. Considering the circumstances that we are in a city that may fall to the Ottomans and have travelled 500 years back in time, I am feeling rather good."

"Hopefully my dear, our new duke and general will prevent that from happening." Anna raised her eye brows when she heard George had been made a general and a duke.

"I have a proposal for you. Would you take the position of

Imperial Physician and train our physicians in your modern medicine? That will also carry the title of duchess."

"Of course your majesty, I am honored to be of assistance."

"Thank you. Now please enjoy the festivities."

George picked up is goblet of wine and spoke to his men, "I would like to make a toast to the emperor; he has promoted me to general and made me a duke. All of you will also be promoted several steps tomorrow. We will have to work hard and pool our knowledge to help save this Christian city and make a home for us here. Everyone will be in the parade ground outside the palace at 0700hrs. Now repeat after me. It means Harrah to the emperor, "Zito O Aftokrator!" Every one repeated the words and raised their glasses to Constantine.

The emperor raised his goblet and asked to have his words translated. "My new friends, I know you are far from your homes and families but please consider us your new friends and family. Whether it was fate or god that brought you here to us, you are the miracle we have been praying for. I drink to your health and our partnership. I am also deeply honored to have you as my soldiers. I also drink to my new general and duke, George Mavrakis and my new Imperial Physician and duchess Anna Marone!" Everyone raised their goblets and drank.

"Now general, I leave you with your troops. I must gather my officers and ministers and brief them on our future. My servants will take you to your quarters. Guards will be posted outside your rooms. I will see you in the morning." With that, the emperor turned around and left.

George turned to Anna. "Well duchess congratulations for your promotion. As a general I'm promoting you to Colonel and my aide de camp."

"Well thank you, sir. I am honored," she said with a big smile. "What did you and the emperor discuss?"

"I will brief you later, if you stop by my quarters where ever that is. I want to discuss a few things and get your advice."

"The great general asking a mere woman for advice?"

"All great men have a good woman beside them."

"Touché, general. I'll be more than happy to discuss our future with you."

"Excuse me for a moment duchess. I need to speak to our new troops." George walked over to Petros who immediately stood up.

"Congratulations, sir on your new titles."

"Thank you Petros. You and your men are now part of my command. I am promoting you to Tagmatarchis, (Byzantine battalion commander) and all your men one level. They will form the new Byzantine rifle corps. I want you and your men outside a little after sunrise to begin training. My soldiers will begin learning Greek and you and your men English. You will also learn to use our weapons. I will brief you more in the morning. Now enjoy yourself."

"Thank you sir. You will find that we will be good students." George was sure of that, he had already overheard some of his troops learning the female anatomy parts in Greek and they teaching them the English equivalent, while they played grab ass with a few of the female servants. No matter what century soldiers are from, they always talk about booze and women.

George walked back to the table where Anna was sitting,

"Are you ready to find out where are rooms are and retire for the night?"

"Yes, I am, my general."

"Let me find out where our rooms are." George called one of the servants over and asked where his and the duchess's rooms were. The servant asked George to follow him. After walking up a flight of stairs and through several hallways they came to an area where there were guards posted.

"Anna, give me about 30-40 minute to wash up."

"That's a good idea I will wash up too."

The servant showed them to their quarters. George's room had a fire going in the fireplace. It was fairly large and was filled with ornate furniture. Up against the wall was a large poster bed. In the center of the room was a large metal tub filled with warm water and a very scantily dressed servant girl standing next to it. "Are you taking a bath, your excellency?"

George smiled, "I think I will."

Approximately forty minutes later he heard a knock on the door. "Come in."

Anna walked in barefoot wearing a low cut maroon dress of the period. Here hair was still a bit damp but had been combed and was hanging to her shoulders. She was simply stunning.

"Well duchess you look ravishing."

She started laughing. "Thank you for the compliment but cut the duchess bull shit and tell me what happened with the emperor."

"In a minute my dear." George walked over and threw a log on the fire and then poured them each a goblet of wine and sat on the bed. "These castles were pretty drafty and it is January. He patted the bed next to him. Please join me I'm sure your feet are cold. You can get under the covers. Don't worry I will behave."

"I am rather cold and I know you will behave," Anna said as she pulled a pistol from a pocket in her dress and flashed it.

"So you are here to assassinate the great new Byzantine general and savior of the empire," George said as he pulled his pistol which he had put under his pillow. They began to laugh but her laughter soon turned to tears.

"What's the matter, Anna?"

"I'm scared." She started crying harder. He went over and hugged her. "We are in a strange land, we're lost in time and in a city that will soon be attacked and sacked."

He held her tight and stroked her head as she sobbed.

"Please don't cry it will be all right. We'll survive."

"I don't know if I can do this?" He looked in her eyes and their lips touched and they kissed. The kissing became more passionate. "I don't want to be alone tonight."

"Don't worry; I will be here with you. He held her tight as he related to her what he had discussed with the emperor. He asked her opinion about selling their knowledge about North America's location, to the other European states for gold, which would help the Byzantine treasury. She agreed with this idea and for several other ones that he had. Finally she fell asleep as held her in his arms. He kissed her on the forehead and rolled over and fell asleep exhausted by the day's events.

Chapter 3

Constantinopolis, Byzantium
11 January 1452

When George woke up early the next morning, he found Anna cuddled up beside him. Sometime during the night she had removed her dress. He could feel her warm breasts pressing on his back. He turned around and stroked her face and hair, she slowly awakened. She put her arms around him and kissed him. "Thank you for being a gentlemen and being kind to me last night."

"I would never take advantage of a lady, when she is in distress. He felt himself stir as she pressed herself on him."

"Well my general, I am now taking advantage of you."

"Mmmm, yes duchess, ravage me."

An hour later, he was out in the parade ground addressing his men. He was carrying the silver baton of a Byzantine general which the servants had brought for him. The morning was brisk; it was still early January in that part of Europe. Anna was next to him as his adjutant. She had removed her captain's rank from her uniform, having been promoted to colonel. Petros and his men had been relieved and told to prepare a classroom to begin English lessons, which he would be giving.

"Good morning ladies and gentlemen, I hope you all slept well. I know that some of you had a rough night and maybe a little under the weather."

"So are some of the servant girls."

"You may be getting married quickly, Green. The Byzantines don't take kindly to baby daddies. Several of them began to laugh. At least their morale was good, considering what had just happened to them.

"You all know our situation. We have somehow been transported back to the year 1452. We have been welcomed to this city and offered a home. There is really nowhere else for us to go. We are surrounded by an expanding hostile Moslem empire. Early next year, the Ottoman Turks will be knocking on the gates of this city. In our history Constantinopolis falls after a brutal two month siege. The emperor dies heroically in battle and the city is pillaged and looted for three days. We ladies and gentlemen, will prevent that from ever happening. We have knowledge and superior weapons, but it isn't going to be easy. We will have a lot of work to do."

"With limited ammo, sir. "

"I am well aware of that, Green. From now on, all brass cartridges will be collected. The only problem for reloading will be developing a primer. We may be able to create mercury fulminate. The ingredients existed in this century. Do we have any chemistry experts?

"I was chemistry major in college, until I ran out of money and enlisted," Sergeant Mary Jones said.

"See what I mean folks. We will pool our collective knowledge and resources and assist our friends in advancing their technology. Some of you may be sailing enthusiast and can help them better their naval vessels. Airman Green I think you said you knew how to sail."

"Yes sir, I grew up learning to sail. As a matter a fact, I have a book on my IPAD on the history of sailing ships and naval warfare. It's called the age of sail. It has ship designs and that of cannon."

George was suddenly elated. "Consider that book invaluable and worth millions in gold and also, Top Secret. It can destroy us, if it falls in the wrong hands. We will need to copy it to the other IPADS."

"Yes, sir."

"I know Sergeant Jenkins is a small arms expert. Our allies need fire arms and cannon. We must develop muskets. I am sure some of you are gun experts yourselves."

"But sir, we need advanced metal working," Staff Sergeant Smith said.

"I know you worked in a machine shop, Smith. There is a machine shop in the underground ex-Soviet base. I know it won't be easy. Most of you have an IPAD along with a solar charger and have books on them we can use. Protect them with your lives. I will have scribes, transcribe all the books. We will all have to think outside the box if we are to survive and win. We are all warriors fighting for our own survival and that of the emperor and this city. If we win we can change history and rebuild this empire. Is that understood?"

"Sir, yes sir," they all yelled in unison.

"Now, the good news. I am promoting everyone. Effective immediately, all Technical Sergeants are promoted to the rank of captain. All staff sergeants are promoted to lieutenant, all Sergeants, to Master Sergeant, all Airman First class, to Staff Sergeant and Airmen to Sergeant. You will be the nucleus of a new army, any questions?" George looked around.

"Okay now the fun part of your training will start immediately. Everyone will quickly learn Greek; there will be three hours of class every day after PT. Major Petros and his men will be there also trying to learn English. You guys will help them with their training. You will give the major the same respect you give me, or as a matter of fact any officer. There is no more UCMJ. Punishments in this era are extremely harsh so don't screw up."

From the corner of his eye he caught site of the emperor approaching. "Flight, atten hut!"

Everyone quickly came to attention as the emperor approached. George did an about face and saluted the emperor.

"Sir, return the salute. This is how we honor senior officers and you are the commander and chief."

The emperor returned the salute. "I am telling the men what we expect of them. They will begin their lessons in Greek and English. Afterwards we will see what knowledge and equipment each of my people has brought with them. Do you have anything to say, sir?"

"Just let them know that we will always be grateful for what they are doing for us. I came to invite you to a meeting with my commanders that will be taking place in the palace."

"I will dismiss the troops so they can begin their duties and I will follow you."

George turned to the troops said a few more words and dismissed them. He left Anna in charge. "Your majesty I am at your service."

"Let's go to the den of vipers. I am sure some of them may initially resent you, especially General Loukas Notaras, a capable man and the commander of the army. I am sure once you have told them your story, they will accept you. We are desperate, we have only 5000 men in the entire army, almost no navy and the treasury is empty."

"We will have to quickly rectify that. I may have some ideas."

When they entered the meeting chamber, the men stood up acknowledging the emperor's presence. Inside the room was a large table and around it sat several men in military garb. A fire was burning in the fire place to provide some warmth in the damp and chilly room. The stone floor was covered with oriental rugs, on the walls hung several religious tapestries depicting several saints and Jesus.

"Good morning gentlemen, may I introduce you to our newest general and imperial adviser, General George Mavrakis."

An older middle aged man stood up also carrying a general's silver baton and pointed at George. "How has this young upstart from the supposed future been appointed a general, without my consultation and approval? Only god knows what demons he brings to us?"

Before the emperor could answer George spoke. "Good morning, sir. You must be General Loukas Notaras. History judged you as a very capable commander and diplomat. But in the end all your skills could not save you or this city. The Ottomans will capture you and have you executed a few days after the city falls, along with the other Byzantine noblemen they have captured. I am the man that might possibly save all your lives and this city. I bring no demons with me, except for 16 of my fellow soldiers and hope."

That had the desired effect on all of them. "Now please listen to him," the emperor commanded.

"Yes your majesty, we are listening"

"Early next year, if all goes according to my time line and nothing changes, the Sultan will decide to attack this city. He will begin moving his heavy guns from Andrianoupolis to here in early March. He will march on this city with approximately 80,000 men." George heard a couple of the officers gasp. "The siege will begin on the 6th of April and the city will fall to the Turk on the 29th of May 1453. Except for a small force of 700 Genovese, you will receive very little help from the other Christian states."

"That's nonsense, our walls will hold back the invaders as

they have in the past," said one of the other officers present.

"Your walls will be knocked down by the heavy cannon they will bring. The age of walled cities and castles is coming to an abrupt end with the use of cannon."

"So what do we do? You don't need us, you can defeat them alone. I am told you bring magical weapons," General Notaras said.

"We do have powerful weapon, sir, but they are not magical, they to use gunpowder and fire bullets. They are the culmination of 500 years of scientific advancement in weaponry. We can't fight them alone, there are just too many and we don't have enough bullets for our guns. We can though influence a battle and events. The best weapon we have is the knowledge we brought with us. With this knowledge we can help you cast bronze cannons and possibly rifled guns. We will immediately improve the quality of your gunpowder through a process called corning, where the powder is wetted and when it dries its put through a sieve. This makes it burn more efficiently. We must manufacture much more gun powder. We can also help improve your technology and scientific knowledge." George momentarily hesitated and looked around him. He now had everyone's attention.

"In my time line General Notaras, men go to war in giant flying machines which can drop a bomb that can destroy an entire city. We have the ability to destroy all life on earth."

"My god. Men in flying machines."

"That would not be for another 500 years, gentlemen. We can though immediately improve the navy. We have a book with us that illustrates the development of wooden warships through the centuries. I am sure your naval architects can copy the designs and we can mount cannon on them."

"That could help us open up our trade routes once again,"

Admiral Spiro Laskaris said.

"If we can harness steam and build steam engines we can power these ships and won't need the wind or rowers."

"Like Hero's engine in Alexandria so long ago," the admiral replied.

"There are machines in the Russian underground base that we can use and additional supplies and weapons stored there, but we must be able to secure that area. It's 30 miles from here."

"We don't have the men to hold an area that far from the city."

"We don't yet, but we will eventually have to. We will need the best minds and craftsmen in Byzantium."

"But we have no money to pay them!" One of the other officers present, blurted out.

"Throughout history men have fought and died to preserve their freedom and beliefs. They will be levied to work for the state. We will develop a patent system. Any man that invents a product will be granted a sole patent for 20 years which means he will receive a set fee for every item that is sold. That gentleman should even encourage innovation."

George could see some of the doubt in their faces beginning to go away. "Another thing, we must do is create the citizen soldier. Every man and woman between the ages of 18-50 will need to serve the armed forces in some capacity, whither as a soldier, a medical orderly or supply clerk."

"We can't feed and equip all those people," General Notaras said.

"I realize that, but we can draft them and train them in batches and have them assigned to units. Once they have received their initial basic training they will report to duty once a month for a weekend of training. Any one that refuses will either pay a large fine or serve a prison sentence of hard labor.

The people that are in prison, unless they are murderers will serve their sentence by working on fortifications and other projects. This way they can serve the state and earn their freedom back."

"I like that idea, we can raise another 8-10,000 troops this way at very minimal cost," Notaras said.

"My country does it and keeps active reserves in case of war."

"Tell us about your kingdom."

"First of all sir, we are not a kingdom, we are a republic and a democracy. The people elect their leaders. My country is called the United Stated of America. It lies about 3500 thousand miles across the Atlantic from the British Isles. It was re-discovered by a Genovese Italian, named Christopher Columbus in 1492, who was looking for a passage to India because the land routes were closed by the Ottomans. He was hired by the queen of Spain. The Viking Norsemen had traveled to America 400 years earlier, but they had no written records. There are great riches of gold and jewels there, controlled by a native empire called the Aztecs who are located on the southern end of the continent of North American. They pray to certain gods that call for human sacrifices.

"Holy mother of Jesus, these idolaters must be exterminated," George turned around and saw a person dressed in church garb who was carrying a bishop's cane. He had walked in unannounced into the room.

"General Mavrakis, let me introduce you to his eminence, the Patriarch Athanasius II," the emperor said.

George took the Patriarch's hand and kissed it in respect. "I am honored to meet you, your eminence."

"As I my son. You are a godsend from the heavens come here to help us in this dark hour."

"We will do as much as we can your holiness."

"Tell me what happens to Aghia Sophia, if the Ottomans take the city."

"Your holiness, there will be many hundreds of people barricaded in the church. The Ottoman soldiers break in and defile the icons, rape women and children on the altar and loot what can be carried away. Many of the people are butchered, others sold into slavery or ransomed. The city is pillaged for three days as is Moslem Ottoman custom. Aghia Sofia is converted into a Mosque and will remain like that for almost 500 years until it is turned into a museum."

"My god, we must try to prevent this at all costs! You will have my support and I will rally the faithful to the cause."

"Thank you your excellency. I will love to see what the holy church looks like today. I saw it as a museum when I visited the city of Istanbul as it was renamed in 1922."

"You are welcomed, any time my son."

"Oh and your holiness as to the Aztecs in the Americas, Spain and the Catholic Church destroyed their empire and looted all their riches. There were enough riches for Spanish kings to finance wars for over 200 years."

"They were heathens my son and deserved to be destroyed." He then took a seat at the table.

"We could do wonders with a couple of shiploads of gold," the emperor commented.

"If we can build an efficient ship like a frigate, it can sail there may be in about 50 days, trade with them and return. We have maps and tools to navigate with."

"That is a future possibility," added the admiral.

"We also need to get Trebizond on board with us. One of America's great leaders during a time of civil war said "either we hang together or hang separately. That stands to reason here also. Within a few years they are also destroyed as is the enclave in the southern Peloponnese. By 1461 the Ottomans rule all of Asia Minor and the Balkans. They even reached the gates of Vienna in the 1500s and again in late 1600s, but are defeated by Christian armies."

"I wise man your leader. Did he win the war?"

"Yes your majesty, but both sides lost over half a million soldiers killed in four years of war and it was 1861-1865, not in my modern times."

"What a senseless slaughter."

"How do we get Trebizond to come along with us?"

"We tell them the truth and demonstrate our weapons."

"That may work," General Notaras said" Even a few hundred more troops can help the cause."

"We must also fill our coffers, gentlemen. We need to start farming more efficiently and export food. We can show you how to do this. This city is almost empty. There are so many fields we can farm. We need to start small manufacturing industries and new cannon foundries. The best product we now have to sell is knowledge." George pulled out an IPAD from his BDU jacket pocket, turned it on and went to an application called world Geography, picked a map of the world and showed them the map. He passed the IPAD around the table.

"This is called a tablet computer. It can do many things such as show pictures, store knowledge and do complex mathematical computations. Computers have been around in many sizes and forms for the last 60 years in my timeline. They are getting smaller and smaller. When first invented, they were the size of a room."

"So our ancestors the ancient Greeks were correct, the earth is a globe. I marvel at the wisdom of god."

"Yes your holiness, they were correct and god was very wise to have created the world in this way."

"We could sell maps to other Christian states. We will keep the secrets of Mexico. The climate there is temperate. We may want to colonize there later, if we survive the Ottoman onslaught. I am sure we will soon come up with more things to trade with the Italian states. Maybe even sell them spy glasses, which are simple to make by grinding pieces of glass and positioning them in a tube to magnify objects at a distance. Astronomers will love them. So gentlemen, there is much to do. We must formulate a long term strategic plan in the weeks to come. My people must learn Greek and your men English, This way we can integrate our forces better."

"Yes, that is a sound plan."

"I do hope that I have your cooperation and most of all I desire your friendship. My goal is to save this city and everyone in it and to keep Byzantium alive. I am not seeking fame or fortune. Are you with me? "

"You sold us," General Mavrakis. "We are with you with everything we have. This city will gear for war," General Notaras said.

"Thank you, gentlemen. One other thing. I am sure by now the Ottomans may have heard something about us from spies in the city. We need to keep our true identity as secure as possible. The sultan will surely hire assassins to have us killed. In the next few days all senior officers in this room will be issued modern guns and will learn how to use them for their personal security."

"That is most gracious of you, general. Let's meet weekly to discuss progress. I will be visiting your classes as will my senior staff officers to learn English."

"Yes, I also agree on the meetings, sir. You and your staff are welcome to come any time. Now I must go back to my training.

"God go with you my son," the patriarch added.

Constantinopolis
12 March 1453

Several weeks later, George and General Notaras were going over the substantial progress that they had so far made. All the Americans were speaking and understanding rudimentary Greek. Petros' men had caught on to English much easier as had the Byzantine General Staff and even the emperor. They had even become proficient with the AK 47, Nagants and the pistols they had been issued. George was even able to convince the Byzantines to change their rank structures to make them match the American one and to even slowly convert to the metric measuring system. During one of General's Notaras' staff meetings, he had brought in a one meter measuring tape and had convinced them to adopt the metric system for the military.

The first attempts at forging and testing Bronze nine pounder guns had already begun under the auspices of Captain Jenkins and Lieutenant Rhodes and were going fairly well. Several guns had been made and were undergoing testing. There had been a couple of accidents with guns exploding; fortunately no one had been seriously hurt. They were hoping to begin mass producing cannon very soon.

George and General Notaras had been invited to the gun range where Lieutenant Rhodes was testing one of the cannons. Rhodes came to attention when the two senior officers approached. "How's it going, Paul?"

"Pretty good, General Mavrakis. I think we finally got the copper and tin ratio correct. We are about to test this gun. It's double loaded with canister. Please move behind the barricade in case the gun explodes, but I doubt it will."

When everyone had taken cover Paul gave the order and one of the workers applied a match to the touch hole from one of the barricades that had been set up for their safety. The gun mounted on its carriage went off with a roar spreading destruction, as hundreds of balls cut down the straw dummies that had been set up to represent infantry.

"We have a winner, gentlemen. We now have artillery. We can probably initially forge twelve to fifteen guns a month until we have the new foundry on line in the next couple of weeks. Then we can easily double production. I have started designing a 12 pounder soon to be followed by an 18 pounder with explosive shells. They should be able to blow any ship out of the water in the strait when they are installed in the forts. Our guns will be much more superior to what the Turks will have."

"Thank you, Paul," General Notaras said. "You just gave this city a chance to survive."

"Thank you, sir, "Lieutenant Rhodes answered in accented Greek.

"Can you start building the naval version?" George asked.

"I've already poured the first gun. It was forged with an eye to be able to secure it on a deck. By the time Sergeant Green has his first two sloops of war launched; we will have the guns for it. "I am also designing a smaller 6 pounder for the galleys but we need more foundries and workers."

"You will have them soon, lieutenant. Now that we have joined forces with Trebizond and they are supplying us with gold, copper, tin and iron, we will be able to build and pay for another foundry."

"Thank you, sir."

"That was a brilliant plan, George, sending a galley with four of your men, plus Major Petros Tomas' detachment with the emperor to Trebizond. They had to have been very convincing to get those fools on board. The emperor used the phrase we either hang together or we hang separately and they took it to heart. Soon they too will be building cannons and hopefully fire arms."

"That is one for the history books," said George laughing.

"President Lincoln will have to now use a borrowed phrase. I am sure they also had a shock, sir, when they saw the troops armed with modern rifles."

General Notaras patted the Makarov Pistol that he had strapped to his side. "These firearms can be very convincing."

"Where's Captain Jenkins?"

"Over in the gun shop, sir."

"Okay, we'll walk over there. Keep those guns coming lieutenant."

"We will have to take a trip soon to the underground base and explore it further and see what else we can find and use. With the metal working machines we found there, according to Captain Jenkins, we could double or triple our Musket production. We are producing about ten a week. We need to increase this by at least two fold for now."

"I'm coming with you when you go."

"Sir, this City can't afford to lose two generals."

"There is no discussion on this point. If you are captured or killed, it's all over anyway."

"Yes, sir."

Both general officers walked the short distance to the Imperial Rifle Works. They found Captain Jenkins checking a finished musket barrel. "How's it going, captain."

Jenkins came to attention and saluted. "Pretty good, Sir."

"How's the work going?" George said.

"It's going, but very slow, sir. It's taking very long to produce barrels with the amount of iron available. We are getting much better at it. If I had those lathes and power tools, we could double or triple production."

George picked up one of the smooth bore match locks. "The work is excellent. How many have you manufactured so far?"

"About 50, sir. I think we will pick up the pace, hopefully to over a 100 a month. Now that we introduced the patent system, I am getting requests from many craftsmen wanting to work here."

"That's good news, Jenkins. How do they shoot?"

"Fairly accurate up to 50 to 75 meters, depending on the skill of the shooter. It usually took iron discipline and massed musket fire to stop an enemy advance. We need to get these out in the field and the infantry trained with them. There is even a bayonet to go with the gun."

Jenkins demonstrated how they bayonet plugged into the weapon. "When the enemy gets close, there is always the bayonet."

"That is almost like a short lance. My men will love this," General Notaras said.

I sent a few examples to Trebizond and two of our crafts men to get them started. Hopefully they will be able to ramp up production too. Sometime in the immediate future we can start building flintlocks. That's a bit more complicated, I do have a design on the drawing board."

"You are doing great work captain. I hope to start training my infantry in the next couple of weeks, if we have enough muskets."

"I am doing my best, sir."

"I know you are, captain."

"We'll leave you to your work, keep them guns coming out," added George.

"Well general Notaras, what do you think?"

"With your help we have made tremendous progress in weaponry. Now we must learn tactics and hopefully begin to fill our coffers with gold and increase the city's population."

"Our trade mission should soon be back from Italy. I hope we can garner some allies. The Venetian fleet will be most useful against the Turk. If we lose, they will end up fighting them for the next 200 years. The mission that went to France should also return in the next few weeks."

"Time will tell, the Latins never had any love for us, neither did their pope. They are responsible for our demise when their 4th crusade sacked the city."

"If I remember my history, imperial infighting was also responsible."

"Yes, that is true."

"Now we are all united under one banner. The state and the people are one. I heard the patriarch's sermon about the people from heaven. That's great for moral but I am sure the sultan has heard about it by now. I am just hoping that he won't believe it and brush it off as just talk to boost morale. We can't begin any military actions just yet. That may tip him off and we will be in trouble. We need a few more months."

"You are so very right, George."

"I will do my best to keep the lid on."

"I am going to the hospital to see how our Imperial Physician is doing. She tells me that deaths by infections have been cut by half and deaths from child birth have also been cut by a quarter."

"Her training of our physicians has had an immediate impact. Just telling us about cleanliness and those tiny animals called germs, has gone a long way in saving lives Our physicians now all clean their instruments and hands before they touch a patient. That will be very important when treating our wounded."

"Yes sir, it will be."

"Give my regards to the doctor."

"I will, sir."

The general took off towards the palace accompanied by his body guards. George had refused one, but the emperor had insisted and George had taken one of the Imperial Guards along. The soldier was armed with an AK47, but George figured the man was just as deadly with a sword. The hospital was located in another district of the city, a brisk fifteen minute walk from his present location. On his way there, he noticed that several cleared areas had been ploughed and fertilized and were waiting spring planting No land near the city would be left unfarmed, they needed food and hoped that they could even export some. When they arrived at the hospital, George walked inside and noticed that the marble floors and corridors smelled of alcohol disinfectant. He spotted Anna arguing in Italian with one of the physicians. When she looked up and saw him she smiled and walked over.

"How's my general, doing today?"

"Very well, actually. How's my pretty duchess doing?"

"I have been trying to talk some common sense to these butchers. Their treatment for anything is to bleed the patient!"

"It takes time to break centuries old habits. Just consider the progress you made in a few short weeks, Anna"

"I know, but it's frustrating."

"Also take into consideration that they are being told what to do by a woman."

Anna began to laugh. "You are right. Let's go into my office, the servants have lunch ready"

When they walked into Anna's office George noticed the food on the table. "You eat like royalty here."

"I am a duchess, silly."

"That is true and I am a Duke." The both began to laugh. "I

am starting to like it here. It seems we are serving a purpose."

"So do I, as do most of our people. I am training Master Sergeant Mary Jones to be a Physician's assistant. She has a degree in chemistry and is proving invaluable to our growing drug industry."

"Speaking of drugs, how is your Penicillin experiment going?"

"Actually, we've been doing pretty darn well. We are making a form of Penicillin tea to be consumed by patients. It has already saved a few lives and cured several infections. It may be a little while before we can actually create a more usable form."

"That would really help the economy if we can begin exporting drugs."

"It would be good for all of humanity. I have my best chemists working on it. We will get there. In the meantime we can export antiseptics and medical equipment. We have made some crude microscopes, but have a long way to go."

"Lieutenant Ross has also made some simple refractor and reflector telescopes. The Byzantine astronomers are having a field day with them. They have already seen the rings of Saturn and moons of Jupiter, discovered Uranus and are looking for Neptune. We will be able to export some of those very soon."

"That would bring in more needed revenue to buy goods and supplies for our infant manufacturing base."

"We will manage, Anna," George said as he gave her a kiss. Their relationship had developed further, where now she was spending most of the nights with him.

"The lunch was great. I need to head back to the palace and plan a trip to the underground base. We really need to explore it further and get some more supplies."

"That's a dangerous trip, my love."

"I know, but we must eventually secure that place. We need

the tools and machine shops."

"Once the Turks get wind of it they will be constantly attacking it. How will you hold out?"

"We can't let that happen until we are better prepared. Anyway, I will see you tonight."

George left the hospital and headed for the palace. Many of the city's citizens greeted him and bowed as he passed. He did not want all this attention, especially if there were Ottoman spies in the city.

After a 20 minute walk, George had reached the palace and was saluted by the sentry. He proceeded into the antechamber where the emperor was talking to the Venetian ambassador.

"Ah, General Mavrakis you are just in time. The good ambassador here was wondering when we will be exporting some of our new goods to his city."

"Probably in the next few weeks, sir. Right after we launch our new warship, the Phoenix. She will make her maiden voyage to Venice, on a trade mission. Her sister, the Aghia Sofia, will be visiting Genova."

"I would be honored to sail with her back to Venice, to speak to the Doge (Duke) about securing sole rights to some of your goods."

"Well sir, I'm sure that can be arranged, but it will be very costly. We want everyone to share some of our latest medical and scientific improvements."

"We are willing to pay top prices."

"In that case, Mr. Ambassador, we may also ask for an alliance with Venice to assist us against the Ottomans."

"I'm sure we can arrange something, sir. Now, I must go back to the embassy. I wish you both a good day."

After the ambassador had departed, the emperor shook his head in disbelief. "That little snake. For the last couple of years,

I have been begging the Venetians for assistance and have been ignored. Now they are kissing out rear ends for a business deal and are even offering to discuss an alliance with us!"

"I am sure the ambassador's spies have been very busy."

"How can anyone not notice the noise of cannon fire and rifle fire?"

"That also goes for the sultan's spies. I'm sure they suspect something."

"I'm sure you're correct, George. But on another note, our patrols have not noticed any increased activity."

"That is a good thing, your majesty. I need to go back into that mine in the next few weeks and see what other things we can find, that may prove useful for our defense. If we had the tools and equipment of that underground base, we could build muskets much faster. Unfortunately, we could not hold the base against a sustained Ottoman attack for very long, unless we have additional forces. I do not want to draw their attention."

"I wish I could come with you."

"Taking General Notaras along is bad enough. If anything happens to me and the general, you and Anna could still save the city. My troops have been integrated well in the new command structure and know what to do. We will soon be producing 30 cannons a month with two foundries going. The new 18 gun corvettes will be immediately outfitted with guns once they launch. They will be the most powerful warships in the Mediterranean if not the world."

"We may even be able to re-establish control of some the off shore islands."

"Very possible, your majesty, but we don't want to antagonize the Ottomans or the Italian states just yet. Once the war ships are outfitted with guns we will be establishing an artillery corps for the army and putting guns in the forts and some on the walls to reinforce the city's defenses."

"I saw the Corvettes that Sergeant Green designed and is supervising their building. They are beautiful ships and can beat anything in the Aegean and Mediterranean"

"They should be, your majesty, they are 200 years ahead of their time. Once they crews are trained to handle the ships and their guns, they will rule the seas."

"I spoke to Admiral Laskaris and he agrees that Green should be promoted and given command of the Phoenix. He has more than earned it."

"I agree with you. Just don't tell him yet, let it be a surprise for when he launches the ship. The admiral must ensure that he gets a crew of competent officers and sailors. We can't afford to lose him or the ship"

"You are right, George. I will speak to the admiral."

Edirne, Eastern Thrace, Ottoman Capital
15 March 1452

Sultan Mehmet II, a short youth of 20, was discussing the latest intelligence reports with Zaganos Pasha, his 2nd Vizier. They were in the palace in the Ottoman capital of Edirne, located in eastern Thrace. He had only been in power for a year and he needed a victory to consolidate his position on the Ottoman throne. Even after having his younger brother killed, removing him as a potential source of discontent, this still left another contender to the throne, Prince Orhan who lived in Constantinopolis as a political refugee. Mehmet was tired of having to put up with the Byzantines. He wanted to be finished with them and claim a great victory to his people.

"Padishah, (sultan's honorific title), my spies tell me the Greeks are up to something. They have been testing guns and are building two ships for their navy. I have also heard rumors that angels from the heavens have come to help them."

"Angels from the heavens! Are you a fool, my vizier? That is but rumors and lies that the infidel spread to their own people to make them believe in their own invincibility. No matter how many guns they build, we can defeat them. What will two ships do against our entire fleet?"

"You are right, my padishah. Nothing will save them when we decide to move against them."

"I know I am right. The ghazwa (holy war) is our basic duty as it was in the case of our fathers. Constantinopolis is situated in the middle of our domains, protects our enemies and incites them against us. The conquest of that city is therefore essential, to the future and the safety of the Ottoman state."

"Yes my padishah, we must rid us once and for all of the infidel."

"I am ordering a fortress to be built on the European side of the Bosporus, at its narrowest point. Work will start in in a few weeks. We will charge a toll for all ships that transit to and from the black sea. This will further choke any remaining Byzantine trade."

"They will not like it, padishah."

'They will not be able to do anything about it. In a year we will attack the city. Now keep your spies busy."

"Yes, my padishah."

Chapter 4

Constantinopolis, Byzantium
9 April, 1452

Spring was in the air, the weather was finally beginning to warm up. George and all the city's top citizens were at the naval wharf to witness the official launching of the Byzantine navy's latest warships, the Phoenix and the Aghia Sofia each weighing about 95 tons, 75 feet in length and carrying 18, nine pounder naval guns. Green had been commissioned as an ensign in the new Byzantine navy. The patriarch had arrived and after a small liturgy, he blessed the two warships and they both set sail to begin their commissioning training. "Well your majesty we did it! Just as I said we would."

"That we did, George. They are beautiful ships and we are building an even larger ship, a 20 gun corvette which will weigh over 100 tons. We will rule the seas once again.

"Yes sir we will. The Phoenix leaves on her shake down voyage with a cargo of goods for Venice in a few days. I am hoping she comes back with several thousand gold ducats."

"The last ship we sent came back with almost 1000. They loved the telescopes and medical supplies."

"Ensign Green will run a hard bargain if the Venetians want to buy maps. Hopefully, our ambassador returns with a treaty of alliance."

"Let's hope so, general we could use the extra manpower, but I don't have my hopes set on it. Ensign Green was told by the admiral to keep the Venetians off the Phoenix, we don't want them learning anything about her armaments and capabilities."

"That was a good call, sir. We want to have the edge even over our own allies, whom I don't trust at all."

"I'm with you on that. They would double cross us if they thought they would benefit from it."

"I do have some more good news, your majesty. We will soon be able to field an entire infantry regiment armed with muskets and cannon. We have already mounted a few guns on the walls."

"That is excellent. We have made great strides, George. My spies are telling me that the sultan is beginning to make plans for capturing the city."

"That is why I going to the underground base tomorrow to see what other items of value we can find. General Notaras insists on coming along."

"I know we have had this discussion before. Just be careful and get back safely."

Russian Underground Base, 25 Miles East of Constantinopolis
10 April 1452

Just before sunrise, the two Humvees and the duce and a half drove through the city gate, hoping to avoid any Turkish patrols that might be in the area. General Notaras still wearing his cuirass armor, rode with George and except for the drivers, the rest of the troops belonged to Major Petros Tomas, who was in command of the second Humvee. An hour and a half later, they reached the entrance to the mine. The trip had been without incident, since they had used night vision googles to avoid driving with the vehicle lights on. The original camouflage hiding the entrance was still there. They entered the mine and quickly covered the entrance again. George had them wait at the entrance until daybreak, to ensure they had not been followed. Once he was sure of that, they drove deeper into to the mine. Ten minutes later they emerged in the large cavern that housed the former Russian base. Within fifteen minutes Master Sergeant Thompson had the generator up and running, along with the base lighting.

All the Byzantines just stood there in awe, looking at the lights. "What great marvels those machines do, making the night become day. How do those glass bulbs provide light?" General Notaras asked.

"There is a small piece of metal in the glass that gets heated up by a force called electricity, which travels through the wires. Lightning is a form of electricity. The electricity in here is made by that other machine that is running. It is called a generator. It generates electricity."

"How long will it run?"

"Until the fuel it uses runs out. Thompson says the underground tank is huge, maybe a million liters, so it will last a while."

"Thank you for the explanation, George. I guess we will have to get used to these lights. Petros, have your men start searching this place I want it turned inside out."

George took the general inside the command center. Before they left, they had disconnected the computers and turned them all off to ensure they had no other accidents happen. He hoped his people could eventually use the mainframe computers. Master Sergeant Mary Jones could write computer code and possibly get some use out of them.

"So this is the place where it all happened. These are the machines you call computers. Are thy not like your laptops and tablets?"

"Yes, sir this is the place. These are computers, but very old ones. The ones we have from my time period are millions of times faster. Even our laptops are a thousand times faster. We disconnected the machines, so nothing happens again when we turn on the electricity."

"I can see how mankind has gone a long way in 500 years, but nothing has really changed. With all your inventions and computers, war still exists and you can destroy all life on earth with your super bombs."

"Yes sir, but we also have done great scientific progress. We travelled to the moon and sent machines looking for life on mars, but have found none so far. We've also sent probes to all the other planets in our solar system but found nothing there either. We have found ice covered seas on the moons of Jupiter and Saturn. I am sure there is life out there and one day we will make contact and man-kind will travel to the stars. Unfortunately, here on earth, we were still fighting religious war between Christians and Moslems even in my time. We have gone a long way but have not learned anything from the past."

"That does not surprise me my friend. So what else is in here?"

"Let's take a look."

George took the general around and showed him the barracks, the machine shops and garages. Inside one of the garages he found an old Soviet BMP 1 which looked like it had seen better days. It needed a lot of work before it could run. The engine compartment was open and it looked that someone had been doing work on it. If they could get it running they could almost defeat any army with it. Its 73mm cannon could destroy any city gate and its machine gun could mow down infantry. Stacked in the back where cases of shells and machine gun ammo. "What is that? It looks like a war machine."

"Yes, it is general. It is called a BMP one. It's a Russian armored fighting machine with small cannon on it and it also holds eight soldiers. If we could get that running we could take any city with it and almost single handedly defeat any Ottoman attack."

The general eyes lit up, "we need this machine George, for our survival."

"We will try, sir. It's been sitting her for 25 years." George took the IPAD out of his pocket and snapped a couple of pictures to show the emperor.

George radioed Staff Sergeant Capone who came over and examined the armored vehicle. "I probably could get it running sir, but would need a few weeks to take the engine apart. Almost everything mechanical on it needs re-lubing after 25 years of standing still. Probably two months till its running."

"Consider this to be your project. I will get you some help."

"Okay, sir. I will do my best. We also found a cave where tens of thousands bats live. There are hundreds, if not thousands of pounds of bat dung just lying around on the ground. That is almost pure potassium nitrate which we can use for gun powder."

"One more reason to secure this cave, general Notaras."

"You are right George, but we don't want to wake the hornet's nest just yet."

"These shops will prove vital in manufacturing steam engines to power our ships and factories and most of all if we are to attempt reloading ammunition. We will need steam if we want to visit the Americas and secure the Aztec gold."

George heard his call sign on the radio, it was Sergeant Davis. He had found something and was asking the two officers to come to his location. They walked to the east end of the base and found him. Davis had found a padlocked metal door. "I don't know what's in there, but whatever it is, it's locked inside and there is a sign with Russian writing. I think it says, "Keep flame making devises out."

"We need to open it."

"Those locks are very thick, sir."

"There is Acetylene cutting torches inside the machine shop. I remember from my metal shop days how to use one."

"What do you think is in there, George?"

"Probably more ammunition and explosives, sir. We will know more when I cut the locks."

Twenty minutes later George had cut through the bottom lock and was ready to open the door. He pushed down the handle and pushed the door open. He turned the light switch and was greeted with a wealth of goodies. The room was 10 by 20 feet and was full of weapons and ammo. Weapons racks lined the walls full of AK47s and Makarov pistols, along with thousands of rounds in filled magazines. Two Soviet 81mm light mortars were also sitting on the armory floor along with several boxes of mortar shells. Next to those were two 12.7 mm DShK heavy machine guns with crates of ammo also stacked against the wall.

"We hit the jackpot, Davis! There are even another couple of crates of RPGs, hand grenades and boxes of 7.62mm ammo."

"I've found more ammo in other areas of the base for the AK47s and Nagants. I also found a few crates of 223 cal. I think they must have either captured it from the Mujahedeen or supplied their allies with it. I also found a metal box containing all sorts of seeds, such as corn, tomatoes and zucchini"

"We can always use that. There was no corn or tomatoes in this era in Europe."

"Wow, no popcorn!"

So far General Notaras had not said a word; he just in looked on and said a silent prayer to the virgin, thanking her for all these gifts that would save his beloved city. "So what are all these other weapons, George?"

"Those two tubes are 81mm mortars, sir. They can lob an explosive bomb almost two miles. The large machine guns can shoot very large bullets over two kilometers, plus we just secured enough weapons and ammo for another ranger company."

"That is wonderful news we should load most of this into your transport machine and take it back to the City"

"We will leave tonight under cover of darkness. Thompson, do you think you can rig something to use the current from the batteries, instead of constantly running the generator and burning up our diesel fuel?"

"I think I can rig a switch."

"Sergeant Capone, what's the possibility of stretching the diesel fuel we have, if we mix it with 10% olive oil?"

"It should work, sir. Actually we can go to 20% bio diesel blend in the winter to 40% blend in summer. Used, but filtered olive oil will work the best. We will need two tanks to ensure the system works better on the vehicles. We will start the vehicle up with regular diesel and then switch over."

"Can you convert the vehicles we got? We need to stretch the fuel we have."

"Yes, but I need the tools that are here in the machine shops to do it."

"We will start collecting the used cooking oil of our citizens immediately and filter it, General Notaras said.

"You can use the tools that are here in the base for that project. We will bring the filtered oil here to mix it. I also need you to start working on the BMP, it may be our salvation. I will be back in a couple of days. We'll leave you the one Humvee and a fire team for security."

"Sure thing, sir."

"Let's start loading the truck so we can get on our way."

Constantinopolis
12 May 1453

A few weeks later spring was in full force, flowers were beginning to blossom and the days were now much longer. The early May morning sun warmed the parade ground. George was inspecting the new ranger company which had been armed with the AK47s they had brought back from the underground base. He was talking to one of the officers when one of the Imperial Guards on a horse came looking for him.

The man dismounted and came running up to George. "Sir, the emperor is requesting your immediate presence."

"Please take me to him."

"Follow me, sir." They walked to the stable where George took a horse and they rode to the city walls facing the Bosporus. Fifteen minutes later they arrived at the emperor's location. George dismounted and climbed the stairs up to the walls were the emperor was gazing out over the waters of the Bosporus with a pair of binoculars.

"You sent for me, your majesty?"

"The Ottoman fleet has sailed in the Bosporus. They have begun building a fort on the European side of the straits, as the Sultan had promised to do." George took the glasses and peered through them. He noticed several war galleys, troops and supply ships.

"They sure are, just as history says they did. They built a fort and charged a toll for ships to pass or they were blown out of the water by the large guns which they will install. We can't let them strangle us like that. I can remove them."

"We can't afford to antagonize them just yet, general. We need more cannons and muskets. The armory is producing 100 muskets a month and that may expand up to 150 very soon. So far we only have a couple of hundred. Your armored fighting machine is not ready and we need a larger navy. Fortunately, another corvette the Holy Trinity will be lunched within a week, with eighteen 12 pounders as armament. I was told that we may even have a few 18 pounder cannon that can shoot explosive shells soon. I don't care as much about the Bosporus as I care about the Sea of Marmara. That is our only life line to the open sea and trade. It may restrict Trebizond but they are also ramping up their production of weapons and ships. So far they have completed two Corvettes and two more are being built."

"Yes, your majesty we will wait as you suggest."

"I don't want to wait either, but we must be ready. I am sick and tired of being humiliated by that young upstart calling himself the sultan. They must not find out about our capabilities just yet. Our trade missions brought back 4000 gold ducats and more will be forthcoming. That is enough to pay our armies and build more cannon and ships. This city is slowly coming back to life we have added over 3000 new residents, many of them craftsmen and scholars."

"We are making good progress."

"Once we attack the fort it may likely lead to war."

"You are right your majesty. I also heard the Venetians are interested in our maps. That will cost them a king's ransom. We should charge 10,000 ducats, plus an alliance."

"They are considering it George. I offered them a couple of islands if they commit. I do want Crete back though."

"You are the politician here your majesty, just know they will try to screw us if they can. The Republic of Venice lasted till 1798, until a then famous French general conquered it. They do take Crete in my history and the Ottomans take it from them sometime in the 1600s and hold it till 1898."

"George, I value your opinion. Ever since you came to us you have proved to be a loyal advisor and a friend to me. You have given us so much and asked for nothing in return. You are like a brother to me. Please call me Constantine when we are alone."

"I am honored, sir. You will always have my loyalty and that of my soldiers. You are an honest man and a fair ruler. History had judged you as such and now I have the privilege to see it with my own eyes. All I ask of you is to return Byzantium to its' rightful glory."

"With your help, we may just do that George, after we have dealt with the Ottoman threat. I do plan to take our lands back. The first city we will take back is Andrianoupolis or Edirne as the Turk calls it."

"We will soon, have a powerful navy to challenge our enemies. Ensign Green has another ship on the drawing boards called a Frigate. It carries double the amount of guns and it will rule the seas. With it we can go to the Americas. We are also working on a steam engine but that will take a bit more time."

"Hopefully, god will give us the time. With an engine on our warships we will not always need the wind."

"On another subject, I remember from the history books that you were looking for a wife. It will be a good thing for the city to have a royal wedding and another ally and you do need an heir. We can't afford any more in fighting and civil wars."

"You are right about that, general. There is a Bulgarian princes available for marriage and I am thinking about it. From her portraits, she looks attractive. I may send a mission there and ask for her hand."

George began to laugh. "What is so funny about me sending for a bride?"

"Not you Constantine. In my time some men used to order brides using a computer from different merchants. They too posted pictures; unfortunately they did not always get what was advertised. Sometimes the bride was three times the size of what she looked like in the picture."

The emperor also began to laugh. "Oh, now I do understand. What about you and the good doctor?"

"I have too many things going on and a future war to fight. But I will think about it. She is a good woman."

"That she is and a beautiful one."

"Let's get back to war planning, sir. We will have to deal with this fort once it's built. If we have the BMP here it would be a plus. Its cannon will rip them to shreds but we must conserve its limited supply of ammo. Sergeant Capone has made a lot of progress; he thinks the vehicle will be ready in a couple of more weeks."

"That would be excellent. I would not worry on taking on the sultan if we had it here."

"The fuel project is also going very well. We have already doubled our fuel supply. With strict conservation, it may last a few years. The craftsmen and scribes you had sent to assist have proven invaluable. The learned quickly are taking notes and are coming out with their own patents. Hopefully we will have a running steam engine by end of the year. I just hope we keep the secrecy around it. The more people knowing about it the easier it can get compromised. We will eventually have to build a port there one day to make transport easier."

"That Russian base was a godsend to this city. The craftsmen and scribes have all been sworn to secrecy under pain of death."

"It is a god send to all of us. Even for my people. We keep finding more things such as weapons and bullets which we need. Most of all is its tools and shops which will help us develop more weapons and other machinery. Sooner or later the Ottomans will find out about the base and we must be prepared to defend it at all costs!"

"What we need to do is to build a fortress around it, with heavy cannons and machine guns to protect it. Unfortunately, we don't have the manpower and equipment to do that yet. We will blow it up first before we let the Ottomans take it."

"I am coming with you on the next trip. That is an Imperial command."

"But your majesty, what will happen if the Turks capture you?"

"They will capture you too, so we will ensure that will not happen. Besides, General Notaras will stay here. He can take my place."

"If you insist, you can come along. We are leaving tomorrow night with a shipment of supplies and musket barrels for the workshops."

"I will be ready."

That night while lying in bed with Anna next to him, he told her that the emperor was thinking about getting married to Bulgarian princes. She too thought that it was a great idea. "I think we would make pretty babies, Anna."

Anna was surprised she sat up on the bed the moon light reflecting off her large breasts. "George is that a proposal?"

"Yes, but after the Ottoman threat is eliminated. I don't want to leave you as a widow."

"I love you George and I will gladly become your wife and have your children. Now let's practice making babies.

Russian Underground Base, 25 Miles West of the City
13 May 1452

The following night, George with the emperor in tow, set out for the mine. The emperor was dressed in a set of tan BDUs and a steel pot helmet that had been designed by Sergeant Janie

Harris. He wore a leather gun belt with the Makarov pistol strapped to his side. He sported the rank of a five star general on a pair of epaulets on his shoulders and George, wore the rank of a three star. The two vehicle convoy reached the mine entrance just before day break. They were met there by the on duty security team who would now be relieved by the new team and would return to the city. They were extremeley surprised when they saw who George had brought with him. They all jumped to attention when the two officers got out of the Humvee.

"At ease men. How's it been going here?" The emperor asked.

"We've seen several Ottoman patrols ride by in the distance, but they have not come this way, your majesty."

"Interesting, they are coming closer to the city. Probably probing and flexing their muscle."

"I suspect so. Mehmet's plans are coming into fruition. Well let's go down. You men cover the entrance."

An hour later, after having breakfast at the small dining facility, George gave the emperor a guided tour of the base. Constantine was amazed at the size of the underground facility, but it was the lights that fascinated him the most. They walked into the workshop where the BMP was being refurbished. George turned the lights on.

"So this is the war machine from the future. It is massive."

"There are many more fighting machines that are much larger. They are called tanks. They were fist used in 1917 during World War one. They had large mounted cannon for destroying other armored fighting machines.

"How can a thing this big ever be stopped?"

"By another armored fighting vehicle or one of the RPGs we have."

"In this age nothing can stop it. With its cannon it can knock down walls and defeat any army."

"It can until its ammunition is gone. Then it's just a big piece of metal."

"That is true. So it must be used wisely and decisively."

"Good morning, gentlemen."

"Sergeant Capone I am promoting you to lieutenant for the excellent work you are doing here."

"Thank you, your majesty."

"How long before this beast is ready?"

"In a couple of weeks, she will be ready, sir."

"That is good to hear."

"How are the rifle barrels going? George asked.

"We have another 50 ready. I think we can start building flintlock rifles very soon, sir."

"That is good to know. I would rather we manufacture some flintlocks pistols for our cavalry first."

"We could do it rather quickly, if we have flints."

"Give me some dimensions and I will get you flints."

"How is Lieutenant Burns steam project going?" It's been a couple of weeks since I was here."

"He's getting there, general. It's just that the poor quality of the metal he is using can cause a boiler explosion. You know he was only a semester short on graduating as a mechanical engineer from Caltech."

"I knew he had gone to collage but not Caltech. I can't believe he left that close to a degree. Let's go see his workshop, your majesty. He should be up by now."

George and the emperor walked into the Lieutenant Burn's workshop. They could smell burning wood. A couple of the craftsmen were adding wood into a fire box under a large metal cauldron. They all stopped what they were doing and came to attention when they noticed George and the emperor walking in. "Continue on gentlemen

I am over here, sir."

Burns got out from behind the contraption. There was oil on his face and hands. "I'm here sir. Oh, your majesty, what a surprise!"

"What do you have here, lieutenant?"

"It's the beginnings of a steam engine, your majesty."

"Does it work?"

"Most of the time, if the pressure does not blow a valve. Please stand back for your safety. She is building up pressure. The quality of the cast iron needs some improving but I solved the bursting boiler problems by riveting it together. Now let's see what she does."

Burns grabbed a rag went up to the machine and turned a couple of valves. There was a hiss and the engine came to life. The steam began to move the piston rods up and down. "She's working. Let's see how long she goes for before she breaks down. Ten hours is the record. I do believe we may have a winner here."

"How long before we have a working model on a ship? George asked"

"You do realize, sir that the ships engine will be at least three times larger than this and a crew will have to be trained to use and maintain the engine, but I think by the end of the year or even possibly even a lot sooner. If I get some of the kinks out, we should have a working steamship engine very soon."

"Imagine a ship that does not need the wind. She could destroy a fleet in a dead calm."

"That is true your majesty. She may be a bit slower than under full sail, but she will keep moving. Just imagine when we build an iron clad, an armored ship."

"Just like the ones I saw on the IPAD?"

"Not exactly your majesty, but she would be protected from any cannon of this period, but that is at least a few years away," George said.

"We may have to machine the pistons and O rings here and have them delivered to the ship yard, probably the boiler too. It may barely fit in the duce and a half. In the future we must build steam engines in the city to power lathes."

"You are right, but first things first. If we can build a few steam gunboats we can wreak havoc on the Ottoman fleet. So keep working on the engine, we could use an operating model a lot sooner."

"Yes sir. This engine might turn out be the one."

"Well keep working on it. I'm sure a mechanical engineer from Caltech can make it work."

"I don't have the degree."

"Why didn't you graduate?"

"I had a fall out with my dad and he threatened to cut me off. I called his bluff and he did. So I joined the air force. I had an assignment back to Vandenberg Air force base; the air force was going to send me back to school to finish my degree and become an officer."

"I'm glad you're here. Finish this engine and the emperor will bestow the degree to you. Once this is over you can teach future engineers, in the new military academy we will open."

"I would love to do that, sir."

"Keep that steam engine running and you may get there sooner than you think.

"I will do my best, gentlemen."

"Ready for some coffee, your majesty?"

"Yes, I really like that drink."

"Thank the Russians for leaving us several hundred cans of coffee. Coffees doesn't come to Europe from Ethiopia for another 200 years or so."

"Oh, I meant to ask what is a mechanical engineer and a degree.

"The lieutenant went to a university and studied how to build machines, engines and other mechanical things. Once a person completes all the necessary lessons they give him a diploma or degree saying he completed his theoretical training."

"Oh I understand now. We can use his valuable knowledge to teach others."

"We will do just that, in the new military academy we must open to train professional officers who will also learn engineering and sciences once the Ottoman threat goes away."

"That is an excellent proposal, George. I will think about that."

For the rest of the day George and the emperor toured the facility. The more the emperor saw the more he believed that it was divine intervention that brought George and his people to Constantinopolis. It was the miracle that they had all prayed for to save the city. By late evening they were ready to return to the city. They loaded the truck with over 50 gun barrels and several barrels of bat dung and headed to the mine entrance. True to his word Lieutenant Burns still had the engine running without any major problems.

When they reached the entrance, George stopped and got out as the sentries cleared the opening. "Be careful, sir. Several Ottoman Sipahi Calvary patrols transited the area earlier this evening just before sun down."

"Thanks we'll keep an eye out for them."

Hassan and his friend Nevzat were siting by the fire sipping hot Tsai (tea) trying to keep the morning chill out. The sky was clear and the moon full. They were part of a 30 man Sipahi patrol encroaching into Byzantine territory. They had departed Edirne a few days ago to scout out the area they were camping in. Rumors had reached Edirne of strange noises that could be heard in the area during the night and of large tracks in the ground that may have been made by very large wagons. They had seen some of the tracks but no sign of horse or oxen tracks.

The two men covered themselves with their blankets and threw more wood into the fire. In a couple of hours it would be daybreak and their guard shift would be over.

"Hassan, I still think this could be the work of demons or Djinn. (Genies) How is it possible for something to leave those tracks on the ground with no animal tracks?"

"I don't know my friend. This place is cursed. Even the infidels that live around here are frightened out of their wits. They lock themselves in their homes at night and talk about demons that travel around here in the night looking for souls to take."

"Schuss, I hear something. It's coming this way!"

"I hear it to. It's coming closer!"

"Hurry and wake everyone. We are being attacked by demons, to arms to arms!"

The camp quickly awake and the men grabbed their weapons and those that could their horses. They all could hear the noise getting louder and coming ever closer. They were all scared that the demons had awakened and were coming to take them to hell. Many of them said a quick prayer for the prophet to watch over them.

"They are almost here. I see the beasts," their officer shouted.

"Allah, Akbar!" With the cry god is great they released their arrows at the coming demons.

The two vehicle convoy had left the mine and was driving with their lights out at a sedate 15 miles an hour through the countryside. The drivers using their night vision goggles to see. George and the emperor were sipping coffee out of a paper cup, when the machine gunner fell into the Humvee with an arrow through his neck. The vehicle having been struck by almost a dozen arrows was now under attack by the rush of charging horsemen.

"Were under attack by Sipahi Calvary, this vehicle is armored but not the truck. Somebody get on that machine gun."

"The emperor jumped up into the cupola."

"Your majesty, get down!" George yelled, worried about the emperor's safety.

The quiet night was rent asunder by the chattering of the M240B machine gun. "Step on it! Get us out of here. George saw one of the riders galloping towards the vehicle. Before he could react the rider jumped on the moving Humvee. Two quick pistol shots sounded out in rapid succession causing the Sipahi to fall off. Another burst of machine gun fire forced the remaining riders to turn around and retreat. A few minutes later the surviving Sipahi were back at their campsite.

"I told you Hassan, those things were demons. Did you see the fire they were spitting out killing men with such ease?"

"You were right, Nevzat. May Allah protect us and save the souls of those lost this night."

After a couple of minutes of fast driving they had left the Ottomans behind them. The emperor dropped down from the machine gun cupola, back into the vehicle. "That was very exciting. That gun can really spit out bullets."

"You are bleeding,"

"Never mind me, how is Stavros?"

"He didn't make it, your majesty."

"God rest his soul. He was one of my Imperial Guards."

"Let me see your arm, sir," George said as he broke out the

first aid kit.

"It's just a flesh wound. He got a chance to swing his sword before I shot him."

"You could have been killed!"

"We all could have been killed, but we were not. It was poor Stavros's time to meet his maker."

"Let me see the arm please."

"If you insist."

"That is a deep gash. It will need a few stiches and cleaning out so it will not get infected. We will stop by the hospital when we get back."

"Okay, general."

Thirty minutes later they were let through the city gates as the sun was beginning to rise. After taking care of their casualty and seeing to the unloading of the truck and their gear, George and the emperor grabbed a horse and road to the hospital followed by two of the emperor's body guards. When they arrived, they found Sergeant Mary Jones a pretty brunet in her mid-twenties, on duty. She was very surprised to see both George and the emperor there, until she noticed the bloody bandage on the emperor's arm. "Your majesty you're hurt!"

"It's just a scratch."

"Let me take you inside the treatment room. You other gentlemen can wait here."

Both George and the body guards began to follow. "You heard the young lady. Wait here," he said with a sly grin.

"Twenty-five minutes later, they both emerged from the treatment room. "Now your majesty, please don't use the arm for a few days, we don't want you ripping any of the stiches. Drink the penicillin tea in the vials every four to six hours. You will need to change the bandages tonight. I will come by the palace to change them for you."

"Thank you, Mary."

After they left the hospital George turned to the emperor.

"Mary?"

"Yes, a very nice young lady, she really took good care of me. She will even come by the palace to personally change my dressings."

"A very pretty young lady."

"Yes, that too."

"Let's get back, sir. I need to get a couple of hours of sleep. I am exhausted after last night's excitement."

Edirne, Sultan's Palace
14 May 1452

The young sultan listened to the story his commander of the Sipahi was relating to him and his two viziers. According to his story, the patrol that had recently been in an area located 30 miles east of Constantinopolis, when it had been attacked in the middle of the night by either demons or Djinn. The demons were spitting fire that killed many of the men that tried to attack them.

"I am supposed to believe this? Demons or Djinn killed ten men?"

"My padishah everyone swears to this. These were experienced warriors. They brought back one of the wounded who died. He had several holes in him."

"This must be some Byzantine trick. Demons and Djinn? Have their priests conjured up demons to protect them?" Zaganos Pasha said.

"I don't care what they have protecting them. I will destroy them and have Constantine's head on a pike!"

"Yes, my padishah."

"I want you to increase our preparations to attack the city.

April of next year is too late. I want this done sooner."

"But it will be winter."

"I don't care! My soldiers will then have to fight harder to defeat the infidel sooner. The more time we give them the more they prepare."

"I will do as you ask."

Chapter 5

Constantinopolis, Byzantium
June 15, 1452

Summer was almost there; the weather was getting hotter and the days much longer. True to his word, Lieutenant Burns had refurbished the BMP 1 and made it operational. The armored fighting vehicle (AFV) had been driven to Constantinopolis and hidden in the palace stables from prying eyes. Burns had also perfected a working model steam engine to be installed in the first gunboat to be launched by July, which only was a couple of weeks away. The ship would be 80 feet long and mount 18 guns, two shell firing eighteen pounders, one on the bow and the other in the stern and the rest would be twelve pounder cannons that could blow any ship of the day out of the water. Even the emperor was now a much happier man, having developed a relationship with Master Sergeant Mary Jones and now given the hope that his city would survive.

George was in his office which was located in the palace reviewing the latest military inventory and weapons projections, with General Notaras the chief of staff. "Sir we are really in good shape. With every month that goes by we are adding a ship to the navy and we now have two companies of musketeers and 100 Calvary armed with flintlock pistols and sabers. We will have another company by the end of the month and another 100 pistols manufactured. We are building an artillery corps, which will have over 50 heavy guns by the end of the summer. By the end of this month, we will have launched our fist steam powered gunboat, the Niki (victory)."

"You and your people have done miracles, George. We have a regiment trained and equipped with muskets and a ranger unit armed with AK47s. By the end of July we will have another regiment. We have even dispatched craftsmen with a few crates of muskets and a couple of nine pounders to our Byzantine brothers in the Moorea, (Peloponnese, Greece) with instructions on how to build them."

"That is great news, sir."

"The army has grown to over 6000 full time men and recruits are joining daily. We have trained several thousand reserves and the navy has grown to over 1000 trained sailors and, based on your suggestions we are beginning to train marines. Each ship will have a 20 man marine contingent. This city has come back to life, George. We have had several thousand new residents arrive in the last couple of months, many of them merchants, which also helped our tax base grow."

"Sir, we brought the knowledge, you helped implement it. Your men are now training the new recruits, after we showed them how. You are also making all this happen. At this point I do believe we can hold this city, especially with that fighting vehicle we now have. The Ottomans are still very dangerous, they have large navy that can cut our supply lines. "

"We have three ship yards and three foundries building ships and casting cannon seven days a week. We can't build any faster we have a shortage of trained manpower.

"Maybe we can recruit some ship builders from the islands, like Limnos?"

"That island is a Byzantine possession and we should start showing the flag. Maybe we can send the Holy Trinity and the Phoenix there. I'll talk to the admiral."

"Good idea, sir. I want to go along on that mission. It will also be a reconnaissance."

"I hate to risk you, but you are right. We need to reconnoiter the straights and the Aegean."

"We should also start garrisoning some of our outlaying towns to protect our populations, sir."

"Yes, we must do that very soon. Ottoman patrols have been encroaching closer to the city. One of our cavalry patrols had an encounter with a Sipahi cavalry patrol, which left three of the enemy dead. The pistols were a big surprise."

"Hopefully, they learned a lesson."

"I doubt that. I learned from my spies that the sultan is moving up his preparations to attack us."

"I feared that. Our arrival here is changing the time line."

"We will do what we must, to prepare our defenses. Our destiny is in god's hands."

"We need more land and a larger population, but we are not quite ready to confront him head on. Soon, very soon, we will be. Ready."

Northeast Aegean Sea
29 June 1452

A couple of week later, George was standing on the deck of the 20 gun flagship, Aghia Helene, enjoying the cool sea breeze against his face. He could see the Phoenix under the command of recently promoted Lieutenant Green, scouting several miles ahead. They had transited through the straits during the night without incident. The two corvettes averaged over nine knots, making it difficult for the three galleasses and a supply ship to keep up with them. The Corvette's captain had his gun crews run out their guns, as George and the admiral watched on. "I hope their gunnery is as good as their speed to general quarters."

"They are very good, Captain, Lieutenant Speliotis, has trained his crew very well in the art of gunnery."

"Let's hope we won't have to test it on this voyage."

"No Turkish vessel can take this ship on and survive without serious damage."

"But they can attack in numbers and overwhelm the ship. If they manage to grapple we will have problems."

"I am glad we now have 20 naval marines on board with muskets and pistols."

"They will help in a difficult situation but not under impossible odds. Our advantage is speed and our guns, admiral."

"You need to forget your old ways of combat. We must now keep the enemy at bay and pound him to bits with our guns. That is the future of naval warfare. When they have been damaged enough, then you can board."

"You are correct about that, George. It will take a bit getting used to."

"We will all have to learn real fast as the clouds of war approach."

"With the launching of the steam gunboat Niki, we hold the naval advantage. We need to still keep that ship a secret."

"For the moment, her commander is only allowed to light her boiler when they are out in the Sea of Marmara. They leave with their sails and return the same way. Her top speed has been eight knots."

"That is fantastic!"

"Our future warships will be even faster, as the engines improve and we can develop screw propulsion. But it will be a while for that."

The island of Limnos soon came to view, an hour and a half later they dropped anchor in Moudros bay in front of a large fortress that dominated the anchorage. Both George the admiral and an escort of ten marines were rowed to the beach were they were met by the forts' commander, an older Byzantine officer, dressed in ceremonial armor along with his honor guard. He introduced himself to the two senior officers. "I am Tagmatarchis (Major) Andronikos."

"I am Admiral Laskaris and this is General Mavrakis."

"We are very pleased to see you. We have not seen a Byzantine warship here in ages. Now we see a fleet with strange looking ships and soldiers armed with even stranger weapons. I thought we were abandoned here to our fates."

"Times are changing. Better days are ahead for Byzantium. We have brought you supplies, money you are owed in back pay and new weapons."

"What type of new weapons, sir?"

"We brought you, firearms, cannon, ammunition, two officers and 30 troops to reinforce you and man the guns. They will also instruct you on the use and maintenance of these weapons and the new structure of the Byzantine army and navy. We will be sending more men and supplies here. With heavy guns installed, this fortress can never be taken without a prolonged siege. You are also being promoted to lieutenant colonel. The new army rank structure will be explained to you."

The garrison commander was stunned. The last time he was in the city several years ago the army was almost nonexistent and could not even man the walls. Well, he would not look a gift horse in the mouth. "Thank you! Please come up to the fort for some food and refreshments. I have been remiss of my hospitality, gentlemen."

"Thank you," George said. "We also have a couple of other things to discuss with you."

"Why of course, gentlemen."

George and the admiral were given mounts and they accompanied the garrison commander to the fort. When they reached the top of fortress, George could view the entire bay. With a few 18 pounders they could blow any ship out of the water. The fort could easily be held with cannon if garrisoned and properly provisioned. The commander took both men inside and gave them fruits to eat and wine to drink. Both men brought him up to speed on the future Ottoman attack. His island would be fortified and used as a naval base by the Byzantine fleet, once the war with the Ottomans began. When the major was asked for shipwrights and craftsmen, he was able to recommend several of the island's ship builders and metal workers to the two men.

After unloading the cannons at the dock, it had taken several days of hard work even with the help of the local population to haul the five heavy two ton, 18 pounder guns up to the fort and install them on the walls facing the bay. The five, nine pounders were easier to haul up since they weighed a lot less. Those were installed facing the land approaches to the fort. With canister rounds they could decimate any enemy infantry attacking from land. When they had finally finished, the islanders held a feast for the crews, happy that once again they were being protected by the Byzantine state.

The next morning the fleet was back out to sea heading for the entrance to the Dardanelles and the Sea of Marmara. The two corvettes were running with reduced sail trying to keep pace with the rest of the convoy. George was on the quarter-deck with the admiral scanning the horizon. "See anything interesting, general?"

"Not at the moment, admiral."

"The Turk must know we are here. We were seen by enough fishing boats on the way over."

"I'm sure they know we're here. The question is will they respond? We are still technically at peace with them."

"They've been much more aggressive lately on land. This is a great spot for them to set an ambush."

"You know admiral, in my time line; 450 years from now, two large naval battles were fought here between the Royal Hellenic navy and the Ottoman fleet. Armored battleships hurled large explosives shells at each other from many miles away. The Hellenic navy was victorious in both these actions. It defeated a superior Ottoman force which gave them control of the Aegean and enabled Greece to be victorious in the Balkan wars and capture enough territory to double her size."

"It's very interesting that the Ottoman scourge remained as a power all those years."

"We could thank the European great powers, France and England for that. They used the Ottomans as a block to prevent the Russians from coming down into the Mediterranean. Had it not been for that reason, the Ottomans would have collapsed much earlier."

"Hopefully, that does not happen in this timeline. We are already changing the future."

"That is very true, sir. Even this voyage never happened in my time. This trip was very productive. We have four shipwrights with us and several metal craftsmen. We even fortified the island.

"Sail, ho."

George put his binoculars to his eyes and looked to the direction the lookout was pointing to. "I count ten sails." He handed his binoculars to the admiral.

"It's the Ottomans and they are out. Signal the fleet, prepare for battle. Do not fire unless fired upon first."

Within thirty minutes the distance had closed to less than a mile. The Ottoman flotilla had taken battle positions. The wind was coming out of the west North West. 'Signal the fleet to turn three points to the south. If they insist on a battle they will have it."

Ten minutes later, the Ottoman commander thinking that the Byzantines were trying to escape, dispatched five of his galleys to attack the corvettes. "It looks like we are not going to avoid the engagement, admiral."

Two galleys each broke off and headed for the Aghia Helene, the other two headed for the Phoenix. "They will attack us on each side as they try to overwhelm our defenses. They will be in for a real surprise," the admiral said. The rest of the Ottoman fleet headed for the transport and the galleasses.

"Here they come, prepare to fire on my command," the ship's captain yelled to his gun captains.

The two Turkish galleys were almost perpendicular to the Aghia Helene and began closing in. Several arrows were shot towards the Byzantine ships, but they were still out of effective bow range.

"Fire!" The ten 12 pounders on each side of the ship belched flame and death. When the smoke cleared the two galleys had been dismasted and smashed to bits. A minute later the same happened to the ones that attacked the Phoenix.

The other galley that had been standing by was now coming at the nimble Corvette at full speed trying to ram, but the corvette had the wind with her. She remained at a safe distance and quickly holed the enemy ship below the waterline with a well-placed shot. "She's done for. Let's go help the galleasses," the admiral commanded.

George was viewing the battle through his binoculars. The Phoenix was well ahead and soon would be in the fray. The Byzantine galleasses despite their guns were having a difficult time, outnumbered two to one, but they were dishing out much more than they were taking.

Captain, head for the enemy galley on the right, she is flying the admirals flag. We'll take her with some old fashion fighting tactics. Send the marines to the tops and prepare to board her."

"Aye, Aye sir."

George watched through his glasses as the Phoenix joined the fray, her guns blasting one of the Ottoman galleys that had latched on to one of the byzantine galleasses. "Load with canister and aim for her decks," The Aghia Helene's captain commanded.

A few minutes later, the Aghia Helene neared the Ottoman admiral's ship. Cross bolts began flying towards them from the enemy galley, one striking a sailor in the shoulder. "Prepare to fire and drop the sails on my command," her captain ordered.

"On the up roll, fire!" The entire starboard side erupted in in smoke and fire as the guns belched out over a thousand musket balls, scything down the Turkish crewmen by the dozens.

"Now launch the grappling hooks." Several of the sailors threw the grappling hooks and pulled the ship closer to the galley, whose scuppers now began to run red with blood.

"Prepare to board her. I want the admiral alive, "The Byzantine commander yelled out to the crew.

Several boarding planks went over the sides onto the enemy galley. "On them men!"

With a yell the Byzantine sailors boarded the enemy ship. George had gone to his cabin and picked up his M4 and followed the admiral who was holding his Makarov pistol in one hand and a sword in another. The enemy crew though decimated by the canister rounds and being shot at from the marines on the Corvettes rigging, still put up a fight. Both George and the admiral had to shoot several of the enemy soldiers before they reached the quarter deck where the Ottoman admiral was being defended by the surviving crew members. George noticed that the enemy officer was sitting down, wounded by a musket ball in the leg.

"Surrender, it's over, no need to spill more blood," Admiral Laskaris cried out in Turkish and Greek.

The ship's captain looked at the admiral who nodded his head, and then he dropped his sword which was followed in turn by the rest of his crew. The Aghia Helene's sailors and marines cheered there victory as they cut down the Ottoman ensign. When the remaining enemy ships saw this they too gave up the fight.

"I am admiral Baltaouglu; You Rum will pay for this dearly when the sultan finds out. Let us go and we may excuse this error of judgement on your part.""

"You attacked us. I'm sure the sultan will have your head for this defeat."

"I have never in my life seen a ship can cause so much destruction."

"Sir, come quick and see what we've found in their hold."

Both George and admiral Laskaris saw the look of dread on the enemy commander's face. After giving orders to treat the wounded and round up the prisoners both men walked down into the hold where much to their amazement they saw chests filled with gold and jewels. "There must be a king's ransom here," the admiral said.

"You're right. There must be at least 100,000 gold pieces in here. What a great addition to the treasury. The sultan will be furious when he finds out."

"We best get back under way admiral. If anyone saw this action they could be on their way to report it back to the Ottomans."

"You are correct, general. I want this gold moved over to the flag ship immediately. We need to sort out the damage and get under way again as quickly as possible."

A few hours later they were underway. Only five of the enemy ships were still seaworthy after the battle. The rest had been either sunk or scuttled. Many of the crews on the captured galleys were Christian slaves and immediately joined the Byzantines. The Byzantine flotilla had lost 30 men and over 50 wounded mainly on the galleasses. They Ottomans had over 400 killed and 200 wounded many of those seriously and many would die enroute, before they reached Constantinopolis. Fortunately for the Byzantines, no one had seen the action and by next morning they were well into the Sea of Marmara, having passed through the straits in the late evening without incident.

George was on the forecastle viewing the horizon with his binoculars. He could barely make out the sails of the Phoenix as she sped ahead to give the news of the naval battle and victory to headquarters. This would also ensure that they were met by ambulances at the wharf, to transport the wounded to the hospital. He heard footsteps and turned. "Good morning admiral."

"Good morning, general. We are almost home. This victory will be a great morale boost to the city. It's been a long time since Byzantium celebrated a naval victory. The ships performed flawlessly, as did their gun crews."

"Lieutenant Green did it, sir along with our well trained crews."

"Yes, his ship designs and the superior training, along with our new guns will ensure us victory!

"With the new steamship and another being built along with a frigate, should guarantee us naval superiority in the entire Mediterranean. This battle proved beyond a doubt, what superior naval power can do."

"I just spoke with Admiral Baltaouglu, he had the musket

ball removed from his leg and is resting in my cabin. It has finally dawned on him, that the sultan would have him immediately executed for the loss of the gold. He has openly declared his alliance for the emperor. His knowledge of the sultan's plans which he said he willingly will volunteer to us to prove his new found loyalty may prove very valuable."

"I'm sure it will, admiral. He knows he is a dead man if the sultan gets his hands on him. So now he throws in with us as does his captain.

"They may prove to be valuable assets. I will take him to my staff. We will have to be much more careful now. The sultan will be furious and want his gold back."

"Did he say what the gold was for?"

"They were going to Egypt to try and buy an alliance with the Mamelukes and use them against the Venetians."

Three hours later the ships had reached the city and docked in the Golden horn area just outside of the eastern walls, where the new naval base was being constructed. They were all surprised when they were met by crowds of people there we wanted to celebrate a much needed victory. A dozen horse pulled ambulances also lined the docks to take off the wounded. George spotted the emperor, the patriarch and Anna waiting for them at dockside. When the gang plank was put down both George and the admiral were first off the flagship to the cheers of the crowed. He could hear the words "Niki" (victory) being yelled by the throngs that lined the quay. Anna rushed to him and gave him a hug and a kiss.

"My hero."

"I feel like a Roman general celebrating his great victory."

"You are one, silly."

"Now that you think of it, I am." They both broke out laughing.

Both men kissed the patriarch's outstretched hand as was Orthodox custom. The emperor then came over and embraced both men. He raised his arms for silence and was handed a cone to speak through which had been designed by one of the Americans.

"Citizens of Byzantium, today we celebrate two things, a victory against the forces of Islam and a rebirth of this great city and Byzantium itself. Most of you must have noticed our city has rebounded in the last year. It is growing once again and business and wealth is coming back. I say this to all. I welcome anyone, regardless of religion or race, as long as they are loyal to the empire, to become a citizen of Byzantium. We may have won a great victory, but the Ottomans will not let this go, they will be back. They will try to take this city and they will by the grace of god fail. So be prepared to fight for your freedom, war is coming my friends, but we will prevail. Now let's celebrate!" The throngs began to yell Niki once again.

Before the emperor's body guards could react, the crowd surged forward and picked up the emperor, George and Admiral Laskaris. They carried them on their shoulders to the palace, shouting long live the emperor and victory. It was a day that had not been seen in Constantinopolis for hundreds of years. When they reached the palace, the emperor thanked the crowd for their patriotism and promised food and drink to the city's citizens, for the official celebration which would be held in two days.

Finally the three men entered the place and went to the emperor's quarters. "Now I know how Julius Cesare felt."

"You could have been killed, your majesty."

"It was a risk I had to take for my people, George."

"Please don't take any more like that. We can't afford to lose you. It only takes one assassin and I'm sure after the sultans finds out what happened there will be plenty of assassins looking for all of us."

"That is true, tell me what happened. Is it's true we have captured all that gold, that Lieutenant Green mentioned?"

"Yes, it is, your majesty," Admiral Laskaris said as he gave a detailed report of their mission and the naval battle that ensued.

"So the ships and guns working together with our superb crews defeated a force twice their size. That's one for the history book as you would say, George."

"Yes your majesty, I would. We need more ships and guns. The Ottomans have many warships available and can overwhelm us as they did against the galleasses."

"I am sure that little spoiled brat Mehmet will be pissed off at losing all that gold and will demand it back. I am not giving it back. That was a godsend. We can pay our military, build more ships and recruit more soldiers."

"Our navy is growing rapidly. The steam gun boat is ready for service. It's being hidden from Mehmet's spies in our new naval base in the Golden Horn. Another gun boat is being built as is a frigate and two more corvettes. Oh, plus the five galleasses we captured and will be added to the navy," the admiral said.

"I remember in my time line, that the Turks managed to capture the Golden Horn by bringing ships over land. But that isn't going to happen now, with 18 and 24 pounder batteries defending it from our new naval base."

"We must speed up our naval construction program."

"We are your majesty," the admiral said. "We brought back several shipwrights and craftsmen from Limnos. We also have a steady supply of lumber coming from the surrounding areas and black sea regions."

"In the next few weeks, we will have to deal with the

sultan's fort that will close the straights. We need them open for trade and supplies, for our war industry. The word is out that we are looking for manpower to work in our new factories. People are starting to arrive from Greek Ottoman occupied villages, in the black sea region."

"You right on that George. We need free passage of the straights. We can't afford to have them closed or pay a tax to the Turks. My customs officials are telling me we are taking in over 500 new immigrants a week. My new chief of police said that many of the new immigrants are taking over abandoned sections of the city, refurbishing them and bringing the districts back to life. We will soon be at over 65,000 inhabitants and by year's end we will be at 100,000."

"That is great news your majesty. We must ensure all our granaries and cisterns are full so we have adequate supplies for the siege."

"We will be ready. The new farming methods you recommended are proving very bountiful. As a matter of fact we will have lots of corn seedlings and the same with the other crops you brought for next seasons planting. I do love the tomatoes."

"We will have lots of cash crops to export, come next year, your majesty."

"The Italians have expressed very much interest in the tomato"

"There cuisine will become one of the best in the world with the use of the tomato, your majesty. Once we have a sufficient quantity Anna will cook some Italian recipes for you."

"I will definitely be looking forward to that."

"On another subject your majesty, as we previously discussed, we must make plans to take that fort in the next few weeks."

"Yes, I know we must George. I want that fort captured before the Ottomans decide to march on the City. I will discuss it with General Notaras.

"I am now going to the hospital to see Anna. She will be very busy with the wounded."

"Mary is there assisting her."

"I have noticed you have grown very fond of her, your majesty."

"Indeed a have. She is a kind lovely young woman. I have called off the Bulgarian princes wedding."

"So you will ask Mary to be your empress?"

"I may just do that, after we have dealt with the Ottomans. I think a union with the past and the future will be good for Byzantium."

"I agree, your majesty," Admiral Laskaris added. "You need an heir."

'I think so to. I will consider this very seriously."

Chapter 6

Constantinopolis
29 July 1452

A few weeks after the sea battle, the sultan's ambassador requested a meeting with the emperor which he granted. George and Constantine waited for the Ottoman envoy in the official throne room. The ambassador arrived near noon and was ushered into the emperor's chambers. The ambassador bowed to the emperor.

"I wish you greetings and good health your majesty. I am here on an urgent request from the all high and glorious Sultan Mehmet II, whom you are a vassal to. The sultan is furious that your tiny and insignificant navy dared to attack an Ottoman convoy and steal a large amount of treasure that belonged to his excellence."

"How dare you accuse us of being thieves?"

The rebuke caught the arrogant Turk by surprise. "I.... I didn't call you a thief your majesty."

"You further accused us of attacking your ten ship flotilla, which in fact attacked a force half its size. Well my insignificant little navy taught you a hard lesson. The gold is now taken as compensation for the attack."

"The sultan demands it back!"

"Tell him, "Melon Lave."

"What's does that mean?"

"He is educated in ancient Greek, he will know."

"The sultan also advises you that as of today any ship passing through the Bosporus must pay a toll to our fort to transit the straits, including your ships. Any ship failing to pay will be sunk."

"May ask why that is?"

"Because he commands it and the Ottomans now own and control the straits."

"I never game him permission to build the fort on my territory. I will not pay him one copper piece! You will also tell the fort's commander that he is on my territory and will take no action. He will also remove every one of his troops in two days."

"You dare challenge the might of the Ottoman sultan? He will crush you and your infidel city like an ant!"

"I am and I will. We had enough of his threats. Now you may leave unless you have something else for me?"

George could see the look of surprise, then rage on the ambassador's face. "You will be hearing from us soon. Good day, your majesty."

Both men waited till the ambassador had been escorted out.

"Well Constantine you tossed a gauntlet in their face. We have to capture that fort. There are about 400 men there under the command of Firuz bey, who will soon be in for a big surprise."

The sultan won't take this lying down. He will attack this city sooner than in your history."

"I am afraid so. That's his plans anyway, according to the intelligence we got from Admiral Baltaouglu. But we are much better prepared. We have a small but superior navy and the army has two full regiments armed and trained with rifles and muskets. We now also have an artillery corps. We can hold this city and defeat the Ottomans."

"I will send out ships to Venice to ask for their assistance. They promised me troops and also to the surrounding islands for recruits."

"Do that your majesty. Have them leave immediately. Even though I don't have high hopes, you never know. Every lit bit of aid will help us. Within couple of months, we may be at war."

Ottoman Fortress Rumeli Hisar
30 July 1452

The following night, George tossed and turned in his bed thinking of next day's battle to capture the fort. Being midsummer, it was very hot and he was sweating profusely. He looked next to him where Anna lay sleeping. He hoped for her sake and the rest of the city, that they could stop the coming Ottoman onslaught. Once the sultan decided to attack he would throw the entire might of his empire at them.

"What is it George? Go to sleep."

"It's hot and I am thinking of tomorrow's battle and what it will mean."

"War is coming sooner or later."

"Much sooner, than in our time line. We could use the extra months to prepare. We're just starting to crank out muskets and cannon."

"We will have to fight with what we have. You do have the BMP."

"That has a finite amount of ammunition. It will have to be used at a decisive moment. It can't win the war single handedly."

"You can take out the sultan with it."

"If you know where he is. But others can take over and still continue the battle."

"We should get married."

"What?"

"You heard."

"Okay, yes. She reached over and gave him a long kiss."

"Maybe if I get tired I will fall asleep," he said as he got on top of her.

The next morning the Byzantine army marched out of the city gates with a regiment of Musketeers, a company of Calvary, several batteries of artillery and some new mortars. It headed towards the Ottoman fortress of Rumeli Hisar, six miles north of the city which overlooked the Bosporus. At the same time two corvettes and five galleys headed toward the fortress to deal with any Ottoman naval threat. When they arrived at the fort, George had his guns setup at 300 yards in order to be out of range of bows and fire arms.

George had another surprise in store for the Turks. Master Sergeant Fulton, an avid glider pilot had constructed a hot air balloon and would use it for artillery spotting. Fulton with his assistants had put the balloon together and was lighting the straw. George under a flag of truce rode up to the fort to offer their terms to the fort's commander, Firuz bey. The gate opened and a middle aged man wearing armor followed by two other officers walked up to George and General Notaras. "How dare you infidel threaten this fortress?"

"This fortress was built without the emperor's permission on Byzantine territory."

"The emperor of one city? He dares to go against the great Sultan Mehmet?"

"You have an hour to surrender and leave, or this fort will be taken by force," General Notaras replied.

The Turk though visibly agitated began to laugh. "You are going to take this fort with what? Seven hundred men and a few pop guns. Get out of her infidel, before I have you all killed with my great cannons."

George gave the signal and the hot air balloon began to rise tethered to the ground by a rope. "What magic is this?"

"Surrender or you will all be destroyed by the Christian god who gives us the ability to fly over those that worship a false prophet."

"I will never surrender to you infidel dogs, no matter what magic you have."

"As you wish, you have an hour to surrender."

After having pulled back to their positions they heard a loud bang followed by a large stone ball landing twenty yards from one of the gun batteries. George gave the order for Jenkins, who had set up the Soviet 81 mm mortar to open fire. The first shell hit the inside of the fort killing several soldiers. Fulton gave corrections, spotting from the balloon. The next round landed by one of the cannons killing the gun crew. The next few shells took out the remainder of the gun crews facing the Byzantines, but not before one of the huge 400 pound cannon balls struck one of the guns, killing two of the gunners and hurling the gun from it carriage.

"Fire."

The Byzantine guns and the three mortars they had brought along opened fire, hurling 18 pound explosive shells over the fortress walls. The three mortars continued to throw shells into the fort taking out the barracks and other structures making the inside of the fort a living hell. From atop the balloon Fulton snipped at the garrison with the Mosin Nagant sniper rifle he had taken aloft. Having had enough, the fortress commander decided to attack the Byzantine formation. Unfortunately for the Ottomans, Fulton had noticed the preparations and radioed George. Several ranks of Byzantine musket men were waiting for them when the fortress gates were opened. Both Turkish cavalry and 200 hundred infantry charged toward the Byzantines, but were met by concentrated musket fire. Having fired a couple of volleys, the infantry were ordered back behind the guns which had been loaded with canister rounds. George gave the order and the guns opened fire shredding the Ottomans with the canister rounds. This broke the back of their attack.

"Fix bayonets!' George screamed out the order.

The 400 musketeers attached the bayonets to their guns.

"Regiment forward! Quick march."

With M4 in hand, George and the 400 Musketeers quickly reached the fortress gates. When they entered, the remaining enemy survivors dropped their weapons and surrendered. Within minutes the Byzantine ensign flew above the fortress, bringing a cheer from the Byzantine infantry. George was soon joined by General Notaras and the rest of the staff. "What's the butcher's bill?"

"Five dead and ten injured," replied George. "The Ottoman commander was also killed."

"We will secure this fort so the Ottomans can't use it again. We need the straights open to shipping and trade. This could also be a good place to stage attacks against the Ottomans if they besiege the city."

"A few 18 and 12 pounders along with a couple of hundred infantry should hold this fort."

"It will hold, sir. We must also build a couple of underground shelters to protect the troops from Ottoman cannon fire and to securely store our powder."

"Understood, George. Your hot air balloon was crucial to the battle. It will revolutionize warfare by giving commanders a view of the enemy positions."

"Hopefully we can keep that secret for a while. I am returning to the city to brief the emperor. We must immediately began fortifying and garrisoning this fort."

"I will come with you," General Notaras replied.

Within the hour they had ridden back the city which was once again jubilant for the victory against the Moslem hordes. George knew their jubilation would not last, once the sultan turned his full attention on the city. They both arrived at the palace to a hero's welcome with the Imperial Guard on parade, Bayonets fixed to their Nagants and steel pot helmets gleaming in the sun.

"Well this is a surprise."

They were met by their commander and chief, the emperor who whisked them into the palace. "I Congratulate you on your victory, gentlemen. This is just one more thing to piss off the sultan with. I hear our casualties were light?"

"Yes your majesty replied General Notaras. "Five dead ten wounded."

"Five too many."

"The fortress commander was killed along with half his men and the rest are our prisoners. We found a chest with 2000 gold coins in the commander's quarters, probably for purchasing supplies and paying the men."

"Each of you will receive a reward of 250 gold coins and each man 1 gold coin. The rest goes to our growing treasury."

"Thank you, your majesty."

"You both earned it. Our navy was also very successful; they sunk two galleasses and captured three others, finding some gold and silver in their holds."

"Your majesty, I think we should rename the fortress we just captured, to fort Justinian in honor of one of Byzantium's greatest emperors," George said.

"That is an excellent suggestion," Notaras said.

"That is in fact, an excellent idea. Now we must wait for the hell that is to come. I heard the young sultan has an extreme temper. I am sure it will boil over after he hears of this slap in the face."

"That is true General Mavrakis the sultan can't sit idly by while we taunt him. His position will be in peril. He will have to act soon."

"I am sure he will. This is too much for him to stomach and not do anything. He will march on the city, much sooner than later," Notaras said.

"I am worried about our underground base, once his army is on the move we won't be able to get our finished musket barrels and flintlock pistols to the City. With the base assisting the manufacturing process, we are making over 250 Muskets a month. We are starting to produce flintlock muskets there in numbers. They are a major improvement over the matchlocks."

"So what are we going to do, George?"

"We may have to do night runs by ship and reinforce the garrison there with Imperial Guards. I have Major Petros Tomas in command there."

"He has proven himself a very competent officer."

"Yes he has and so have all his men."

"I want an additional company there, Notaras said."

"Let's wait a bit until we know what the sultan is doing.

Edirne, Western Thrace, Sultan's Palace
5 August 1452

In Edirne a hundred miles to the east, Sultan Mehmet II was sitting in counsel with his two most trusted advisors, Candarli Halil and Zaganos Pasha, contemplating their next move against the Byzantines. The sultan was incensed about the loss of his 100,000 pieces of gold. If he could get his hands on Admiral Baltaouglu he would have him skinned alive and his head on a pike. "Padishah our ambassador is here from Constantinopolis. He wishes to see you."

"Send him in."

The ambassador walked in and prostrated himself to the sultan. "What news have you from the city" Asked the sultan letting the ambassador sweat in fear.

My padishah, on the way here we ran into a wounded cavalry officer from the Rumeli Hisar fortress. It has fallen to the infidel."

"What? I just left there a few days ago. Where is this man?"

"He died just before we arrived in Edirne. He also spoke of a flying demon and explosive bombs that killed many of the forts defenders."

"Flying demons? Do you take me as a fool?"

"No my padishah. This is what the dying man told us."

"Did you get the gold back and an apology?"

"No, my padishah, the emperor said we attacked him and the gold is his for compensation and damages."

"Did you tell him he will face my wrath?"

The ambassador was trembling to in fear for his life. The sultan did not take lightly to bearers of bad news. "Yes I did my padishah."

"What did he say?"

"Melon Lave." I did not understand what he said, but he said you would."

That was all that was needed to set the young sultan off. In a rage he struck the ambassador knocking him to the ground. We are marching on Constantinopolis. "Melon lave! He will pay for this."

"Guards get this fool out of here and have him flogged."

The now ex ambassador, was relieved that he would not be killed and was getting off with only a flogging.

"I want our army in front of the city gates no later than 60 days from today. Send word and have all our vassals send their levees."

"Yes, my padishah, but 60 days is a bit early. Our guns may not be ready."

"I want our Hungarian friend working around the clock. Pay him more gold. Those guns must be finished."

"Yes, my padishah."

"I also want more patrols attacking and harassing the Byzantines, especially in the area where these Djinn or demons were seen. I also want to take all their towns and forts leading to the city.

"It will be done, my padishah."

"My padishah, what does Melon Lave mean?" Candarli Halil asked.

"It is ancient Greek. When the Persian king asked king Leonidas of Sparta to give him the pass at Thermopolis to spare their lives, King Leonidas replied "Melone Lave," come and take it!

"I will come and take it Constantine," he yelled in rage "and your head too!"

Constantinopolis
8 October 1452

Within eight weeks of capturing the Ottoman fort, the defenses of the captured Rumeli Hisar fortress had been upgraded with 12 and 18 pounder guns. Additionally, a 300 man garrison armed with a combination of Muskets, Mosin Nagant rifles and mortars was stationed there to hold the fort in case the Ottomans attempted to take it back. Underground bunkers to protect troops resting, from cannon fire, had also been built. The fort would be a hard nut to crack if the Ottomans decided to try and take it back. The obsolete Ottoman cannon had been removed and melted down to create hundreds of gun barrels for the new flint lock muskets and pistols.

The Byzantines had not been sitting idle either. Once famous for their spy networks they had begun to rebuild it with their new found wealth. Intelligence had been coming in that the sultan had been collecting thousands of troops in and around his capital Edirne, 100 miles to the west. The city walls had been strengthened and cannon added to the defenses. Volunteers were pouring in from the Italian states and outlying areas to join the Byzantine military. A weapons industry had taken root and was operating 24/7. It had grown to several factories, powder mills, and foundries, producing cannons, guns and swords.

The Byzantine military had also done many improvements to their fighting abilities. Another regiment of Musketeers had been formed, this one armed with Flintlock rifles that were able to shoot accurately up to 200 yards, thanks to the underground soviet machine shop which was now at risk. The new Golden Horn naval base was protected by 24 pounder gun batteries and a 24/7 naval patrol. Additionally, a barracks housing 200 naval marines had been built there. The Byzantine navy had grown to 5 corvettes, 15 galleys and the steam gunboat, which was docked in remote location not to be seen. The frigate that was being built would have a steam engine but would mostly rely on sail for very long trips. It would not be ready till the next year. The surrounding fields had been harvested and the food stored and all the water cisterns filled. Every day that went buy the city's defenses became stronger but everyone knew time was running out. The Ottomans would soon be on the march.

Underground Base
15 October 1452

A week later, George had decided to visit the underground base and brought along with him an additional 30 men of the

Imperial Guard, to forty its defense. They had all been sworn to secrecy and briefed on the existence of the base. The men were armed with bolt action Mosin Nagants that outclassed anything the Ottomans had. Fortunately ammo for them was still very abundant and stored at the underground armory. Even though it was mid-October, the weather was still good, making the short sea voyage by galley pleasant. At the beach they were met by the duce and a half and the Humvee. The truck was quickly unloaded of 100 machined gun barrels and parts for the new frigate's steam engine which were hoisted and loaded aboard the ships to take back to the city. George had brought extra rations and supplies for the troops garrisoning the base and another load of un-machined rifle barrels. Several barrels of used olive for processing into usable bio fuel, was also loaded into the truck for processing. One day in the future they would have to drill for oil, possibly in Rumania, in the Ploesti region where in the future oil would be found. When the unloading and loading had finished, the ships immediately left for the city.

The short drive to the underground base had been incident free. Upon arrival George was greeted there by his old friend Petros whom he had appointed as the base commander. George had not been to the base for many weeks, but was sure not much had changed. The major saluted and gave him a hug.

"How are you, my friend?" Petros said in accented English.

"Just fine, major. How is everything going here?"

"Good general. We are producing many rifles and the lieutenant is making great progress on the newer version of his steam engine for the new frigate that is being built."

"That's very good news. I too have some good news; we now have two regiments armed with Match lock muskets and flintlocks. The Calvary is now armed with pistols and sabers."

"That is great news general. This will enables us to better

fight the more numerous Ottomans. The enemy will soon be on the march. They have increased their patrol activity here. I sent out scouts and they've seen Ottoman engineers cutting trees and widening some of the roads. Sooner or later, we will run into their patrols or navy and we will have to fight "

"They're prepping the roads to handle their huge siege guns. You are to avoid contact with them at all costs. If they find this mine shaft we are in deep trouble."

"I need to rest for a few hours to clear my head, it was a long day."

"Sure, we have lots of space, sir."

Several hours later George had awakened from his nap and was having breakfast with Petros and both Lieutenants Burns and Rhodes. He was discussing the progress of their programs. He had gone into Burns' workshop and seen the progress on the new engine. Rhodes had come along to check on his craftsmen who were refining the rifle barrels. "Sir, I wish we could build the weapons faster, but we are limited to just the workshops here," Rhodes said.

"We will produce a steam engine to run a lathe, after I get the new frigate's engine finished. That will help speedup production."

"How's that going, Burns?"

"Pretty much on schedule, sir. Will be sending out the last parts tonight with you. I will be coming along to supervise the installation. The ship wrights are ready for it."

"It's a lot larger than the gunboat's engine."

"She's about 50% bigger but much more efficient. We learned a lot since our first model went out. She should be able to propel the frigate at a steady 9 knots. She will only be limited to the fuel carried on board."

"I plan to send her on an expedition to Mexico, to get the

Aztec gold before the Europeans do. We will be kinder to them then the Spanish, but I promised the patriarch that the human sacrifices will be stopped. Hopefully, we can convert them to Christianity and make them allies. But that's a long way down the road."

"We have to first survive the Ottoman onslaught, before we deal with them."

"We will, Burns."

"Sir, we've also completed several more crates of the metal grenades that were sent to us for finishing. All they need to do is fill them with powder and screw in the cap and fuse. They should be pretty nasty."

"Great news! We'll use anything to take out the sultan's troops."

"With three gun foundries running, we are producing over 50 cannon a month. We are even making small two pounder anti-personnel swivel guns. We have begun installing them on the city walls and the fleet. Each one is a big two pounder shotgun."

"That should be able to take out lots of infantry."

"Yes sir. We've started putting nine pounders between the walls in case of breaches. They will be loaded with canister."

"You've done a great job Rhodes; I don't know what I would have done without you. I don't know what I would have done without all of you. By the way, how is your pretty little clerk Despina? I know she has been doing a great job for you keeping track of everything."

"I was meaning to talk to you about that, sir."

"Well what is the problem?"

"I would like your permission to marry her."

"Why of course and when?"

"Immediately, sir."

"We would like you to be the best man and the godfather of our coming child."

George started to laugh and hit Rhodes on the back. "Of course, Paul I am honored. It will be the first union of the old world with the new world."

"I will have a word with the patriarch to schedule your weeding."

"Thank you very much, sir."

"Now will you and Lieutenant Burns please stand over here in the position of attention."

The two young officers both obeyed. George nodded to Major Tomas who stepped out of the room. Now follow me please. The three men marched outside into the large cavern area. The major had assembled all the men there. Petros came to attention turned around, "Company atten hut," Petros commanded.

George and the two men marched up to the formation and stood facing it. Petros saluted George. George turned and faced the formation. "By order of Emperor Constantine Paleologos, commander and chief of the Byzantine Army, Lieutenants Burns and Rhodes are hereby promoted to the rank of captain, for services rendered to the empire."

George turned, faced the two officers and pinned the new rank on each man.

"Congratulations, gentlemen. You have well-earned this promotion." George began clapping, soon followed by clapping and cheers by everyone present. Morale was good he thought they would need it for the hell that would soon be bestowed upon them.

By nightfall they had loaded the truck with the grenades, gun barrels and steam engine parts. They had received a radio message from the other Humvee located in the city that the ships were on their way to meet them at the rendezvous place. According to the guards at the entrance, there had been lots of activity. Several Ottoman cavalry patrols had been seen in the area. Besides the normal escort, George requested that ten Imperial Guards come along on the duce and a half for force protection. The night sky was cloudy, with the full moon making occasional appearances, as it went in and out of the clouds. Twenty minutes after leaving the mine entrance, they reached the beach. A galley was waiting for them along with the Phoenix, which had dropped anchor in deeper water off shore.

The crew of the galley quickly helped to unload the truck and took the cargo onboard. After being unloaded, the two vehicles set off back for the mine. Lieutenant Green the Phoenix's captain had sent the ship's long boat to pick up George and row him out to the warship. As he stepped on the deck, George was piped on board. He saluted the ship's ensign and was greeted by the twenty-three year old Lieutenant Green. He noticed that the ship was prepared for battle. "We need to get out of here quickly, sir. Raise the anchor and takes us home, men."

George could see that the galley had pulled off the beach and was heading out to open water. The Phoenix began to slowly pick up speed as the wind filled her sails "What's going on, Green?"

"It's started, sir. We heard from some of our patrol ships that the Ottomans have begun attacking some of our outlying towns and forts. The Ottoman navy is out in force and trying to clear the sea of our ships."

"We all knew it would happen sooner or later. The sultan chose to attack us several months sooner than our timeline. Guess he is pretty pissed off, losing all that gold and his fort. He does have a hot temper and this is also better for us. He has had less time to prepare."

"He has a lot of ships, but we are superior in gunfire and training. The only threat is if we get swarmed by several ships at once. If that happens, then we have a problem. We can run fast with the wind, but going against it or lack of wind, can be deadly for us. Those galleys are pretty fast in short spurts."

"That is true. We can only do our best and use our advantage where ever and whenever we can. So how are you doing anyway, Green?"

"I miss my parents, but otherwise, I love it. My dream come true, sir. I always wondered after reading all those Horatio Horn blower novels, how it will be to fight a sailing ship with cannon. Well now I got my chance."

"I am sure you will have many more opportunities, lieutenant."

The quiet of the night was punctured with a gunshot, coming from the shore. They could hear the distant pop, pop of rifle fire and the occasional burst of automatic weapon fire.

"They've must of run into an Ottoman patrol probably scouting the area."

"Sails ho. Three enemy galleys coming from the portside, captain. They're Less than half a mile away. I believe they've spotted us."

Both Byzantine ships were silhouetted against the coast by the occasional moonlight shining through the clouds. The corvette could run north with the wind and easily lose the three galleys, but it would leave the other galley alone to fight three ships. Besides, they could not lose that ship. It had the finished parts to the new steam frigate's engine in her hold. If the enemy managed to capture that galley they would find the engine, machined rifle barrels and grenades. Someone in the crew would be made to talk, and then they would find the mine shaft.

"We can't let them capture that galley at any cost, lieutenant."

"Yes, sir. Helmsman, take us across their bow."

"Aye, aye captain." Having lost the wind advantage the Phoenix slowed to less than five knots giving the speed advantage to the galleys. Thinking her as easy prey, two of the galley's headed for the Phoenix, the other one headed towards the Byzantine galleass.

"We're going to cross their T. Prepare to fire."

Thirty seconds later the Phoenix was crossing the T of the two enemy warships that were sailing abreast of each other. Green waited till he knew he would get maximum effect. Fire" The starboard side nine pounders fired in unison. The iron balls traveled straight down the length of the crowded enemy decks of both ships tearing men to piece, smashing into wooden structures and sending out deadly wooden splinters that killed scores of soldiers and crew. One of the balls hit the mast of the second galley sending it into the sea which acted as a giant sea anchor.

"Load with canister."

The other galley hurt, though not serious was trying to catch and board the Phoenix.

"They're going to catch us in a few minutes," George Said.

"They are, but not before they get a load of canister to better our odds."

"We'll give them all we got, Green."

"Prepare to repel boarders. Marines, fix bayonets."

The remainder of the ship's crew grabbed whatever weapon they felt comfortable fighting with and waited for the enemy. The marines stood by with loaded flintlock rifles and fixed bayonets gleaming in the moonlight. The enemy ship was less than 100 yards away, well within projectile range. Several arrows and cross bolts struck the Phoenix, killing one man and injuring two others.

"Prepare to fire. Helmsman, hard to starboard." The Phoenix began to turn to the left exposing her entire side to the enemy ship.

"Fire." Nine guns belched out canister shot, raking the deck of the enemy ship, Killing and maiming dozens. At the same time, several grappling hooks came over the side to hold the Phoenix as the two ships crashed together. Scores of enemy sailors and soldiers swarmed aboard the Phoenix, many of them being cut down by the marines' musket fire or gutted by their bayonets. Both George and Green jumped into the fray with 9mm Berettas in hand. George spotted a giant baldheaded enemy sailor armed with an axe running towards Green. He raised the pistol and fired two shots hitting the man in the torso. The dying sailor crashed into Green knocking him to the deck. George reached down and helped up the dazed lieutenant.

"Thanks sir, you saved my ass."

"On them, men!"

The Phoenix crew lunged forward and began pushing the enemy back. The two Americans took down over twenty men, with their automatic pistols, breaking the impetus of the attack. When George's Beretta ejected its last round he reached for his M4 which was slung across his shoulders, but an enemy sailor seeing the opportunity, rushed toward him with a drawn Ottoman Calvary saber. George caught the movement from the corner of his eye and was just able to pull the rifle free to partially block the sabre cut. The blade scraped the rifle barrel and glanced off his left arm. George felt a sharp pain, but could do nothing as he almost dropped the rifle. Fortunately, he had installed the bayonet. Holding the small rifle like a spear with his good arm he plunged it into the enemy sailor's gut, as he came around for another swing with the sword. Pulling the rifle out, he pulled the trigger.

Less than a minute later, they felt a bump and heard a loud cheer. Seeing they were now outflanked and did not stand any chance, the enemy soldiers and sailors dropped their weapons and surrendered. The Byzantine galley having dealt with the enemy ship had come to assist the Phoenix.

"We beat them, sir." Green said bleeding form a gash to his temple.

"Yes we did and captured a prize in the process."

"You're wounded."

"It's nothing, just a cut. I'll have the ship's doctor take a look at it. I hope Captain Rhodes is okay. He was on the galley."

Forty-five minutes later having secured the prisoners they were back underway. They had lost over 20 men in the battle. The other galley had not received any casualties. Not willing to risk boarding the enemy ship, they had pounded the Ottoman galley with cannon fire until it sank. They reached the city just as the sun rose. George noticed that the base was on alert, several gun batteries were manned and picket ships were challenging shipping in the Bosporus.

At the dockside, he was met by admiral Laskaris and several ambulances. Being the senior officer, George was first off the ship. "Good morning George, I see you have another ship for our navy."

"Yes, admiral, I'm sure she will make a fine addition. It did cost us 20 lives though. We also sank two of their ships."

"We will lose many more lives before this war is over. I see that you were injured."

"Just a sword cut. I will have Anna stitch it up. We were attacked by two galleys. We sank one with gunfire and the other managed to board us. I saw our marines in action. They are really a valuable addition to the ship's company."

"Creating a marine corps was an excellent suggestion. We now have 500 marines and growing."

"I'm sure we will use them before this is over, admiral. Is there any news on the sultan's army?"

"Or intelligence sources said they are on the move. The advance guards are moving their heavy guns. Tens of thousands of men have mustered in and around Edirne and will soon be on the march. Within two weeks, they will be here in force. We also had a contingent of 700 Genovese arrive last night, under the command of a professional soldier, Giustiaianini Longo."

"I see their ships in port. Just like the history books said it occurred, only this is happening earlier. He is a brave man and an excellent fighter. In my timeline, he was given command of all the land forces. He was mortally wounded by a bullet on the last night of the siege and died a few days later on his way back to Genova."

"Hopefully, he does not meet the same fate."

"We brought back over a hundred Musket Barrels. If we finish these rifles in the next couple of days, we can give some of the matchlocks to the Italians."

"I'm going to the hospital to get this cut treated and then to the palace. I will see you later, sir."

"May god be with you."

"May god be with all of us, sir."

George rode along with one of the ambulances, to the hospital carrying the wounded from the previous night's battle. They were met there by Anna and recently promoted Lieutenant Mary Jones, the emperor's new fiancée. Anna was totally surprised to see George. "My god George, are you hurt?"

"Yes, my love, only a small sword cut. I will live."

"Small cuts in this era can kill."

"Tend to the more serious wounded. I can wait."

"Mary is doing the triages. Come with me, this will only take ten minutes."

George followed her into the office and she closed the door, hugged and kissed him. She was crying. "You could have been killed."

"But I wasn't. Many will be killed before this war is over."

"I don't want our child without a father."

"Child? What do you mean? Are you are pregnant?"

"I ran out of birth control pills months ago. Sooner or later, having unprotected sex would cause that."

"It does not matter my, dear. I am so happy. We must get married this week. I want my child born out of wedlock especially in this era, in case something happens to me."

"The answer is yes. You forgot to ask me."

"George kissed her. I will talk to the emperor and patriarch to do the wedding in Aghia Sofia."

"That would be wonderful. Now let me look at that wound."

Ten minutes later she had stitched up the wound. The experience had been rather painful, without the modern numbing medicine like Novocain. "Now drink this nasty Penicillin tea to word off any infection."

George gulped it down. "It tastes horrible."

"But it works and it's the best we got for now."

"Now go tend to the more serious wounded. I'm going to the palace and talk to Constantine and afterwards get some rest."

George kissed her goodbye and escorted by his body guards was transported to the palace.

Chapter 7

Constantinopolis
17 October 1452

When George arrived at the palace, he noticed lots of activity. He immediately went to the command center and found the emperor and General Notaras having a discussion with a middle-aged short and stocky man, dressed in armor of the period. The emperor noticed George enter the room and motioned him to come over. He saw the bandages on George's arm and looked concerned. "General you were wounded?"

"Just a slight wound, your majesty, during last night's naval action. I will be fine. It was just a small sword cut. Anna stitched it up for me."

"I heard of the battle. Congratulations to you and Lieutenant Green."

"It's the lieutenant, that that should get all the credit, sir."

"You are too modest, general. Let me introduce you to Giovanni Giustiniani Longo, from Genova. He and the 700 men he brought along have graciously volunteered to join our fight against the Ottomans. I am bestowing the rank of colonel, to him. He will fight under your command and has been fully briefed about you and sworn to secrecy."

"I am honored to meet you, colonel. I had read so much about you and your exploits during the siege in my history."

The man's eyes lit up and his grip was strong. "Really? I am honored. I hope it was all good. I am very honored to have made the history books and awed to meet you, sir."

"You were very brave during the siege and stopped the enemy's advances on numerous occasions, until you were mortally wounded by an enemy bullet, on the last night of the siege. The wound proved fatal, a few days later, after you left the city for home. Hopefully that will not happen in this time frame."

"Hopefully not, but thank you anyway for the insight. I am really astounded to hear about you and your troops. Your weapons are amazing. They will make a difference."

"Let's hope so, Giovanni. There will be many of the enemy and our ammunition is limited."

"Can you not make more?"

"Not immediately, we must make some industrial and chemical break through before we can manufacture more ammunition for our weapons."

"I see. So they must be used wisely and decisively."

George was surprised at the astuteness of the man. "You are correct Colonel Longo. We can kill many, but it must be during a decisive moment of the battle, when our intervention will mean victory or defeat."

"Please call me John."

"We are all glad you are here and we could use all the help we can get. We will equip some of your men with better fire arms. I will ensure that you and your officers receive training and fire arms of my period."

"I will be very grateful, for that sir."

"The enemy is on the march and we must do anything we can to slow them down."

"Yes, we need to plan something against them, sir."

"Excuse me for a minute, John. "Your majesty, I need to speak to you and General Notaras."

"Please accompany me to my private office," General Notaras said.

Once inside the office George briefed them on what had happened after leaving the underground base. "So will the base be secure, George?"

"If the enemy finds it, our troops can only hold out until overwhelmed by sheer numbers. The last radio call said that a large concentration of enemy forces were in the area moving heavy artillery."

"Must be their advance guard," Notaras said.

"I remember in the history books, that they had huge siege guns that shot a stone ball weighing as much as eight men. They battered down the walls with those guns."

"Anything we can do to slow them down and damage them will help. I sent a galley to Trebizond to ask for assistance. Hopefully they will send us some help by the next week," the emperor said.

"I expect their fleet will arrive in the next few days. They will most likely attempt to secure the Bosporus so they can cross troops. Our fort should give them a surprise," George said.

"I have also sent out word to the people in outlying areas to come into the city. I put all out forces, on level Two alert."

"That is a good, sir. It will take us a couple of days to mobilize. On another matter your majesty, Anna and I would like to get married in Aghia Sofia this Saturday, which is five days from now. Would you be our best man?"

"Congratulations and I am honored you are asking me, but what is the rush? Can't it wait till after the battle?"

"Not really. She is with child."

"The emperor smiled. Why of course, you have my blessing. You know what? Maybe Mary and I should also marry. This city needs an empress. It will show the people that even with a siege imminent, we are not really worried about it. It will greatly improve every ones' morale. I will tell the patriarch to plan for a double wedding and a celebration this city has not witnessed in a very long time."

"Thank you, your majesty, now I do need to get some rest so I can later show John around. I have not slept in two days."

"Why of course. We will see you and the good doctor for dinner in honor of our alley and friend, Colonel Longo."

A few hours later, one of the servants knocked on George's door to notify him that Colonel Longo was waiting for him. George put on his uniform and went out to meet the man. George noticed that Longo was wearing a field cap with an eagle's insignia on it, denoting colonel's rank. This man learned fast, he thought to himself.

"General, I hope I did not disturb your sleep?"

"No, I rested enough, John. There is work to be done and little time to prepare. Let's go to the armory."

George left his body guard behind, since he had the colonel with him. They both walked the short distance to the armory, which was under one of the palace wings. They found Master Sergeant Davis there. "Hi Davis, I want to check out Colonel Longo on a Makarov. He just arrived with 700 troops from Italy."

"Pleased to meet you, sir."

"Thank you, sergeant." Davis let the two men inside. "This is very impressive," Longo commented when he saw all the weapons.

Dozens of AK47 as well as M16 and Nagant rifles were stored in racks. On another wall were stacked matchlock and flintlock rifles.

"You will learn to shoot both the pistol and AK47 colonel."

Davis brought over a Makarov pistol with a holster, an extra magazine and a box of 50 rounds of ammo. He then brought over an AK47 with a one magazine and a hundred rounds of ammo. George showed him how to put on the gun belt and holster and carry the pistol. Then he picked up the rifle and ammunition.

"Let's go shooting, colonel"

They walked the short distance to the firing range. After they arrived, George showed Longo how to take apart the Makarov and load the magazine with eight rounds. George put up a cloth target over the wooden silhouette of a body. "You must have shot a firearm before, John?"

"Yes, I haves shot hand guns before."

"Well this a bit different. Every time you pull the trigger it shoots. So it's fast and accurate, if you aim properly. Let me give you a demonstration."

George loaded the pistol and showed the colonel how to hold it and then he fired off the full eight rounds that were in the mag. "That is magic!"

"No John. That is the future." George put a new magazine in the pistol. "Here you try it. Squeeze the trigger."

He squeezed the trigger and the Makarov fired. "Do it again till the gun is empty and reload like I showed you."

After firing a few magazines George felt that the colonel was familiar with the weapon. "You are hitting the target in the center. How do you like the pistol?"

"It is an excellent weapon, general."

"I am glad you like it. After you clean the pistol like I showed you, it is yours to use."

"Thank you, very much general."

"Now let me show you how this AK47 rifles works. The principle is the same only you can kill someone at a longer distance. It can reach out to almost 500 paces with these sights."

"That is amazing my friend."

"There are other weapons that can hit a target, much, much farther." George showed him how to take apart and reassemble the weapon.

After having Longo practice several times with dissembling and assembling the AK47, George went through the basics of shooting and using the iron sights on the rifle. George shot one magazine demonstrating the basics of marksmanship then he had Longo try it. The man was a natural with a weapon. After a few shots he was able to hit the target center from 100 meters almost every shot. When the rifle was empty he handed it back to George. "Let me show you what else this s capable of."

George loaded a magazine flipped the selector on auto and emptied the magazine downrange with slow bursts of automatic fire."

"In god's name that is amazing! With a thousand of those guns, any army in the world can be defeated."

"We don't have a thousand rifles and the ammunition is limited. We can't reproduce it yet. The bullets need a special chemical and we are working to make it, but it may take a while."

"I can find the best chemists in the world and bring them here."

"That may have to be done after this battle, John. But now we must survive it. This rifle will be yours once the siege starts. We have another older rifle from my time. It too can shoot very far, but it's not semi-automatic like the AK47. These rifles were created just before our first great world war and also used in our second world war."

"A world war? How is that possible?"

"In the next several hundred years, many of the great European powers will create empires around the world for resources. Even Italy, which is what your future nation will be called, will have an empire. When all the city states are united on the Italian Peninsula, 400 years from now, she will capture several small nations in the Meditereanean basin and have a small empire. People will be able to rapidly communicate with one another, anyplace in the world, by using a machine. There will be many new political movements, some good some bad. Many monarchies will no longer exist. Do to these movements and ideas, a war will break out engulfing Europe and all her allies on a global level. Over 50 million people will die during our second great war and 17 million in our first world war."

"That is almost all the population of Europe."

"Russia lost 25 million and Germany almost seven. Giant flying machines would fly missions many hundreds of miles, to drop explosives and fire bombs on cities. Finally we created the ultimate weapon, which could destroy an entire city and kill tens of thousands. We built thousands of those bombs, hundreds of times more powerful and put them on large rockets that could fly to anywhere on earth in 30 minutes. We could destroy all life on earth. That is the future of war my friend. It's hard to believe but it's true."

"Mankind has much to look forward to, but also much war and destruction."

"Yes my friend, now I want to show you some of our defenses." George selected one of the Nagant sniper rifles and walked over to the stables with Longo and grabbed two horses. Fifteen minutes later they arrived at the south west walls and he took the colonel through a tour of the defenses. George inspected the troops manning the guns and showed the colonel the new, 18 and 24 pounder guns.

"I have never seen cannon like these"

"They are about 200 years before their time. They will blow any ship coming into their range out of the water. Our ships have been equipped with the same type of cannon, only some have smaller guns."

"What's their range?" Their max range is about a mile and a half and their effective range, anything less than a mile."

"The Ottomans have nothing like these."

"No, their cannon are huge, taking many men to handle them and a long time to load them. Their largest gun, as I said before will shoot a stone weighing as much as eight men. They will be very effective in knocking down these walls. That's how they won the siege. They had knocked down a section of the wall and you had gone over to stop them. You were shot and mortally wounded, but you did not know it at the time. You withdrew and your men followed you and the Janissaries attacked and took the walls. The rest is history."

"The colonel looked very surprised. The city is lost because of my action?"

"It was one of the causes, my friend."

"Hopefully that never happens. We can't let those guns get in range."

"Let's go inspect the western walls. This is where most of the action will take place during the siege. Before we go there, let's stop by the city hospital. I want to introduce you to someone there."

Twenty minutes later, they tied their horses to a post outside the hospital and walked inside. He observed Anna treating one of the wounded men from the previous night's sea battle. George waited till she was finished bandaging the man. She looked up and noticed George with another soldier beside him. She went over to him and he gave her a hug and a peck on the cheek. "This is my fiancée, Doctor of medicine and Duchess Anna Marone. Anna, this is Colonel Giustiaianini Longo from Genova, Italy. He arrived yesterday with 700 men to assist us."

"I am honored to meet you duchess," he said in Italian.

"As I colonel," she replied in Italian.

"You have a beautiful and charming fiancée, general."

"Thank you, colonel. Yes, I am a very lucky man. We are getting married this Saturday and you are most welcome to come."

"Yes, please do and sit at our table."

"I will be honored, duchess."

"Has the emperor proposed to Mary?"

"Why yes, he has. There will be a double wedding in the cathedral and a wild party afterwards. He will announce it tonight at dinner."

"That will be great for the morale of the City."

"I asked Constantine to be our best man and he agreed."

"Well I will be giving away the bride, too him," she added.

"We are making history my dear in more ways than one. I will see you later my love. I am taking the good colonel here for a tour. "

"Stay out of danger, please."

"It was nice to meet you, duchess."

"The pleasure is mine, also. See you tonight."

Fifteen minutes later, they were touring the defenses of the western walls. The gun batteries were manned with a skeleton crew, the rest were resting in the towers and could be called out in a minute's notice. George demonstrated this to the colonel. He had one of the officers in charge of a battery of 18 pounders call an alert drill. Within five minutes the guns were manned and ready to fire. George had one of the guns fire an explosive shell. "That is very impressive general. These are large guns and those shells can do some damage."

"They are 18 pounders and can hurl an explosive shell a mile. We have smaller 12 and 9 pounders installed on the walls. Those can be loaded as well as these guns, with canister rounds."

"What is that?"

"A bag full off little balls and pieces of iron. When fired, it can kill over a dozen men."

"Very impressive, general. These guns along with the new rifles and muskets give us an excellent chance of surviving the siege and in the process inflecting horrendous casualties on the attacker."

"That is our intentions, John. Not only to defeat them but to cripple and destroy them as a military organization."

"We will find out very soon my friend."

"Sir, There is an Ottoman Calvary patrol outside the walls," the battery commander said as he observed them through his spy glass which had been issued to him and every gun captain on the walls.

George peered through his binoculars at the Turkish patrol.

"It looks like there is a high ranking officer with them. He is on the second horse. They have stopped and he is pointing at the city. They must have heard the gun fire. I estimate that they are about, a half mile away. Here John, have a look."

"I see them too, General. Yes there is a very senior officer with them."

George took the Mosin Nagant sniper rifle and laid it on the walls edge. He kneeled down and set the distance on the scope.

"That is very far, my friend."

"A good shooter could kill a man much farther."

He peered through the scope, took a couple of breaths and stopped breathing, as he squeezed the trigger. The rifle went off with a loud bang. George quickly pulled the bolt back, ejected the spent casing, put the bolt forward and took another quick shot.

A second later Longo exclaimed out loud, "You got him! But you missed with the second shot. That was an amazing shot, by the way."

"That's one less Ottoman general, we have to worry about."

The riders got off their horses to see what happened to their charge. No one in the 15th century could ever imagine, that a bullet could strike and kill, from the city walls over 700 yards distant. Thus they did not have the slightest inkling what had happened, giving George the opportunity to shoot one more.

"I'll stop shooting for now; we don't want them to know our capabilities. Maybe we can knock off some more of them later."

"They are searching the surrounding area thinking the shots came from nearby," John said.

"It would be nice if we get the sultan in our sights."

"Who knows what fate has in store in the next few weeks?"

They watched as a Byzantine cavalry patrol, exited the city gates and chased after the Turkish unit which departed the area in haste. "They'll be back in force very soon," George said.

"Let's head back to headquarters."

When they reached the palace the Byzantine cavalry patrol had returned with the body of the dead senior officer and a prisoner. The other man that George had shot was still alive. The bullet had hit him in thigh and he was receiving first aid from a medical orderly. General Notaras and his staff, was outside the palace, talking to the wounded man. George and Colonel Longo both saluted, George having shown Longo how. The General noticed George with the Nagant. "Did you do this?"

George smiled. "Yes, sir, I'm guilty."

Notaras returned the smile. "Good job General, those rifles are amazing, taking them down at almost half a mile from the walls. It seems you took out one of their top commanders."

"Wish we can get some more of them, before that battle starts. I stopped shooting so they would not suspect that they were hit from the walls. We may want to snipe some more of them. Maybe even the sultan if he shows his face."

"So did you like what you have seen of our defenses, colonel?"

"Yes sir. The city has very impressive defenses, especially now, with those guns on the walls."

"Hopefully they can help save the city. Your men are being trained on many of our new weapons and being integrated into our forces. They are being assigned to units with Italian speaking officers."

"Many of my officers also know Greek."

"Yes we have noticed and that will greatly help with the integration and training."

They walked over where the injured Ottoman prisoner was being treated. "Has he said anything?" Notaras asked one of the officers interrogating the prisoner.

The Turkish officer noticed the general's rank. "I speak Greek, infidel. Your heads will soon adorn the sultan's court. You dare attack and kill Karaca Bey, one of the sultan's senior commanders and sneak away?"

"No one snuck away."

"Then how was the commander killed, infidel?"

"I shot him and then I shot you," George said.

He noticed George's rank. "Another gavur, (unbeliever) general? Shot me with what? Nothing can shoot that far."

"But you are wrong. I shot you with this weapon." George showed him the Nagant.

"What trickery is this?"

"No trickery, look through that tube at that man on the wall about 300 paces from here."

The Turk picked up the empty rifle and looked through the scope. "In the name of Allah, this is Satan's work."

"No, it's called better weapons and a gift from the Christian god. We will defeat and destroy you."

The Ottoman officer quickly lost all his bravado and one could see genuine fear in his eyes. "Take this man to the hospital for treatment of his wound."

After they had taken the Turk away, they all went to army headquarters. There they found Staff Sergeant Janie Harris, an attractive blond haired girl in her early twenties, on her apple tablet taking notes from a senior officer. When she saw George, she got up and snapped to attention as did the other officers present. "At ease everyone," George said.

"Good afternoon, sir."

"How's it going Janie? George said in English."

"Taking notes on our inventory, sir. We added another hundred flintlocks, several more mortars and some more 12 pounders."

"That's good news. Now let me introduce you to Colonel Giustiaianini Longo from Genova, Italy. Or John for short," George said in Greek."

Janie gave her hand to the colonel who kissed it. "This beautiful woman, must be from your country or future country, America" the colonel replied in accented Greek."

Janie blushed, "Thank you, sir. Yes, I am American."

"What is that machine you are using?"

"It a tablet, a computer, sir. It does work for us and can do many other things such as take pictures and movies."

George could see that Longo was totally confused at the concept of a computer. "Let me barrow it for a second."

Janie handed the IPAD to George. "John, please stand next to Janie." George snapped a couple of photos.

"Now say something."

"What a lovely lady I am standing next to."

"Now hear yourself talk and take a look at your ugly face." George showed the picture to John and played the recording.

"That is magic, it stole my soul."

"No, John. That is also the future. George showed him the maps that were stored on the IPAD of the world. He showed him where America is and also pictures of airplanes and war ships."

"So the world is round after all? The Greeks were correct."

"Yes colonel and a fellow country man of yours and also from Genova, Christopher Columbus will find America in 1492, for the Spanish crown. At least he was supposed to in my old time line. Once this war is over we will go there and colonize it and benefit from its vast riches. That is if we are still alive."

"There is a very interesting world out there my friend, with a very interesting future for all of us."

"You are correct about that, John. Now let's go into my office. George's office was nothing special even though he was a general. He had a desk, a leather chair, a sofa and his laptop which was kept fully charged by a solar charger. Various pictures of saints and of past Byzantine battles adorned the walls. There was even a small fireplace for the winter. His most prized possession was a solar powered coffee maker. It had been found in the supply truck along with a couple of solar printers, extra batteries and battery chargers amid various other office supplies. The solar printers needed no ink since they tanned the paper with heat. George made them both a cup of coffee. Fortunately the duce and a half had several boxes of coffee grounds, along with coffee mate and sugar packets. Plus the several cases of Russian coffee we found in the underground base."

"Here John, try this beverage, it is called coffee."

The colonel took a sip. This is delicious!"

"The coffee bean is now grown in Africa and Ethiopia. It's roasted then ground up and boiled. The Turks will bring it to Europe, in about 200 years from now."

"That would be a good business to bring coffee to Europe

now."

"Yes, it will."

"I see that you have a have a different computer?"

"Yes, mine is a bit different. It's called a laptop and can do almost the same except take pictures." He did not want to even explain what a smart phone could do with the right apps. George brought up a map of the area on his laptop screen and showed it to the colonel.

"We will need to try and slow the Ottomans down. I propose that we conduct a raid and try and destroy some of their guns and bridges along their marching route. Here is a map of eastern Thrace. If we land five miles west of Heraclea and march about five miles north, we will reach the bridge at Corlu. If we destroy that bridge, it will take them at least a week to rebuild it strong enough to bring their heavy guns across. We will also look for any guns to wreck, while we are there. Once the mission is completed we'll travel to our underground base. Hopefully, the following night we will be picked up by ship and transported back to the city."

"Sounds very interesting, how are we getting there?"

"The mission will launch the day after tomorrow. We will depart at sunset, using the steam gunboat for transport. I would like you to come along and see how we operate and besides, I can use your combat expertise. We will be armed with modern weapons. Is there anyone you would like to bring along?

"Yes, he one of my captains and second in command, Niko Garibaldi. He is an excellent soldier and would be an assist if he comes along."

"Excellent, we will get him weapons certified immediately. You may want to shoot off a few more bullets if you think you need too?"

"I just may."

"Our secret naval weapon will transport us there."

"A secret naval weapon? You did say something about a steam gunboat."

"It's a steam powered gunboat armed with ten 18 pounder shell firing guns."

"Steam powered?"

"Yes, it requires no wind to move. It does have sails when it can use the wind and save fuel and for emergencies."

"That is amazing. Do you have any flying machines like the pictures in your computer, or any other surprises?"

"No, but we have a hot air balloon that rises into the sky using hot air. It is for observing enemy positions and movements. Maybe in the future, we can build a lighter than air flying machine."

"A flying machine! My god the world will be totally changed with these new weapons of war. Small powers will be able to quickly defeat larger powers that lack the new instruments of war."

"That is true, colonel. When flying machines were first invented they were supposed to help mankind travel faster. Within 10 years during the First World War, they were being used as weapons of war. Men were fighting each other like the old Knights, only in the sky. The concept of honor quickly disappeared as the war became a blood bath and the flying machines improved, become faster and carried more bombs and guns."

"Mankind will never change, "Longo said.

"We do have a few more surprises that we brought along from our time period. We have several rapid firing guns and some light mortars that can throw a small explosive bomb a mile and a half, but we have limited ammunition. We also have a secret armored fighting machine you will soon see. Our Navy is also building a large steam warship, called a frigate. It will not be ready for several more months. We will use it to go to America."

"If we all survive this coming siege, I want to come with you to the new world."

"Of course, you are welcome to come along with us there. We intend to survive and win this war. Hopefully this mission can buy us some more, time to reinforce and arm the army with more flintlock rifles. Maybe we can even find and destroy an enemy gun or two."

"Sound like a plan, my friend. I will go check on my men and see you tonight for dinner, general."

Eastern Thrace
24 October 1452

Sultan Mehmet II sat atop his white steed and scanned the horizon. Men, material of war and horses filled the fields and roads as far as he could see. His great army was on the march towards Constantinopolis and destiny. He had over 60,000 men with him and when the army from Anatolia joined his forces it would be close to 100,000, nothing could save the infidel. The Ottoman navy would soon destroy the few ships the Byzantines had and would then blockade and starve the city. Mehmet was still seething from the insults heaped on him from the so called Byzantine emperor; within a week, his forces would surround the Byzantine capital and put it under siege. His great guns, which he had already sent ahead, would batter down the walls and his Janissaries would surge through the gaps to take the city. He would soon have Constantine's head on a pike to parade around his capital. A great victory would guarantee his position as sultan, amongst the Ottoman nobility and his army. He would show mercy to the Greek and Christian population.

Mehmet would need their loyalty to combat the Latin states and other Christian kingdoms as he spread his empire. Aghia Sophia was another matter. He would turn the Christian house of god into a mosque and worship Allah and his prophet Mohamed, as it should be.

Mehmet looked up at the sun, it was beginning to set. They would have to stop soon for evening prayers and to rest for the night. He was tired, hungry and dirty, he was looking forward for his bath and rub down by his slave girls. Mehmet would pray and ask the prophet to make their journey on this great jihad safe and speedy. Not that he thought the Byzantines would or could do anything to hamper their drive towards the city walls. They were but a shell of their once great glory. He had heard reports of new weapons and magicians from the future, Yes probably the Byzantines had picked up some new gunpowder weapons, but soldiers or Djinn from the future that was ridiculous. Within a week, he would see what the Byzantines truly had.

Constantinopolis
24 November 1452

George, Anna and most of the city's nobility sat around the emperor's table enjoying the delicious local foods and wines. George had taken a seat to the left of the emperor and General Notaras, the senior Byzantine commander to the right of the emperor. Colonel Longo was sitting beside Anna, where he was having a lively discussion with his pretty date, Staff Sergeant Janie Harris. George could not keep a straight, face as he heard Janie trying to teach John some English words and his Italian pronunciations of them.

"George, stop laughing and making fun of him! At least he is trying to learn English. He already speaks a few languages.

Most Americans can't even speak proper English," Anna said.

"Yeah, so he can get into Janie's pants faster. Typical Italian lover boy."

"Well you got into mine pretty fast."

"Remember? I was a gentleman our first night and did not take advantage of you my dear duchess. You took advantage of me the next morning and thereafter. Look at your condition as a result of it."

"Oh shut up. I can't win with you," she said planting a kiss on his check.

"It's your Italian genes, darling." She just shook her head and laughed.

The emperor stood up from the table. "First of all, I want to welcome you all here my dear friends. In the next few weeks, this city and all of us will be tested very hard. Some of us here may even lose our lives. In the long run we will prevail. We have all been working very hard these last months to prepare for what we all knew was coming. Everyone in this city needs a break to let out some steam. So I am announcing tonight, my marriage to the lovely Mary Jones, who will be by my side as the next empress of Byzantium. Our marriage will take place this Sunday in the cathedral, along with the marriage of my esteemed friend and my Imperial Military security advisor, General George Mavrakis and his beautiful fiancée doctor and duchess, Anna Marone. Afterwards we will feast and enjoy ourselves. Hopefully the occasion will bring some joy to this great city, which will soon see a rebirth of the great Byzantine Empire."

The emperor picked up his goblet. "Long live the empire!"

Everyone picked up their goblets and shouted the toast.

A toast that had not been heard for several centuries. "Long live the empire, "echoed through the hallways. George prayed that it just wasn't all wishful thinking.

Chapter 8

Eastern Thrace, 30 miles west of Constantinopolis 27 October 1453

The steam powered gunboat Niki (Victory) was cutting through the swells of the sea of the Marmara at a sedate 6 knots. She could do almost 9 knots in an emergency, but Green was not pressing her tonight. He had been given command of Byzantium's new flagship and for that, the world's first and only steamship. He had relinquished command of the Phoenix to his second in command the other day. He would miss the sleek warship which was now shadowing the steam ship a couple of miles further out to sea. The Niki was carrying General Mavrakis and five other commandos on a mission to destroy a key bridge and slow down the Ottoman advance.

The Niki had just passed the small Byzantine port of Heraclea. The town was now under siege by the sultan's advance guard. They Phoenix and a transport had earlier landed some extra supplies and troops to try and hold the small port. The Byzantines had been transporting supplies there, but it had been getting more dangerous due to large numbers of Ottoman ships in the area. The day before, they had lost a transport as it was returning to Constantinopolis. Hopefully, they would not meet any Ottoman ships on this trip. They could not risk the loss or the capture of the Niki. The longer the Turks did not see it, the better the surprise would be in the large naval battle, which would soon be fought for mastery of the sea lanes.

Not that Green would let it fall into their hands; he would burn and scuttle her first.

Green looked at his watch, it was almost one in the morning he would wake the general and the rest of the team. "Yiannis take the com. I am going below."

"Yes captain," the Nicki's executive officer said.

Lieutenant Green went below, but he found everyone already awake, smearing charcoal on their faces and preparing their gear. "Sir, we'll be arriving in about 15 minutes. We haven't seen any of the enemy all night. I did hear some guns booming when we passed Heraclea about an hour ago."

"Thanks Green, we're ready. Just be there to pick us up."

"I will be there, sir."

The all felt the ship begin to slow down as they entered shallow water. "Let's go up guys, we need to get off quickly."

A few minutes later, the Niki dropped her anchor about a hundred yards from the shore. The six man team got into the ship's longboat and was quickly rowed to shore. The team included Colonel Longo, Captain Garibaldi, Lieutenant Larry Williams their explosive expert, Master Sergeant Ron Thompson and Sergeant Leroy Davis each also carrying a Russian RPG. The men watched as the longboat returned to the Niki and the ship disappeared into the darkness.

"Well let's start walking gentlemen; we got about 5 miles to go. I want to get there before daylight. Remember, no shooting unless necessary and only the M4s are to be used since they are suppressed."

With George using night gear and a compass to navigate, they made quick time toward their objective. So far he had been impressed with Captain Garibaldi. The man was a competent soldier only a few years younger than Colonel Longo. Besides the AK47, he also carried a crossbow with him. Fortunately, they did not run into any enemy activity, until they hit the main road three hours later. They followed the road and arrived at the bridge. Finding a good hiding spot overlooking the road, they waited until Sergeant Davis returned from scouting the target.

"What did you see, Davis?"

"There are no guards on the bridge, Sir. But there are many troops all around the place, mostly sleeping."

"I kind of expected that. Who would blow up a bridge in the 15th century? They would need a ton of gunpowder to destroy a stone bridge."

"See any patrols?"

"No, sir."

"Well let's get moving gents."

Ten minutes later they were on the bridge. It was a solid stone structure spanning a river that did have a small stream of running water, which troops could easily cross, but not heavy cannon. "The bridge is built very well. It will take a couple of charges to wreck the road," Lieutenant Williams said.

"Well let's get moving then. Two of you secure each end of the bridge. I will go help Williams with the charges."

"I'll take the west end with Captain Garibaldi," Davis said.

"Remember everyone, if you can avoid it, no shooting."

"Sir, this bridge is pretty strong. I need to chisel couple of holes under the arch over the side of the bridge to place the charges. Fortunately I brought a hammer and chisel, considering I had a stone bridge to deal with."

Williams pulled out some rope and tied himself to it. "Sir, lower me down till I can get to the road bed."

George wrapped the rope around him and lowered Williams a few feet till he was under the arch. He could hear him chiseling. "Jesus Williams, you are making too much racket they will hear us."

"I can't help it sir. This bridge is made out of stone."

"Well, hurry up."

"I'm trying, but this is hard going."

Sound travels better in the quiet of the night. One of the sentries of an infantry encampment a couple hundred yards west of the bridge heard a sound of metal banging. He woke his officer. "Effendi, I am sorry to wake you but listen, you can hear it too."

"Yes I can hear it also. Something is going on. Wake the men."

Both Sergeant Davis and Captain Garibaldi were having a heated conversation about women in the US military, when they heard a horn blaring just west of them. The yelling of officers waking up their men echoed through the enemy camp. They had seen the campfires and new it was an Ottoman encampment "Damn, the shit has hit the fan," Davis said.

"What is that, Davis?"

"Means everything just went to ka ka."

"Ah yes, you are correct on that. I think we will have lots of company very soon," Garibaldi said.

George also heard the horn and subsequent yelling.

"Williams we don't have much time."

"Almost there sir, need another five to ten minutes."

"Davis you need to hold there for at least ten minutes," George yelled.

"We'll do our best," Davis shouted back.

"Stay here, captain, be right back. I will send them a few surprises."

"Be careful, Davis."

Leroy Davis was pretty good with the M203 grenade launcher. He could usually hit a target at 150 meters and more. In this instance the entire enemy encampment was the target. At

150 meters he loaded the grenade launcher with a M406 High-Explosive Round. When fired the shell needs to travel between 14 and 27 meters to arm. It produces a ground burst that causes casualties within a 130-meter radius, and has a kill radius of 5 meters. Davis took aim and fired. The first round landed amongst a group of soldiers, who had just grabbed their weapons and were being organized by their officers. The grenade killed five of them including two officers and wounding another six. Davis waited ten seconds before he fired his next round, which also landed amongst a group of soldiers running to help the injured, killing four and wounding eight.

Davis could now hear screams of panic coming from the camp. It would take at least ten minutes for their officers to organize them back into a coherent fighting force. Davis ran back to the bridge. "Don't shoot! It's me, Leroy."

"What happened back their?"

"I sent the Turks a few surprises. It should buy us another ten minutes."

George had heard the explosions and figured out that Davis was trying to buy them some time. "Hurry up Williams. We don't have much time before the Turks come pouring through here."

"Almost done sir. I am setting the charge now."

"About time."

"Well sir, when these guys build bridges they build them to last!"

Sergeant Davis had hoped that he bought them all ten minutes, but unfortunately it had been an elite janissary unit that he had hit. Within five minutes their officers had organized everyone and were heading towards the bridge. Many of the enemy soldiers were carrying torches so they could better see in the darkness.

"Here they come."

The enemy troops were approximately 100 yards from the bridge when Niko fired his crossbow, hitting one of the enemy soldiers in the chest. Sergeant Davis also fired his suppressed M4, killing one of the Janissary officers. "Don't shoot your rifle yet. They don't know our position. " Davis fired again dropping another soldier. This caused the Janissaries to momentarily seek cover.

George could hear the suppressed M4 firing. "I am done, sir pull me up." George pulled on the rope and hoisted Williams up. Williams was holding a role of wire in his hand. They ran towards the eastern end of the bridge Williams cut the wire and connected the firing mechanism.

"Anytime, sir."

"I am going to get Davis and Garibaldi."

George ran over to where the two men were hunkering down. "Shit! Here they come," Davis yelled.

The Janissaries had drawn their swords and charged the bridge yelling, "Allah Akbar" at the top of their lungs. Everyone opened fire taking the first rank out. "Run to the other end," George yelled.

The three men turned and ran across the bridge as quickly as they could, followed by the Janissaries who were no more than fifty yards behind them. When they reached the other end George turned around and saw the janissaries had reached the middle of the span. "Blow it! Hit the deck."

"Fire in the hole," Williams yelled as he pressed the button, setting off the charge. A large flash lit up the night sending stones and body parts sky high. Over 50 of the Janissaries were killed instantly.

When the dust settled over 30 feet of the span had fallen into the river. "Let's get out of here. That explosion must have awakened every Turk within a five mile radius," George said.

By sunrise, they had put about six miles distance behind them while avoiding the main road and Ottoman troop concentrations. Finally by mid-morning, they came upon a convoy consisting of a large wagon train and a huge siege gun. Taking cover in the forest they observed the huge gun tethered to over 50 oxen being pulled along, on the road. If George remembered his history correctly, a gun that size could fire a stone ball weighing over half a ton and could breach a wall.

"Wow look at the size of that thing," said Thompson.

"We need to destroy that gun."

"How in god's name are we going to do that?"

"With one of those, colonel" Davis said pointing to the RPG7.

"How far can that thing shoot?"

"About 200 meters effectively," George replied.

"I'll do it, Sir." Davis said.

"Okay, we will cover you. Try not to be seen. Hit them and clear out and don't shot unless you have to. There are too many to fight."

"I know, sir."

"I keep repeating it because one may forget. Yes we do have weapon superiority and it may make you seem invincible but they have numbers, horses and their bows can shoot over 100 yards pretty accurately."

"Yes, sir. I will remember that."

"We'll meet you back here, Good luck." With that Davis grabbed an extra RPG round and took off running through the trees. George and the rest of the team slowly followed the slow moving convoy for about another 50 yards. A rocket zoomed out of the tree line and struck the gun ripping it from its sled and destroying the barrel and in the process killing several of the men around it.

"Yes! He did it," shouted George.

Suddenly another rocket flew out of the forest and hit one of the wagons. There was a bright flash, immediately followed by a huge explosion as the gun powder in several of the adjacent wagons also blew up, setting off a chain reaction. The explosions knocked over nearby trees and slammed George and the rest of the team into the ground. Pieces of wagons, oxen and bodies rained down on them. By the time the explosions had ended, over 1000 Ottoman soldiers and laborers had been killed and hundreds horribly burned. Several smaller guns had been destroyed along with almost 6 tons of valuable gun powder.

"Wow, what the hell just happened?"

"Hell was just visited upon our enemies. It seems Davis just took out an entire regiment and their munitions."

"Davis should have been back. Let's go find him."

Ten minutes later, they found Davis. He was lying under several branches that had been blown apart by the explosion. He had been only 150 yards away when the powder train was set off by the RPG. They quickly pulled the branches off him and George checked for pulse. "Thank god, he's alive."

A branch had struck him on the head but fortunately he had been wearing his helmet which partially protected him from the impact. They quickly checked to see if he had any other injuries evident, but could not find any. "He's coming too," said Captain Garibaldi.

"What happened? Jesus, my head. I have a terrible headache."

"The wagon you hit was carrying gun powder. When it blew, that set off a chain reaction that wrecked the entire convoy." George said. "The explosion was huge. You killed hundred and wrecked several of their big guns."

"Yeah, I remember a bright flash, then I was knocked into the dirt, but it felt like I was kicked in the head."

"That was the concussion and branches falling on your head. The helmet saved your ass. Can you get up and walk?"

"Davis tried to get up."

"Wow, my head is spinning."

"You probably have a slight concussion," Said George.

"Let's make a liter and carry him till he feels better. There are lots of branches around to make one," said Thompson.

Fifteen minutes later they were back on the road. The going was much harder, as they carried the stretcher through rough ground. After a few hours they stopped on a tree covered hill to rest and have something to eat. Davis was feeling a bit better. George had some Tylenol left in his first aid pouch and gave him a couple for his headache. They could still observe the smoke rising in the distance from the destroyed supply column. They had hurt the Ottomans bad, but not enough. George lit a small fire and warmed the MRES. When the rations were all heated up, he put the fire out so the smoke would not give them away.

"How do you like the MREs guys? This is what future American soldiers will eat in the field."

"This pasta and red meat sauce is not bad," Longo said.

"That brought a laugh from the Americans."

"What's so funny?"

"So typical Italian when it comes to pasta dishes. In our time Italy is famous for its cuisine, especially pasta. The red sauce is made with a fruit called tomatoes. It originally came from the new world. This is what makes the red sauce. Europe is missing much on its cuisine. We discovered lots of packaged seeds in the Russian base including tomatoes. We have planted them to create a seed base for next year's planting. We will soon have many new vegetables to improve your diet."

"This chili with beans is very good and so is the fruit desert. The chili is a bit spicy, but very tasty." Garibaldi said.

"That is future Mexican and Texan cuisine. After this war I want to go on an expedition to Mexico. There are many riches in Mexico, but a cruel people called the Aztecs live there. They sacrifice humans to their gods and rip out their still beating hearts."

"Mother of Jesus!"

"We will show them Christianity and hopefully make them our friends and potential allies. But that is in the future."

"We will have a future, my friend. We will with gods' help defeat the Turks and free these lands," Longo said.

"How are you feeling, Davis?"

"A bit better, sir, the food and coffee helped some."

"Can you walk?"

"I think so."

"We have about another five miles to go."

"I think I can make it, sir."

"Okay, you guys each grab some of his gear and let's move out."

Over the next few hours they slowly made their way towards the mine entrance, bypassing many Ottoman troops. They could hear the cannon fire coming from Heraclea seven miles to the southwest. George prayed it could hold out. The small city had been reinforced, but not to his liking. He was sure that after today, the Turks would not be in the mood for taking prisoners. The one good thing was that there were no witnesses left alive to blame the Byzantines for the destruction of the cannon and ammunition convoy. Fifteenth century gunpowder was very unstable and accidents occurred very frequently.

By late afternoon they had reached the vicinity of the mine.

They had run into several enemy horse patrols, but managed to avoid them. George sent Thompson, to make contact with the sentries. He returned 30 minutes later, giving the green light for the rest of them to proceed to the mine. At the entrance, they were met by Major Petros Tomas. "Welcome back, General Mavrakis."

George introduced both Captain Garibaldi and Colonel Longo to Petros. George noticed that Petros was becoming more fluent with English. He must be practicing with Captain Rhodes, thought George. "How's everything going here, Petros? I also see that your English is really improving."

"We've all been practicing, English. Captain Rhodes has been kind enough to give all of us daily lessons and I've been having conversations with him on Byzantine history and culture and he's been telling me about the future."

"Have you noticed any enemy activity?"

"After that loud thunder this morning, activity has slowed a bit."

"That was us. Our hero here, Davis destroyed one of their cannon with a RPG rocket, then he hit a wagon filled with gun powder, causing the entire wagon train do blow up. Hundreds of enemy soldiers were killed and tons of equipment and supplies wrecked. Hundreds more were injured. I suspect many of the enemy troops rushed there to aid the wounded.

"That should slow them a bit. How did the other mission go?"

"We seriously damaged the bridge. That should hopefully slow them up for a few days until they figure out a way over or around it."

"Any bit to slow them down helps. We have another 50 rifle barrels made to take back with you."

"This maybe is the last trip here for a while."

"We know that, sir, but we are ready to sacrifice our lives to hold or destroy this place if we have to."

"How are you on supplies?"

"We're okay for now. We hunted a couple of wild boars the other night and smoked some of the meat and froze the rest."

"Hopefully, some more supplies arrive tonight."

"Let's go down to the base."

"This transportation machine is just like the one in the city that you showed me?" Longo asked.

"Yes it is. Now, Niko and John, are you ready for a real surprise?" George said as they got into the Humvee for the ride to the main base.

"Surprise us, general? I don't think after what we've seen so far there are any more real surprises."

Ten minutes later they had reached the main base. To conserve power and lighting they had turned off many of the lights, but the two Italians were in total shock when they saw the lights and the huge cavern housing the base. "Mother, Mary of god, what is this? Have you taken us down to hell?"

George began laughing. "What is it that makes primitive societies relate everything to religion and heaven or hell?"

"I am not primitive."

"You sound like it sometimes. This is a base from 500 years in the future. You have seen only a tiny bit of our capabilities, John."

Colonel Longo began to laugh. "Now that I think of it, you are right." That brought a laugh from everyone there.

When they got out of the vehicle, they were met by Captain Rhodes. "Welcome back to hell, sir."

Every one of the Americans began laughing, which made Longo and Garibaldi have a look of terror on their faces. "Did I say something wrong, sir?"

"No, captain, just an inside joke."

"Davis, get something to eat and lay down. You did get a pretty hard bump on the head."

"Yes, sir."

"Need you in decent shape when we leave tonight. We may have to fight our way out of here."

"Niko, John, do you guys want a tour of hell?"

"Sure, show us the devil."

George took the two soldiers around and showed them the work-shops. Both men were confused, but very amazed with what they saw, especially with Rhodes' workshop. They were especially awed with the construction of the rifle barrels and the theory behind rifling. Rhodes had another surprise for George. He had found several gasoline car motors that had been covered with canvas tarps along with several Russian army short wave radios. Also found were additional crates of ammo, explosives and shells for the BMP.

"I see you've been busy, captain. Those motors may come in handy later on."

"If we could develop a fuel for them, I could get them to run and maybe construct a crude airplane."

"Great idea, it will have to wait till after the war."

"We are going to get something to eat."

"I will meet you two there in a little bit. Save me some food."

George watched the two Italians leave the work shop and thought of the future. "I wonder what else is hidden here for us to find."

"Who knows, sir? This cavern is huge I'm sure we may find more stuff. We've found a couple of minor shafts that have suffered cave ins. Who knows what's in there. One thing we're lucky, is that the Russians built a huge underground fuel storage area. With the bio diesel conversion we've been doing, we now have fuel for years."

"We need to really stretch that fuel. Once it's used that's it. We have no more."

"Have you made any progress on developing mercury fulminate for percussion caps and reloading our ammo?

"Some sir, we're working with Master Sergeant Mary Jones and some of her chemists. We're beginning to separate the needed ingredients. Probably be six months to a year."

"You mean the future empress and recently promoted lieutenant. The emperor asked her to marry him. The wedding is Sunday"

"Wow, an American empress of Byzantium. Isn't that another one for the history books? Wish I could make the wedding, but I'm needed here."

"Mary will understand your responsibility to duty. Even as the empress, she will still be working with us."

"Do you think we have a chance to beat them, sir? There are an awful lot of them"

"With all the work that you and others have done, not only will we beat them, we'll throw their asses out of Europe. We are slowly changing history here. It will be a totally new world. Maybe we can shape it better than our ancestors did, knowing the mistakes they made."

"I hope to expand the empire and take some of Asia Minor back from the Ottomans and eventually colonize the new world. We can build an empire with colonies and trade. We can't be fighting reckless wars in Europe, as our ancestors did. We must have education, technology military superiority and allies we can trust."

"That will be hard in this period, sir."

"Yes it will. That's why we must be strong. I want us to establish universities. The knowledge we brought with use can't be lost. Mankind has a chance to profit from it. We will all be instructors. The Byzantines have many scholars and craftsmen that can learn the theories and put them to effect."

"Yes, I have seen some of them here in action. They've already found better ways to manufacture the barrels and flintlock pistols and they are documenting every step which will be transcribed into future technical manuals."

Let's go grab something to eat at the dining hall, before it's all gone."

They both walked to the dining area. Petros and much of the garrison was there having diner. Petros got up in respect to George. "No, sit down. I'll join you." George grabbed some food and sat down.

"We received call, the Niki is on its way, she will be here in a few hours," Said Petros. "She is loaded with supplies."

"Hopefully, they won't have any problems on the way here. The Ottoman's are out in force. I expect their fleet in the Bosporus by next week. With its speed advantage, the Niki should easily slip through." George Said.

"We'll hold out here as long as necessary. We've already started rationing and hunting to supplement our food. The pig you are eating was hunted by us. Fortunately there are those cold rooms that can store lots of meat. We'll be fine here, sir."

"You guys are resourceful. This wild pig by the way is excellent. Just be very careful and don't be seen or followed back here."

"We are careful, sir."

"I'm going to lay down for a couple of hours. Wake me when it's time to leave. I am exhausted and can't think straight."

Sea of Marmara
28 October 1452

The steam powered gunship and pride of the Byzantine Navy, the Niki, was making a comfortable six knots through the Sea of Marmara. Lieutenant Green stood in her bridge gazing out at the horizon, looking for enemy vessels. He was wearing his night gear and with the help of a three quarter moon he could see a long way. Green had spotted a few sails earlier, but had steered well clear to avoid them. In an hour they would be arriving at their destination. His ship was full of supplies for the base and he was bringing along few extra Imperial Guards, to shore up the underground base's garrison. Green had been teaching navigation part time in the budding naval academy. He had instructed most of the officers and helmsmen to use of the points of a compass to steer. Fortunately, all the Americans that had come over had a compass with them and that certainly helped his students. Everyone knew a circle was 360 degrees and that north was zero or three sixty. There were even beginning to install crude magnetic compasses on some of the ships.

"Sir, the engine room reports that they are having a pressure leak and will have to replace the valve. They are asking us to slow down."

Green took his eyes off the horizon. "How much?"

"Half speed, sir"

"For how long?"

"Probably an hour, captain."

"What if we don't slow down?"

"We can blow the engine and lose all steam power."

"No, that would not be a good thing. Tell Burns to fix it quickly."

"Yes, sir."

Fortunately for the Niki, Captain Burns, the inventor of her engine had wanted to come along for the ride. If anyone could fix it, it was Burns, Green thought to himself. He felt the ship slow as Burns let out steam. They were now down to about four knots the average speed of a sailing ship and galleass. Green scanned the horizon again and noticed a couple of sails. Giorgos steer a couple of points to the North. He would hug the coast and hopefully they would not be seen, since he did not have any sails up. Thirty minutes later, Green spotted another galleass. This one was inshore on a parallel course with the Niki. There was no way he could head out to sea and escape, they would be seen by the off shore ships. Green yelled down the copper tube that was connected to the engine room. "All stop." He turned to his executive officer, "Ensign Stamatis, you have the bridge."

The ship glided to a stop as the paddles stopped turning. Green ran down to the engine room and found Captain Burns working on the engine. "Jay, how much longer? There is an enemy galley near-by."

"Probably another 20 minutes."

"Hurry up, I need the engine. If I use the sails we'll be seen, plus the wind is against us."

"I'm doing the best I can."

"I know you are, just hurry it up!"

Burns ran back up to the bridge. Ensign Stamatis was observing the enemy vessel. He's turned and now heading west, sir. He's no longer headed this way."

"That's okay for now, but bad for later, since he is heading down the coast towards the same place where we want to go."

Several minutes later, Burns finally gave the order to get back under way. Having restored full power, Burns joined

Lieutenant Green on the bridge. "I told you I would fix it. Now take it easy with her."

"We're screwed if she breaks down again."

The Niki was cruising at a sedate five knots trying not to make too much of a wake and be seen. "The fix should hold until we reach the yard then we can do a better repair once the engine cools. Don't force her."

"Hopefully we won't have to. We've been playing cat and mouse all night with the Ottoman navy and anything can happen. Anyway we've arrived once we get around that point. A few minutes later Green gave the light signal towards the shore and it was immediately returned.

"Depth?" Green shouted.

"Three fathoms, sir."

"All ahead dead slow."

"Two fathoms, sir."

"Drop the anchor and give me reverse."

The heavy sea anchor splashed into the shallow bay as the paddles reversed to stop the Niki's forward motion. "All stop."

"All stop, sir."

"Ensign Stamatis, I want all guns manned and ready to cut the anchor if we have to. Now drop the boats and off load the supplies, make it quick."

"Aye, Aye, captain." Green got a rush every time he heard that phrase, having taught it to his Byzantine crew.

"Be ready to give us full speed if we needed, Burns. Something tells me we will."

"You don't want to blow the engine, so you will be lucky to get seven knots."

Within a few minutes they had loaded the two longboats and headed for the shore to dump their cargo and return for more. They had brought another few Imperial Guards for the garrison and a couple of light 6 pounder guns.

George had seen the light flashes and had returned the signal. It had only taken a few minutes for the Niki's crew to drop the long boats in the water and begin loading them with cargo. The trip from the mine had been uneventful and they did not see any enemy patrols on the way; he had a suspicion they were still recovering from this morning's blast.

They all heard the splash of the oars as the longboats got closer and the scrape of their bottoms as they hit the beach. "Come on guys give them hand to unload we can't stay here all night."

After a half an hour of hard work they had loaded up the all supplies that the Niki had brought on the truck. The 60 completed musket barrels, a box of grenades and a couple of the Russian radios brought from the base were loaded on the Niki.

"General, I wish you luck and I will pray for our victory," said Petros.

"Our prayers will also be with you. Please be careful, avoid any contact with the enemy. That base must remain secure. It is our future."

"We will general. I will also have the entrance camouflaged even better than before. May god go with you my friend and may he keep you safe."

The two men embraced and George entered the long boat for the short row to the Niki. George was piped aboard and he saluted the Byzantine ensign as he got off the stairs. Both Burns and green were there to meet him. "Welcome aboard, sir."

"Thanks Green. How was the trip?"

"Except for a bit of engine trouble that Burns quickly repaired, the voyage was not too bad."

"Good job, Burns. Let's hope nothing breaks down going home."

"Thanks, Sir. As long as we don't tax the engine the repairs should hold till we get back to the yard."

"Raise the anchor and take us home, Stamatis."

"Aye, aye, captain.

George laughed. "You're eating this up, Roger. Who would ever dream that a 23 year old kid from Jacksonville, Florida would be commanding a warship in the age of sail?"

Both Burns and Green laughed. "Not in my wildest dreams or fantasies. When as a kid I was reading novels of sailing ships and naval battles. I always tried to fantasize how this would really be. Well sir, it's nothing like I ever imagined. It's really pretty cool, but people get killed and I have become very good in killing our enemies."

"Yes, you are good at this, but you can also get hurt or killed."

"That is true, sir. Now on the other side of the coin, who would ever imagine that a Greek American, US Air Force Master Sergeant, would become a general in the Imperial Byzantine army?"

"You make a good point there, Green."

They heard the anchor being raised. "I am going down to the engine room," Burns said.

"Keep that engine going, Burns."

"Let's go to the bridge, sir."

"I'm right behind you."

"Ahead three quarters," Green ordered the helmsman.

"Ahead three quarters," Ensign Stamatis yelled into the engine room com tube.

The paddles began to turn and the gun boat gradually picked up speed. "Steer south, southwest."

"Turning to a heading of south, south west, sir."

"I want the crew to remain in general quarters, Stamatis. The men can go and grab something to eat or take a break from the guns one at a time. Go relay my orders to the gunnery officer."

"Aye, aye, captain."

The Niki came about and headed out into the Sea of Marmara. She made a hard target to find in the dark, when she was not using her sails. "There's been lots of enemy naval activity on the way here, sir. So far we were able to avoid them with our superior speed."

"They will force a naval battle on us for sure in the next few days. They need to have control of the straights in order to get troops and supplies across to enforce a total blockade of the city."

"Yes you are probably correct, on that one, sir. That's what I would do if I was their admiral."

"Let's make it back in one piece for now. My wedding is the day after tomorrow."

"Yeah and the emperor's too. I can't believe Mary is going to become the empress of Byzantium. Now that's another one for the history books."

"It sure is, Green."

Two hours later as they neared the straits, the lookout reported sales in the horizon. Through the night vision gear they observed more than a dozen ships blocking the entrance to the straits. There was no way they could run the blockade with so many enemy ships on station. They would have to fight and break through to reach the city and safety. "Stand by to give me full speed, "Green hollered into the speaker tube.

They were finally spotted, several galleys began an attempt to cut the gun boat off and trap her between them. "Helmsman, steer for the opening where these galleys were on station."

"Aye, Aye, captain."

"Gunners, prepare to fire as we pass and reload with explosive shells."

"They're going to cut us off, Green."

"Give me all she's got now," Green yelled down the tube.

The paddles started going faster and the Niki picked up speed." Hard to port and fire as you bare."

The gunboat was doing almost eight and a half knot as the wheel was spun hard to the right bringing her starboard 18 pounders to bear. Three of the galleasses were attempting to sandwich the Niki between them. Each one of the guns captained by a petty officer started to fire as the first target came into range, less than 100 yards away. Several hits were scored on the middle galley, the eighteen pound balls smashing into men and bulwarks causing death and destruction. One of the balls hit the galley on the waterline causing a serious hull breach. The gunboat's well trained gun crew quickly loaded the guns and fired as the outside enemy ship came in range. Three of the explosive shells hit the enemy ship below deck causing a fire that rapidly got out of control. Fire at sea is the worst thing that could happen to any ship. Ships of the period were tinder boxes made with wood and tar. They could hear screams and see men on fire jump into the sea with others joining them, preferring to drown then be burned alive.

Almost as quickly as it started, the battle was over. With her superior speed the Niki was able to avoid the other enemy ships and easily slip through the blockade. She left one ship in flames and another one sinking. The cannon fire and the burning enemy ship had been seen by the soldiers manning the seaside city walls. The rumble of the guns had also been heard by many of the city's inhabitants. When the Niki entered the straights, she lit her lanterns to be seen by the garrison. The men on the walls began to cheer, seeing her safe return and were soon joined by many of the city's inhabitants. By the time she docked at the naval base they could hear the cheering all the way to the dock side.

When they finally docked George was first off the ship. He was met at dockside by both the emperor and Admiral Laskaris. George saluted the two officers but instead of returning the salute, the emperor embraced George to the cheers of hundreds of sailors and soldiers at the naval base. "You made it back in one piece my friend. I had been praying for your success and safe return."

"We not only seriously damaged the bridge; we took out one of their wagon trains carrying ammunition and cannon. The huge explosion killed many hundreds of enemy soldiers."

"That is excellent news."

"The cannon shells work well. We destroyed a galleass with them. I'm sure we will be involved a major naval battle soon."

"Ah, here is Lieutenant Green and the rest of our Americans."

"The men saluted their commander and chief."

"I heard of your success these last couple of days ending with tonight's small naval victory. I thank you from the bottom of my heart. Each one of you will receive 50 gold coins as a reward. Sergeant Davis is also promoted to Staff Sergeant for his gallantry, in destroying the enemy supply train. Now go back to the palace and get some rest."

"Squad, atten hut!" Lieutenant Green turned saluted the emperor and did another about face. "Troops dismissed!"

"Long live the emperor!" Screamed the newly promoted Davis. The cry was taken up by most of the men in dock yard.

"Our men's morale is excellent and the troops love you, your majesty," Admiral Laskaris said with a smile.

"Let's see how much they still love me once the battle and the dying starts. Anyway let's go back to the palace. I'm sure General Mavrakis wants to get some rest and see his bride to be as I do mine."

Eastern Thrace
29 October 1452

The young sultan was livid, as he toured the devastation which had been caused by the massive gun powder explosion. The destruction of the convoy had been complete. Tons of valuable gun powder had gone up in smoke and several siege guns along with some smaller cannon wrecked. Over a thousand men had been killed and hundreds horribly burned or maimed. Because there had been no survivors that witnessed the initial explosion, there was no way they could find out if this was an accident or caused by enemy action. To top it all off, a key bridge had been wrecked by the enemy, which would now cause a few days delay in getting his heavy guns across. To make an example to the rest of the army he had the surviving officers of the ill-fated weapons convoy flogged to death and their heads mounted on spears. He could no longer afford incompetency. Mehmet heard a man screaming nearby and went to see what was going on. A man was tied to a branch and was being flogged.

The sultan turned to the officer in charge. "What has this man done?"

"We found him in the woods, my padishah. He said that he had been part of the convoy, but had gone to the woods to relieve himself. He saw a black man dressed in strange cloths carrying a rod that spit fire, which caused this destruction."

"Cut this man down immediately."

"The man was cut down and kissed the sultan's feet."

"Thank you my sultan for showing me mercy."

"Get up man, what is your name and tell me what happened here."

"My name is Nuri. It is true, my, padishah. I was relieving

myself in the woods about 150 paces from the road, when this strangely dressed black man appeared. He was carrying a staff with a small object on the end. Before I could get up, the man pointed the rod toward the convoy and a flame shot out of the top towards the road. That is all I remember. I was knocked out by the tremendous blast."

"How is that possible? The bump on your head made you imagine it."

"No my sultan, I swear by Allah, this is the truth"

"The sultan considered himself an educated man. He had read stories of Marco Polo's trip to China and how the Italian traveler had described the Chinese using flaming rockets as weapons of war. To a man that had never seen this before it would look like a rod spitting fire. Had the Byzantines acquired rockets? This could complicate his battle plans."

"Free this man. He will join my household guard."

"Yes my padishah," said the officer.

Mehmet was not superstitious, but if this man was the only survivor, maybe he could bring him some luck. The sultan addressed one of his senior engineers. "You have three days to repair this bridge or your head will be displayed here for all to see."

"It will be as you ask, my padishah."

His army could not be delayed any longer. Each day that went by gave the Byzantines added time to prepare their defenses. Not that it would save them in the long run, but it would cost time and many more casualties for the Ottomans.

Chapter 9

Constantinopolis, Aghia Sofia Cathedral
31 October 1452

George was truly amazed at the splendor of the 900 year old cathedral built by the great Byzantine Emperor Justinian. The beautiful icons and holy relics were displayed for all Christian believers to see and worship. The ancient Byzantine church hymns that George remembered as an altar boy were actually being sung by a real Byzantine choir. The great church was filled to the brims with the city's nobility, wealthy and military elite. Even outside, thousands of the city's residents came to wish the emperor and their miracle general well. Anna looked very beautiful in her silk wedding dress. She was wearing a beautiful gold crucifix that was encrusted with precious jewels, a gift from the emperor. George was dressed in a general's military uniform and wearing a breastplate given to him by the emperor of beautiful well shined armor, also decorated with gold and precious jewels. Three gold stars were on each shoulder epilate. The wedding would be a Greek Orthodox ceremony. Anna had been baptized Orthodox earlier, by the patriarch as had Mary.

When the liturgy officiated by the patriarch started, the emperor as the best man, walked up to the alter and exchanged the bride and groom's head crowns. When the ceremony was over, both George and Anna stepped outside the huge church. They quickly walked down the steps passing under the swords of his American honor guard, commanded by his friend General Longo, to the cheers of thousands, yelling "long live the miracle general" and "long live the emperor."

"You are very popular, my dear husband."

"Hope it lasts," George said as he kissed his bride to the cheers of thousands of soldiers and civilians who had come to see the weddings.

"Let's go in and change, its Mary and Constantine's turn next."

Twenty minutes later to the joy of thousands the Imperial bride was taken to the cathedral in a splendid carriage escorted by the Imperial Guard Calvary. The guards formed to her sides and escorted their future empress up the steps of the cathedral where the emperor was waiting for her. The couple approached the alter, where the patriarch and Anna were waiting. Mary was also dressed in a similar type wedding gown, but she was also wearing a solid gold and jeweled encrusted tiara. The emperor was also wearing the uniform of a Byzantine senior commander, his shinny breast plate studded with jewels, showing off the new wealth of the city. On each shoulder epilate was a circle of five gold stars denoting him as commander and chief. He was also wearing his side arm to denote that the empire was at war.

The ceremony began and Anna repeated the steps the emperor had done for her earlier ceremony. When the wedding was finally over the bells of Aghia Sofia began to ring, soon picked up by all the other churches in the city. A 21 Gun salute was fired in honor for the imperial couple, by the Niki, the navy's flagship.

The emperor and his bride walked down the aisle of the old cathedral, to the outside cheers of thousands and cries of "long live the imperial couple!" George, Anna and Colonel Longo stood to the right of the imperial couple. The emperor was handed a bullhorn and raised his arms for silence. When the crowed had quieted down enough, he began to speak.

"Citizens of Byzantium, today is one of the happiest days of my life and I am sure it is a joyous moment for this city. In the past ten months we have accomplished many things and have made tremendous progress in preparing this city for the storm, we all knew was coming. With the help of my dear friend General George Mavrakis and his people, who came to us from a far off land, we have been able to build new weapons and ships that will defeat the Ottoman scourge that has been slowly devouring this once great land. After this is all over I will settle once and for all the rumors you have heard. No, they are not angels but flesh and blood like us. Could you call their arrival to our city a miracle? I would say it was. Suffice to say they have sacrificed everything to be here with us. The final battle with our age old enemies will begin in the next few days. I expect every one of you to do your duty, not just for me but for your city and neighbors, to your religion and culture. Now my friends enjoy the food and festivities."

A huge applause followed by cheering broke out amongst the thousands who started chanting, "Niki". (Victory)

"That also was definitely one for the history books, your majesty."

"Yes it was. Now I have a scribe transcribing all these moments for that very reason," said the emperor.

"Good for you, sir. Just be careful what you say. It can be used against you if it's written down. This was done many times to discredit popular and unpopular politicians by the news media."

"Yes but in this age I can have their head." The emperor tried to look serious but began to laugh.

"I hear the small pro imperial party newspaper that was started by Lieutenant Ross, has taken off. Especially now, with the introduction of the printing press giving the ability to print the news much faster."

"Yes it has and we've sold several presses and their patents to the Italians at a pretty penny."

"Learning will now spread faster throughout the world. That is one positive step we accomplished with our arrival."

"Yes my friend and we will open several schools and universities once the Ottoman threat is over. Constantinopolis will once again become a great learning center for the world."

"Maybe we will go to the moon 200 years earlier in this time line."

The emperor turned to his bride. "Do you want to go back to the palace my love, or get some of your American foods? I do love those hamburgers as you call them and spare ribs with the spice rubs. The fried chicken is great too. There are even new stands opening up selling ribs and feta cheese burgers throughout the city."

"I never say no to spare ribs and fried chicken, Constantine. Wait till we begin harvesting tomatoes and potatoes. Nothing beats a burger with fries and tomato ketchup."

Let's go grab some food then."

Throughout the city many food stands had been set in honor of the wedding to feed the populace. They were cooking local dishes and the new American foods. Needless to say almost everyone opted for the "American delicacies."

After they had finished eating, the imperial couple got up and started walking toward their carriage, followed by George and Anna. The Imperial Guards, busy keeping the crowds back did not immediately notice a man about 10 yards away, pushing through the crowd holding what appeared to be a small cross bow. He brought up the bow to fire. Mary noticed the assassin, "watch out Constantine." she yelled. The assassin fired, and the empress jumped in front of the emperor taking the bolt in her side. The man saw that he hit the empress instead of his intended target. He quickly pulled out a dagger, but was shot dead by Colonel Longo, before he could take another step.

The emperor held Mary in his arms as Anna rushed over.

"My love, why did you do that?"

"Because without you Constantine, there would be no Byzantium. Your death would cause chaos, since there is no heir in such a crucial moment and besides I love you."

"Move over, "Anna said the doctor in her quickly taking over. "Take her immediately to the hospital. I must perform surgery at once. George, you have A positive blood, find out who else has it. She will need blood."

After the assassination attempt the crowed began screaming and running. The Imperial Guards fired their guns in the air and yelling at the crowd to settle down. The emperor finally stood up and the people saw he was unhurt and order was quickly re-established.

"How is she Anna?" George asked.

"Not good. I don't have an x ray machine or MRI to see what has been damaged and how deep the bolt went. I will have to operate in the blind."

"If anyone can do it, you can my love."

"I will do my best. Anna turned to the patriarch who had arrived to see what had happened. "Please start praying your holiness. She and I will need all the help we can get."

"I will my child."

Mary was put into the carriage and transported along with Anna to the hospital. George and the emperor followed on horseback. When the carriage arrived they took Mary into the crude operating room and prepped her for surgery. Anna came over and stuck a needle into George's vein and the other line into Mary. "We are lucky I still have some of these I kept for extreme emergencies like this. I also have a few IVs left. But I'm going in blind, George."

"She's lucky to have you Anna. You specialized in internal medicine and did some surgeries."

"She's in pain and shock. All I have is a couple of vials of anesthesia and some morphine.

"You're all she's got. Now do your best and save her."

Anna washed her hands and sterilized them with alcohol as she did with her instruments. She gave Mary some anesthesia through her IV and with the help of two local doctors she had been training, began the difficult surgery. After George had given over a pint and a half of blood the needle was removed and sterilized by one of the nurses and quickly placed into Master Sergeant Fulton's vain. George was given some water to drink and he stepped out of the operating room and into the hallway. There he found the emperor, with several body guards and General Notaras sitting in the hallway.

"The emperor got up and embraced George. "Thank you my friend for giving your blood to help my wife. How is she doing?"

"Anna is still working on her. If anyone can help her in this world, it's Anna."

"She took the bolt for me!"

George could see tears in his eyes. "She did it out of love, Constantine. You would have done the same for her."

"Yes, I would have."

"She knows without your leadership, this city is done for."

"Without her I am done for."

"She will make it, if Anna has anything to do about it."

"Anna is not god. She can only do so much."

"That is true, her life is in god's hand but Anna was trained in modern medicine and she has treated much more serious combat wounds in our time line."

A while later, the surgery room door opened and Anna stepped out. She removed her mask. "I've done all I could do. The bolt had nicked her lung and just missed her heart. I repaired all the damage, but's she's lost a lot of blood."

"Will she live?"

"The next 24 hours will be crucial your majesty. She's young and strong and I have high hopes that she will pull through."

"When can I see her?"

"Possibly in a few hours, Constantine. She's still under the anesthesia, so not until she wakes."

The emperor hugged and kissed Anna on the cheek. "Thank you doctor, for saving my wife."

"She's also my friend. She's not out of danger yet."

"But without you, she would be already dead."

"Go get some rest, Constantine. I'll be here watching over Mary. I have my nurses in there monitoring her condition."

"I can't leave with my wife hovering between life and death."

"Okay, as you wish. I understand."

"Your majesty you should make an official news announcement to the people. There are thousands of citizens gathered outside," George said.

"Yes, yes, you are right, George."

The emperor walked to the hospital entrance followed by the Imperial Guards. Thousands were gathered outside, many praying. When they saw the emperor come out the crowed became quiet and the emperor began to speak. "My citizens, today was supposed to be a great day of joy for this city. It would be a new beginning, a new dynasty in the making, the old joining the future. Instead it became a day of pain and despair. Well I am here to tell you all that the empress is alive, thanks to doctor Mavrakis and her surgical skills. The empress's prognosis is guarded and the next 24 hours will be crucial, so please keep her in your prayers. To our enemies all I have to say is that you will pay for what you attempted to do to the people of this great city. You may want to destroy this city's will to fight and make it citizens cower from fear. What you really did is show them the evil you truly are. We will fight to the last and we will defeat you." With that the emperor turned and went back into the hospital.

"That was an excellent speech, your majesty. You showed the people you are in command and that the empress is alive."

"Let's hope we can back our words, George."

Constantinopolis
1 November 1492

The next morning the city was awakened by the loud booming of cannon fire. The Ottoman army of Anatolia under the command of Ishak Pasha the Beylerbeyi (governor) of Anatolia was attempting to cross the straights with small boats to invest Constantinopolis from the Northeast and join up with the forces coming from Edirne. His crossing was being prevented by the guns of fort Justinian and the navy. A long range gun dual had erupted between the crude but very large Ottoman guns and the cannon of the fort. In shear throw weight the Ottoman projectiles were massive weighing over 400pounds and when one hit, it did tremendous damage. The Byzantine guns were far more accurate and could be loaded much faster and the explosive shells much more deadly to the enemy gun crews. This came as a complete shock to the Ottoman commander having been told his enemy lacked heavy cannon.

After a couple of hours, the Ottomans pulled back out of

range having suffered many casualties to their valuable gun crews. One Byzantine shell had also set off a powder wagon destroying the adjacent guns. The fort had also taken a couple of hits, damaging the walls and one large projectile, taking out an 18 pounder and its crew. Repair details trained for just that occasion, quickly fixed the breaches to the walls. Ishak Pasha the Ottoman commander would wait until the navy cleared the sea lanes and cross the straights with his troops, out of the range of the Byzantine guns.

The emperor having spent the night at his wife's side was given his daily intelligence briefing by George, who had gone to the hospital for that occasion and to visit his wife and Mary. The empress had awakened sometime in the night which was a good sign towards her recovery. She had been in pain and Anna had given her a homemade opium brew to relieve her discomfort and some antibiotics she still had left. So far Anna had observed no infection which could ultimately kill her patient.

George hugged and kissed his wife."You look exhausted, Anna. You need to also get some rest. Remember you are pregnant."

"I know. I've thrown up enough times to remind me. I will get some rest soon. I think she is out of danger. There is no sign of infection and she is resting on her own."

"So she is better, Anna?"

"I would say so. Her youth helps the healing process and she is in great shape. She jogs daily several miles."

"After what happened, that may have to change once she is better."

"Thank god that I had saved a few boxes of IV drip, some anesthesia drugs and antibiotics for real emergencies."

"There will be many emergencies coming in soon."

"I'm saving those for the Americans and the emperor. We need to stay alive to help these people. Plus, I'm a little selfish. After all we've done I think we deserve it."

"I won't argue that point with you. But we will have to start manufacturing our own soon."

"We have plans to start. Mary is heading up that project. We are reusing our needles but we will need to start making some, one of these days. "

"That may be a long way off. I need to talk to Constantine."

"He's been at her side most of the night."

"What a way to spend your honeymoon."

"Look at us."

"When all this is over, I'll take you to Mykonos for our honeymoon."

"Yeah, Mykonos in the 1450s."

"We can get a jump on everyone and build the first nudist resort."

"I'll look so sexy, all pregnant." George started laughing.

"Let's go see Constantine and Mary."

They walked to the room were Mary was recuperating. Two Imperial Guards armed with AK-47s with fixed bayonets stood guard at the entrance. When they spotted George they came to attention. Walking into the room George observed the emperor who was sitting next to his wife had dozed off holding her hand. The room was nice and toasty with a fire going in the fireplace to keep the patient warm since it was November. Mary was hooked to an IV and sleeping. Her color had improved from when George had last seen her. "Your majesty I hate to wake you since you must be exhausted being up all night, but I need to brief you on the latest events."

"I did get a couple of hours rest dozing off."

"The empress looks much better since I last saw her."

"Thanks to Anna being by her side for most of the night. She is better."

"She is a strong girl. She will pull through."

"I'm going to my office and lay down for a while. If Mary awakens let me know."

"We will Anna. Now go get some rest," George said.

"So general it's begun. I heard the gun fire earlier."

Its beginning, Constantine. Almost like the history books, only in my timeline the Turks were able to cross from Anatolia to the European side with thousands of troops, because they controlled the fort we now own. Unfortunately for them, we control the fort and our navy controls the Bosporus for now."

"Where is General Notaras?"

"He took a Humvee and went over to the fortress to observe the enemy."

"The fool can get killed or captured and we lose a valuable fighting machine and also one of your men."

"Don't worry, he's safe I sent John to keep an eye on him and get him back here quickly. He should be back any minute."

As if on cue General Notaras walked in the room. "How is the empress?"

"Much better. Anna thinks she will be okay."

"Thank god. The wholes city is praying for her. The patriarch held a special sermon for her."

"Well maybe god heard all their prayers. Let's step outside so we don't wake her. She needs to rest."

The three men stepped outside and one of the nurses went inside to keep an eye on Mary. "So has the main body been sighted?"

"Yes your majesty, one of our cavalry patrol said the Ottomans are encamped five miles from the walls and have their artillery with them," General Notaras said.

"It seems they were able to repair the damaged bridge rather quickly."

"Anything is possible, when enough heads roll."

"Fear only works so much, your majesty. Its loyalty, patriotism and the desire to fight for your home and ideals that really motivates people," George said.

"We are fighting for our survival and freedom. As one of your early founding fathers said," give me freedom or give me death."

"That was Patrick Henry giving a speech."

"Yes, I read it on Mary's IPAD."

"Remember, your majesty that they too believe in the ideals of Islam and jihad (holy war) so they will be ideologically motivated to fight us as holy warriors seeking an instant pathway to heaven."

"That is true. They believe that in a jihad. If they die in battle against the infidel they will go to heaven and have 70 virgins and mountains of food to eat."

"Not a bad place to go if it's true," Notaras added.

"We'll never know. Anyway, tell me General Notaras, how did the gun duel with the Turks go?"

"We gave a lot more then we got. Those huge stone balls are something else. One of them dismounted a gun and killed three men. We forced them to give up their attempt to cross. A couple hit the walls knocking down a small section but our rapid repair teams quickly fixed the damage. General Mavrakis' suggestion to form those teams worked wonders."

"Hopefully they perform just as good on the city walls. Those guns are much bigger and will do a lot more damage."

"That's what caused the city to fall in my time line. There were just too many breaches to the walls. Hopefully we can keep those guns silent for most of the time and limit the damage."

"I think your majesty, that by tomorrow we will be surrounded and their navy will attempt to wrest control of the straights from us, so they can bring their Anatolian forces across the Bosporus. That's what I would do in the sultan's place."

"You are probably correct. Tomorrow may be decisive for our navy, if the Ottomans decided to give battle, General Notaras."

"In my timeline, the Turks eventually defeated the allied navy and brought ships overland into the Golden Horn."

"I remember you telling us that, George. Well we have several surprises in store for them if they reach the Golden Horn. Our heavy gun batteries should blow them out of the water."

"I am counting on that, your majesty, as is Admiral Laskaris."

"Yes, he is even happier now that two Corvettes from Trebizond have joined the fleet."

"I hope the Venetians will come through on their alliance agreement with us."

"In my time line they never did. A good portion of their fleet waited in the Aegean, just outside the entrance to the Dardanelles straights, due to bad weather and in their minds, they had also written off the city."

"Then tomorrow may in fact be a decisive day for us. If not the next couple will surely be and determine our fate."

Ottoman Camp,
Outside the Walls of Constantinopolis
1 November 1452

The sultan looked up at the setting sun. He had just finished his evening prayer to the one god and only god Allah and to his prophet Mohamed. He had asked Allah to grant him victory against the infidels. He had issued his final orders to his commanders. His heavy guns were on the move and would in the next few hours be in position. The attack would begin just before daybreak, with a massive bombardment against the city walls. Once the walls were breached, his army would charge forward. To his surprise the Byzantines had built cannon and put them on the fort they had captured from his army. This prevented his Anatolian reinforcement s from coming across the straits and reinforcing his main force. No matter, he still had over 60000 troops and 60 heavy guns to bring to bear; he would crush them and make them pay for the humiliations they had caused him. In the next couple of days he would also unleash his navy to destroy the enemy fleet and blockade the city to submission. His victory would forever spell his greatness and rule of over the Turkic tribes. After the Byzantines were finally destroyed, his power would stretch from the depths of Anatolia to the borders of central Europe. Given time and opportunity he would conquer the middle-east, take Mecca and Medina and be caliph for the entire Islamic world. He would show his enemies his greatness once and for all.

Mehmet walked out of his tent and was met by his advisor, Al din Pasha. "My padishah the guns will be in place in the next few hours. I have given commands that no fires will be lit, so we can give the infidels a surprise."

"Excellent! If we can knock down the walls I want the auxiliaries in the breach immediately!"

"Yes my padishah it will happen as you say."

"Any news on the assassin?"

Aldin Pasha was hoping the sultan would not ask. "Yes my padishah the attempt failed. The empress was wounded instead. She jumped in front of the emperor and took the cross bolt."

"Does she still live?"

"Yes she does."

"Good, I may take her as one of my wives."

"As you wish, my padishah."

"I will now rest. Wake me a couple of hours before the attack is to begin. I wish to be there."

"By your command it will be so. May the Prophet watch over you in your sleep."

Several hours later, the sultan had been awakened. He had a breakfast of bread cheese, olives and tea and then rode on his white stallion to the front lines. He was met by his commanders who waited to begin the attack. The sultan rode up to one of the great cannons it was loaded and ready to fire. He got off his horse and rode up to the gun captain. The gun crew prostrated themselves in front of the sultan.

"Rise! Are you ready to die in this great jihad?"

"We are all ready to give our lives, killing the infidels, my padishah," the gun captain said.

"Then fire your gun and begin this great jihad."

The gun captain put his lit match to the touch hole and the great gun fired, hurling the huge 1200pound stone ball over half a mile, so it could strike one of the center walls. The siege had finally begun.

Constantinopolis, city walls
2 November 1452

All through the night the Byzantines had been hearing the Ottomans surrounding the city and beginning the preparations for the siege. Except for some vital Americans whose knowledge could not afford to be lost, George had distributed his American troops thought out the walls to help stiffen the defenses. The sky was dark and cloudy, making it difficult to see much even with the night vision googles. He had been up on the outer walls since 4am waiting for the attack to begin. The gun batteries on the outer and inner walls had been manned and response forces redistributed throughout the walls to quickly respond if there was a breach. Colonel Longo had taken command of several units in the outer ramparts, armed with match locks and 9 pounder guns. His mission was to bleed the enemy as much as possibly, before he would retreat behind the walls.

George looked to the east, it would be sunrise soon. He prayed that they had done enough to save the city. Granted he still had a couple of surprises for the Turks and he would save them for the appropriate time. George saw a bright flash that momentarily blinded him as it was amplified through the night vision googles he was wearing. He heard the thunderous report of a large gun firing. A couple of seconds later he felt a shock that knocked him to the ground. A huge stone ball weighing over half a ton had struck the wall 50 feet away, knocking down a small section and killing four men. Several more stone balls hit various sections of the wall killing and maiming several of the defenders. The barrage lasted for several minutes, damaging several sections of the wall. George heard cheering and saw Constantine arriving with several of his Imperial Guards

"Good morning, your majesty. How is the empress?"

"She is doing just fine. She is off her IV and eating some soup. She will fully recover."

"That is at least some good news. We've taken several hits on the wall and some casualties."

"Those stone balls are huge. They damaged several sections."

The cry of Allah Akbar from the throats of thousands was heard coming from the Ottoman lines. "Here they come. Every second gun will load with round shot," George yelled. The order was also relayed to the other gun batteries on the wall. The sun was beginning to rise, and they could see a line of several thousand Ottoman irregular infantry about 500 yards distant charging towards the wall breaches.

"Fire!"

The Byzantine cannons belched flame and smoke as they sent their 18 pound round shot and explosive shells plowing into the packed infantry. Each ball ripped through the packed formations killing and maiming several men at a time. But they still came. The troops in the ramparts commanded by Colonel Longo began firing their smaller cannons that had been loaded with canister when the advancing hoards entered the cleared kill zone that had been prepared days before the battle. The hundreds of musket balls ripped through the advancing infantry killing and maiming scores. Finally Longo gave his musketeers the order to fire, adding to the blood bath. Even the best trained infantry could not take that kind of punishment for long. The undisciplined irregulars broke under the combined cannon and musket fire and rapidly retreated back to the Ottoman lines leaving hundreds dead on the field. The first round had gone to the Byzantines.

"They are retreating. We beat them back!"

"That was too easy. Those were not the sultan's best soldiers. They are probing our defenses. They will be back."

George ordered counter battery fire against the Ottoman gunners using explosive shells. The 18 pounders hurled their explosive shells at the huge Turkish cannon, but their crude fuses were not always effective. Nevertheless they did manage to knock out one large gun by setting off the powder train and for the most part, kept the gun crews from firing at maximum efficiency. Sometime in the afternoon the Turkish smaller guns switched their targets from the walls to the outside ramparts which Colonel Longo was holding. After an hour barrage the Ottoman infantry attacked. This time they were driven forward by officers welding whips. Even though they suffered horrendous casualties they managed to reach the ramparts. Longo gave the order to fix bayonets and met the reckless Ottoman charge. His men fought like lions cutting and slashing at the enemy. Emptying his assault rifle, Longo pulled his Makarov to make his last stand, but the enemy charge had reached its zenith and they began retreating.

"Forward men! After them!"

The Byzantine troops poured out of the ramparts and chased the irregulars to the Turkish lines, in the process capturing and wrecking a couple of the enemy's smaller guns. Finally after meeting stiffened resistance and beginning to suffer casualties, Longo gave the order to pull back to their lines. They had won the day, but they knew they could not stay at the ramparts much longer, they would get pounded to pieces by the enemy cannons and eventually over run, there just was too many. Longo would bleed them as long as he could. The sun was beginning to set. He needed to attend the evening briefing at headquarters. Leaving his second in command the newly promoted Major Garibaldi, he was let back into the city and transported to the palace. Longo entered headquarters where he was greeted by the emperor and the general staff.

"Good evening, gentlemen."

"What you did was brave and very foolish, colonel. You could have been killed and all your men lost. A loss we can ill afford," General Notaras said."

"We killed hundreds and took out two of their guns."

"That you did and put the fear of god in them. But they have thousands of men to lose, we don't. You weren't even fighting their best troops. Please colonel, don't do anything foolish again, we can't afford to lose you."

"I apologize. I just got caught up in the fray, I thought I was a dead man when they breached the ramparts and when they broke all we wanted to do was to kill them. I will be more careful in the future."

"I probably would have done the same, colonel. Tell us, what were your casualties?" George asked.

"Twenty two killed and 15 wounded some seriously."

"We've had ten killed on the walls today and the same number wounded. The enemy may have had hundreds killed but we can't afford these casualties in the long run."

"We've called up the reserves, so we can count on almost 15000 troops which is a substantial amount for a defender. That was a brilliant idea, General Mavrakis. This way we have doubled the troops we have," said General Notaras the Army Chief of Staff.

They could hear the dull boom of the enemy siege guns firing here and there and the Byzantine counter battery fire.

"What about the damage to the walls?"

"Our civil engineering teams, led by Lieutenant Ross, will repair and shore up the damaged walls tonight, your majesty."

"We have to find a way to somehow silence those huge guns."

"Our counter battery fire is semi effective, Colonel. We are having timing issues with the fuses."

"You do have those Russian mortars you can use."

"I can, colonel, but we have a very limited amount of bombs. Now, less than a hundred. We used a bunch of shells to take the fort."

"We may use them to take out the crews and silence the big guns, those monsters that fire 500 kilo stone balls."

"They will just keep replacing the gun crews until we run out of shells. Those mortars may be more useful taking out their infantry if they breach the walls."

"We may fire a few shots and harass them starting in the morning, we can put the balloon aloft."

"That's a good idea, George. It will also help the city's morale if they see the balloon overhead."

"Yes, your majesty."

"We do have our secret weapon in an emergency, "Notaras said.

"The ultimate war chariot, the BMP," the emperor added.

"True sir, but it too, has limited ammunition. It must be used in a crucial moment where it will make a difference. It's also to protect you and the empress your majesty. In an emergency if the walls are breached you and the empress will go in it and be evacuated to a safe location."

"I will never take the coward's way out, General Mavrakis."

"It's not the coward's way and you were never known as a coward in history. In my timeline you were killed fighting the enemy and Byzantium died with you. If you are killed in this timeline, there will be no Byzantium. You will be safe in the armored vehicle until we regroup and throw them out of the city."

"Hopefully that time and decision will never come. The empress though, is to be protected at all costs."

"Of course, your majesty," George replied. "Now let's get back to the war. Colonel Longo, your position at the ramparts in the next day or two will become untenable. They will pound you to pieces with their guns. Be prepared to evacuate at a moment's notice and take your guns with you. If we can prevent it, we don't want them falling into enemy hands."

"I will keep half the men in the dugouts we've built and bleed the Mohammedians as long as possible, before we evacuate."

"Make sure you do that. As I reiterated before, we can't afford to lose you or your men. That is an order, colonel."

"Yes, sir.

The guards at the briefing room entrance opened the doors and Admiral Laskaris, dressed in a dark blue US civil war era naval uniform, with three stars on his lapel, entered with one of his aides, who was carrying a stack of parchments. The admiral had been viewing pictures of civil war era naval uniforms a couple of months ago, in one of the naval history books on Lieutenant Green's IPAD. He liked them so much, that he decided to adapt them for the Byzantine navy. Thank god, General Notaras did not ask to copy the SS uniforms he saw on Burns IPAD for the army. He had thought they were very cool.

"Good evening gentlemen, sorry I'm late but I have been out inspecting the fleet and issuing orders for the upcoming battle."

"Yes, yes, admiral. Please take a seat," the emperor said.

"You have all met my aid, commander Stavropoulos."

"I have not had the pleasure," George said as he shook the portly middle aged officer's hand, who was also dressed in a civil war period naval uniform."

"What is the status of the fleet, admiral?"

"Our five Corvettes, the steam gunboat Niki and 12 galleasses have been resupplied and are combat ready. Two corvettes from Trebizond have also joined the fleet."

"What is the size of the enemy fleet, Admiral?

"We estimate 15 large war galleys, 40-50 smaller galliots and 30-40 smaller rowing craft. It's a manageable number, as long as our ships are not swarmed by several craft at the same time. Our guns should make short work of the galliots and smaller craft. Our marines should be able to handle any boarders."

"Tomorrow may be the decisive day for the fleet, admiral. The Ottomans need control of the Bosporus, so they can move their Anatolian troops across the straits and encircle the city."

"Yes, I am aware, your majesty. Hopefully by tomorrow

night, if the Ottomans chose to fight, our navy will rule the sea lanes, or be at the bottom of the sea!"

"We will have losses your majesty, but if we can draw them into the Golden Horn our gun batteries will wreak havoc on them."

"I want one of us on the walls at all hours, gentlemen. This battle just started and will go on for some while. We all need to get enough rest, so we can think with a clear mind and be able to make decisions quickly."

"Yes sir I will draw up a roster. In the mean-time I will take the first shift," said General Notaras.

"In my timeline, the Turks tried to mine under the walls using Serbian miners. We were able to stop all their attempts. So we need to be on alert."

"Good point, General Mavrakis. I will have my engineers monitor for any mining." Notaras commented.

"Any news from our supposed allies, the Venetians?" Asked Longo.

"Last news we had was they were mobilizing their navy, answered General Notaras."

"Don't hold your breath, general. The Venetians are snakes. They will wait and see how the battle goes before they do anything."

"I'm hoping they show up George, but I'm not counting on them."

"I have the same sentiments, general," The emperor said.

"Let's call it a night and get some food and rest. Gentlemen, please thank your staff for a job well done so far. George you have the walls at sun up."

"I'll be there, sir."

The meeting was adjourned and George went to his quarters where Anna was waiting for him, with dinner on the table.

After getting married they were given a larger apartment. Food was still cooked by the palace staff and was brought in to them.

"Hello my love, how was your day"

"We were very busy, lots of wounded were brought in. Mostly sword and arrow injuries. Mary is much better. I think I will have her moved to the palace. We will need the bed space very shortly."

"That's very god news, the emperor will be happy."

"She should be up and walking in a few days."

"You are a great doctor my dear. You saved her life."

"We were lucky; another inch to the right and the bolt would have pierced her lung and heart."

"Let's eat. This chicken looks good. I'm hungry and exhausted and have duty on the walls in the morning. I'm sure they'll be attacking again."

"Be careful my love. I don't want anything to happen to you."

"I will do my best Anna, but I am a soldier. This city can't be allowed to fall and if it's my fate to die defending it so you and our child can live to be free of Ottoman rule, so be it."

"This chicken is great why aren't you eating?"

"I'm not so hungry, let's go to bed, George."

"Sounds like a great suggestion, a couple of more bites and I will be with you."

Chapter 10

Constantinopolis
02 November, 1452

George buttoned his BDU jacket trying to keep the early morning chill out. The three golden stars of a Lieutenant general were prominent on his lapels and the men on the walls saluted as he made his rounds. He looked to the east as the sun began to rise. The firing of the enemy guns had begun to increase in tempo. One of the larger enemy stone balls hit a nearby guard tower and shattered in hundreds of pieces, killing several of the men that were stationed in the tower. Even more cannon balls began to land on the ramparts; fortunately many of the men there were taking shelter in the dugout and trenches.

The Byzantine guns fired back sending 18 and 24 pound explosive shells toward the enemy gunners. George looked through his binoculars seeing several shells land near the enemy guns but failing to explode. The nearby gun battery fired, George watched the shell land amongst several enemy wagons, causing a very large explosion that hurled one of the big guns into a formation of enemy troops crushing dozens to death. Loud cheers erupted from the soldiers on the walls. Unfortunately that would be only a temporary respite, since the enemy had many more guns.

The sun had finally risen and its golden rays were beginning to warm the cool November morning air. George walked down to one of the empty fields, where the hot air balloon was being readied by newly promoted Lieutenant Mike Fulton and his crew. He had since made two other balloons for his fledging observation corps. The men all came to attention and saluted, when George and his two body guards walked up to the balloon. "Good morning, sir."

"Good morning lieutenant, are you ready to go aloft and make history again."

"My men and I are ready to serve, sir."

"I see you have your handy Nagant sniper rifle with you."

"I should have many targets to shoot at from 500 feet in the air."

"If you have clear shots, take out their officers and then the gun crews. Don't waste bullets on ordinary soldiers."

"I will try my best to get the gun crews, sir."

"We need to drop harassing rounds on them, but we don't have many mortar shells, so make each one count. Good luck!"

"Thanks, sir."

"Okay men, raise the balloon."

The ground crew slowly let out the rope as the hot air balloon quietly rose over the city. The city's inhabitants saw the hot air balloon and began cheering. A silence spread over the battle field once the enemy spotted the rising balloon. They had no idea what to make of it. Lieutenant Fulton used his binoculars and spotted a group of men coming out of several large tents, which had many banners flying from them. He figured it had to be some type of headquarters with senior officers. "

"Captain Jenkins, I have a fire mission for you. At one hundred and ten degrees Looks like some kind of headquarters unit. Range is approximately 2000 meters. I will be standing by with corrections."

Ottoman Camp
2 November 1452

Sultan Mehmet was enjoying a breakfast of cheese, olives bread and tea with his senior commanders and discussing strategy for the day's battle. "I want those ramparts taken. They are a thorn in our side. Reduce them with cannon fire."

"Yes, my sultan. It will be done," Said one of the senior KapiKulu Suvaris (sultan's household cavalry) commanders.

All of a sudden they heard a commotion and shouting coming from outside. "What is going on here," he yelled to one of his servants."

"My padishah, the men are saying that there is a strange smoking demon flying above the city."

"That is nonsense." The sultan got up and walked outside the tent followed by most of his staff."

"There! Look, my padishah."

Lo and behold, there was something in the sky above the infidel city. "It's a dragon, conjured up by the Christians to kill us all." One of the officers yelled out.

"Silence you fool. Do you want to panic the men?" But panic began to spread and a silence suddenly came over the battle field. All of a sudden a strange whistling sound could be heard coming closer.

"What is that, my padishah?" One of the officers asked.

Before the sultan could reply, there was a loud explosion as an 81mm high explosive mortar round crashed into the tent they had just left and exploded, sending shrapnel flying in all directions and cutting down several men. Mehmet felt a burning in his right thigh, as a small piece of shrapnel struck him. Soon they heard another whistling sound coming towards them. "Take cover you fools," the sultan screamed at the top of his lungs. Mehmet dived onto the ground landing in mud and horse manure, just as the shell hit nearby, killing several of his senior staff.

The great Sultan Mehmet lay in the mud, terrified of his mortality, just like a common soldier. Several more mortar shells landed nearby killing men and horses and spraying him with blood and body parts. He was astonished that the enemy had weapons that could shoot so far and kill so effectively. When the bombardment finally ended, he got up dripping mud and dirty water. He could hear the screams of the wounded. He could hear the bombs dropping on his gunners now. The Byzantines were full of surprises, he thought.

Several of his surviving officers ran towards him to see if he needed assistance. "Are you okay? You are bleeding my padishah," said Zaganos Pasha. "Get the physician."

"I am fine. It is only a flesh wound I will have my physician treat it after I clean up. What are our casualties?"

"I don't know, there are several men down. I came here immediately to check on you."

The both walked over to one of the bodies. Shrapnel had taken off the top of his head and he was unrecognizable except from the clothes he wore. "The Grand Vizier, Candarli Halil, is dead," Shihab al Din Pasha, the sultan's second vizier, said as he looked at the body."

"That is a great loss, my padishah," Zaganos Pasha said

"Not really. I did have my doubts about his loyalty to me."

"Who will take his place in this crucial moment?" asked Shihab al Din Pasha.

"I appoint Zaganos Pasha as my new grand vizier," the sultan said loud enough to be heard by all the senior officers that had gathered around.

"Thank you, my padishah for this great honor to serve you.

I pledge my life and total loyalty to you."

"Is there anyone that has an objection?" No one said a word.

"Then it is done."

"I will not expect any less of you my grand vizier, nor from anyone here."

"We are all at your command my sultan."

"It seems the Byzantines have some type of explosive rockets or bombs. I had heard that the Chinese and Mongols have used these types of weapons in the past. Their range is astonishing. They were fired from inside the walls."

"What is that devilish thing in the air above the city my sultan? Can their Christian prophet be helping them fly?" One of the cavalry commanders asked.

"Don't be a fool. There is only one god and his prophet is Mohammed. There has to be some type of explanation. I want our spies in the city to find out how they are flying."

"Yes, my padishah.

"Also find me competent replacements for the men that were killed here. I am going to wash and change."

"Please, take my tent till your new one is up."

"Yes, I do need to clean up and change clothes. We will move my tent further back out of range of those weapons. I was almost killed today."

"It will be done immediately my padishah."

Constantinopolis
2 November 1452

Lieutenant Fulton watched through his field glasses as the mortar shells exploded, causing confusion in the enemy camp. He hoped he had killed a few important officers with the precious few mortar shells they had to use. He soon switched his targets and began harassing the gunners by dropping a few mortar bombs amongst them causing the guns to go silent. Unfortunately, they had to stop the shelling after using up a good chunk of their 81mm mortar bomb supply. He tried taking some shots at the gunners and officers but the balloon was bouncing too much in the morning air for him to be very accurate, managing only to hit one gunner after firing ten rounds. The effort was not worth the expenditure of their precious remaining ammo.

Fulton scanned the horizon and looked out into the Sea of Marmara. The mid-morning mist was lifting and what he did see gave him the shivers. Scores of white sails dotted the sea. The Ottoman fleet had arrived in force, to challenge the Byzantines for control of the sea. He gave the order to lower the balloon basket. When he reached the ground, he was met there by Captain Jenkins and by General Mavrakis, who had been observing the operation. "So how did it go, lieutenant?"

"Pretty good, sir. Wish we had a bit more ammo to use. We plastered what looked to be a command area. There were lots of flags and tents there."

"I wish we did have more, but that's all we have for now. We need to keep the rest of this ammo for an emergency, in case the walls are breached and the enemy gets inside the city."

"I did manage though, to silence their guns for the time being, but they will be back in action."

"I'm sure they will be, as soon as they see the firing against them, has slackened."

"I did spot the sails of many ships on the horizon. Seems like the entire Ottoman navy, is out there."

"I will let the admiral know immediately."

"I'll go back up later, sir and try to take shots with the Nagant and do some artillery spotting."

"Okay, just be careful up there. You are our future air force commander."

"Will do, sir."

George took Captain Jenkins's horse, leaving his protesting body guards behind and galloped towards the naval yard. At the gate, he was let in by a marine sentry, who was armed with a bayonet tipped Mosin Nagant bolt action rifle. George wished they had found more of those rifles, as he raced to naval headquarters, a two story stone and tile roofed building by the quay. Upon arriving, he tied the horse to the building and went inside the admirals office

The admiral was talking to several of his staff members, when George interrupted the conversation. "Admiral the Ottoman fleet has been sighted by our balloon observer, many sails to the east."

"Will you excuse us for a moment gentlemen?"

After the officers had left, the admiral turned to George with a worried look on his face. "Well the base and ships are on full alert and they can sally at a moment's notice. I will send a few galleys out and see if the take the bait and lead them into our guns."

"That would be much to our advantage, admiral.

"Put the word out, that no one is to fire on the enemy ships unless I give the order. Sinking or damaging a couple of ships is not enough. The rest of the fleet will be on standby. If they don't take the bait or just partially, we will have to give them battle with the Niki leading the attack."

"Yes, sir. I will relay your orders to the garrison commander."

"A victory at sea, does not guarantee we win the war. We are still in danger. If they manage to keep breaching the walls with those massive guns, then we are in deep trouble."

They heard the tempo of enemy gun fire suddenly pick up again. "There they go again."

Both men waited silently for a crash of a giant stone ball hitting the walls, but heard nothing. "It seems that they are not attacking the walls, admiral. There attacking the ramparts. We only have a regiment there with some light artillery."

"I heard Colonel Longo gave them a severe beating the other day."

"That's true, but he only has a regiment of musketeers and some light guns. He can't hold out there forever, especially if they are pounding him with their artillery."

"The longer he holds out, the more we bleed them."

"Wish we had more time so we could have had several regiments with rifles"

"We're lucky to have what we got, General."

"I am going to the walls to see what's going on at the ramparts and see if they need any help."

"Good luck, general."

The enemy guns were pouring heavy concentrated fire on the Byzantine positions. Both Colonel Longo and Major Garibaldi stood at the ramparts with fifty men, while the rest took shelter from the enemy gunfire. They both knew, that the enemy would soon be assaulting in strength. The ramparts were a thorn in their side and they would take it at all costs. Once the ramparts fell, they could assault the breaches made to the walls, by their heavy guns without impedance. The enemy guns finally fell silent. "They will be attacking us soon, colonel."

"Bugler, call the men out." The bugler sounded the call and the troops poured out of the dug outs and took their positions on the ramparts.

The sultan's elite KapiKulu Suvaris cavalry were charging the ramparts. "Here they come. Gunners load with canister. Musketeers take aim and fire!" The guns roared and the musketeers fired on the charging cavalry taking out the first couple of ranks, but the rest kept coming.

George observed the attack on the ramparts unfolding. He ordered the guns on the walls to provide supporting fire raking the enemy flanks with explosive shells. It was possible that Colonel Longo's force could stop the cavalry, but what was coming behind them would roll over Longo. He had to do something to prevent them from being overrun. George jumped on his horse and galloped towards the armory.

Longo watched mesmerized as the cavalry men fired their bows at the ramparts striking several of his musketeers and gunners. The horse men then grabbed their lances and continued the charge. "Fix bayonets and prepare for cavalry."

The men quickly fixed the bayonets to their muskets and waited for the Calvary. Longo and Garibaldi continued to fire their assault rifles aided by several men that had a few Nagant bolt action rifles. Several of the mounted archers became impaled on the stakes in front of the ramparts when they were thrown from their horses screaming their lungs out in agony begging to be put out of their misery. One of the cannons fired a load of canister, taking out a dozen riders with their mounts, before the horseman reached the gun and killed the crew. Slowly but surely Longo and his men beat the sultan's elite cavalry back. Suffering heavy losses, the Ottoman horsemen pulled back for the next attacking wave, the sultan's elite infantry corps, the famed Janissaries.

Longo was exhausted and almost out of ammo, as were many most of them men that fired the modern rifles. He was amazed at their ammunition consumption. Modern wars would be won on who had the most efficient supply system, not solely on a soldier's bravery and fighting ability alone. They had barely beaten off the cavalry fighting like madmen. He had many men down and as he looked at the next wave, he doubted they could hold them off. Everyone looked across the battlefield at the smartly dressed infantry marching to Ottoman military music. Most of them carried fire arms and swords. "They are the Janissary corps," said one of the Byzantine captains in Colonel Longo's command.

"What are the janissaries?"

"They are mainly Christian youth taken from their families, converted to Islam and trained to be the elite soldiers for the sultan. They are treated special, receiving the best food, women and pay. They fight like madmen."

"I guess we will see if they live up to their reputation. Load with canister," Longo shouted.

Several of the smaller Ottoman guns opened fire to support the Janissary attack. The sultan's patience was running out and the Janissary commander had been told to not come back alive, if they failed to take the ramparts. The Janissaries were now within 150 yards of the ramparts and were starting to taunt the Byzantines. A couple of shots rang out from the ramparts taking out a couple of the enemy troops with accurate fire from the Russian Nagant rifles. The janissaries halted for a moment. An imam (Moslem holy man) came out and started to preach to them, telling them that this was a jihad against the infidel and if they died they would be in heaven with the prophet, eating food and enjoying 70 virgins. The Janissaries began yelling "Allah Akbar," (god is great) as they were stirred up by the imam.

"What are they saying?"

"God is great, sir."

Longo took aim with the AK 47 and shot the imam dead.

"Indeed he is!" Longo commented bringing laughter from the men in the ramparts.

The Janissaries seeing the imam shot down became further

incensed and could not be controlled by their officers. Wanting blood, they charged towards the ramparts. "This is it men. Make every shot count. Fire!"

The nine pounders barked, sending hundreds of canister rounds downfield dropping dozens of the charging enemy. The colonel could see that these were much better troops; they did not charge bunched together making them easier targets for their guns. They ran, fired their weapons and reloaded and charged forward again, forcing the defenders to keep their heads down. Though not as accurate as the Byzantine rifles, several of the defenders had been struck in the head by enemy bullets and killed. The enemy had learned quickly and adopted accordingly. No matter how hard they fought, the enemy continued to advance and finally reached the ramparts.

The Byzantine defenders had already fixed their bayonets and a close quarters struggle had begun which only could have one outcome since the enemy force outnumbered the defenders five to one. Slowly but surely, Longo's men were being pushed back. Ottoman pennants soon were flying over the ramparts. Longo and his friend Garibaldi fought like lions, firing off all their ammunition in their assault rifles, then drew their pistols, shooting down 10 more of the enemy soldiers, before both pistols clicked empty. Both men cut and bleeding from several minor wounds, drew their swords, crossed themselves and prepared to die.

"This is it my friend. I will see you in heaven. At least we will die standing as ..." Before Colonel Longo could finish his sentence he heard the rapid firing of what his friend George had called a machine gun. The enemy ranks turned in their tracks and began and to run back towards their lines in terror. Both men heard the sound of horse hooves and that of a vehicle engine approaching.

"I think heaven will have to wait a bit longer, my friend."

"I believe you are correct, Niko."

"John, Niko, are you guys okay."

Both men ran towards the sound of George's voice. Running over bodies of friend and foe, many locked in embraces of death as they had fallen. When they reached George they could see that he had taken the Humvee and used its machine gun to save their asses. He had also brought along a unit of cavalry and several wagons to transport the dead and wounded back to the city. "General, you arrived just in time to save our asses."

"Well let's make it quick and get out of here, before they recover. We don't have that many rounds to spare for that gun. I don't want any weapons left behind for the enemy. Hitch the guns to the spare horses and load your dead and wounded on the wagons."

"Longo had tears in his eyes. "Are we pulling back, General? We beat the heathen bastards!"

"Yes, my friend we did. But you saw what happened. Every one of you would have been killed, had we not arrived and saved you. You fought very bravely and bleed them enough. Longo watched as the dead were piled onto the wagons and George's words finally sunk in. "We just can't afford to lose you John and suffer so many casualties in just one day's battle."

The Colonel quickly calmed down, his adrenalin rush over. He looked at the hundreds of enemy dead that littered the battlefield. "Yes, you are right general. We have in fact bled them. We were not defeated; we will march out of here proudly with our heads up in the air."

"Yes you can, John."

"You men heard the general. Leave nothing and no one behind. Move it!"

Having loaded their dead and wounded on to the carts,

hitched the guns and picked up all their weapons, Longo had the men form into ranks and marched them back into the city, leaving the battlefield to the enemy. The Ottomans jeered as the Byzantines left their positions. It may have been a tactical success for the Ottomans, but it had been a pyric victory at best. The cost had been heavy, an elite cavalry unit had been decimated and the Janissaries had suffered over 300 casualties. But the cost to the defenders had also been steep, over 40 men killed and 50 wounded.

Ottoman Camp
02 November, 1452

The young sultan had watched the assault unfold before his eyes. The KapiKulu Suvaris Calvary had attacked, but were driven back having suffered horrendous casualties in the fighting. Their sacrifices had opened the way for the Janissaries to finally take the ramparts. Victory had seemed complete, when a huge horseless machine came roaring out of the city, spitting death and destruction, causing his elite Janissaries to flee in panic, back towards their lines. He could not blame them; he probably would have done the same.

That infernal machine had saved the rampart defenders and enabled them to march back to the city unopposed; it was a slap in his face. They were even able take all their equipment with them. He would have loved to examine their guns and firearms. The firearms loaded faster and fired more accurately then his. Some of the cavalry survivors had even said that the weapons could be fired repeatedly, without reloading. How was that even possible? Their cannon were so efficient and mounted on wheels and could be quickly moved to different locations. He was impressed on how quickly they were evacuated back into the city. It seems that his nemesis, the

Byzantine Emperor had found a better gun builder, then the young Hungarian that had built his guns. Still he had given them a defeat, if he could call it one. His forces had paid dearly.

"My padishah, I'm sorry to disturb you."

"What is grand vizier?"

"Our commanders are asking if you want to continue the bombardment on the walls and assault them tonight, while out victory is still fresh in our soldier's hearts."

"This was a very costly victory."

"But we still won the day."

"At this rate we will be bled dry. We will not attack tonight. Let the men rest. I want harassment fire on the walls. If we manage to damage them, so much the better."

"As you wish my sultan."

"Had it not been for that infernal satanic machine they used we would have slaughtered their men and handed them a great defeat."

"What was that devilish contraption, my padishah? We can't fight demons."

"That was no demon. That was a machine. I don't know how it was powered. I remember reading ancient Greek texts on how the Greeks had harnessed steam, to power simple machines."

"But it was spitting out death and cutting down our troops."

"They have some type of rapid firing guns. Now I know what those fools had seen a couple of months back when they thought they had run into Djinn while on patrol east of here."

"Yes, I do remember my padishah. But why have they not used these machines before. They can defeat us with a few of those."

"Good question my Grand Vizier. They only thing I can think of, is that they have a limited number, with limited abilities, to be used in emergencies like the one they were facing today."

"That does explain a lot, my padishah."

"If we make a large breach to their walls, I want it exploited immediately. The more forces we can pour in, might overwhelm their defenses."

"If we send a large number of men, followed by the Janissaries, we may succeed my sultan."

That is another reason. I need those Anatolian forces. The enemy controls the straits and they can't cross."

"We can have them march further down on the south coast and use our navy to transport them here."

"No, not until we destroy their navy and we have total control of the seas. We will attack them tomorrow with our fleet and destroy the few ships they have. I too, have a few surprises for our Byzantine friends." Summon the admiral."

"As you command, my padishah."

Constantinopolis, Military Headquarters
02 November, 1452

After the almost debacle at the ramparts, Colonel Longo and his friend Garibaldi, cleaned themselves up went to the hospital to check on their wounded and afterwards to headquarters to meet with the general staff. They were surprised that the emperor was also attending the meeting. When they walked inside everyone in the room stood up. "Welcome gentlemen. I saw your brave exploits. You are both to be commended for your bravery in the face of superior odds.

"The men did best they could, your majesty."

"True, but your leadership inspired them to fight. I have been told our total casualties in the two days of fighting were heavy, 60 men killed and over 100 wounded. The wounded are receiving treatment at the hospital, by doctor Mavrakis and her staff. Many of them will be back to duty in a few days, thanks to her skills. We have though killed many hundreds of the enemy.

"Yes, we did your majesty. We probably killed over a thousand. The battlefield is littered with their rotting corpses, but there are so many of them and so few of us."

"That is another reason I ordered you pulled out of the ramparts. There are just too many and the sultan does not care about his losses at the moment. So we will now fight them from the walls."

"With the weapons we have, we can kill them at a distance. I personally have killed scores of them with this wonderful weapon."

"Our ammunition though is finite, George said. "We can be expending it at the rate we are. We used almost 700 rounds rescuing you, colonel and I would do it again. We must save it for an emergency, in case there is a major breach to the walls."

"How are we on munitions?"

"We are fine on powder and shot and 80% remaining on cross bow bolts and arrows. We have only 90 mortar rounds left," General Notaras said.

"Thank you general. So admiral, how is the fleet?"

"We are ready to sally if they enter the straights. The crews are on standby, keeping the ships ready to sail. We are short on 18 pounder shells so I have had those issued to the Niki."

"Jenkins, how is our weapons production going?"

"We are operating at 100% capacity, with three shifts going. We will have another 50 flintlock rifles ready for issue by tomorrow. The matchlocks are being issued to the remainder of Colonel Longo's troops. We will also have 50 more 18 pounder shells ready, plus 100 grenades."

"What about bullets?"

"We will have our first batch of 2000 rounds of .58 caliber minie balls for the flintlocks delivered by tomorrow. The

Imperial Guards will receive them first."

"What are minie balls?" Longo asked.

Jenkins took one out of his pocket and showed it to the colonel. Longo twirled it in his fingers. "This is a strange looking ball. It's not round."

"You are correct, sir. It's almost the shape of a modern bullet, like you are using in your pistol. It takes longer, loading a large round ball in a rifled musket, than a smooth bore musket, because of the rifling. The minie bullet is slightly smaller than the bore of the rifle, loading the weapon is quick and easy. The minie ball is actually hollow inside and has grooves around the outside. As pressure builds in the chamber from expanding gas, the projectile would actually deform slightly and expand and engage the rifling groves giving it a spin and a much faster muzzle velocity. This will also make the rifle very accurate up to 300 meters and much more deadly. Three times more accurate and more deadly than a regular smooth bore musket. These bullets will shatter bone and cause horrendous wounds. I am estimating velocity around 1000 feet per versus 850 FPS or 240mps of a smoothbore."

"Thank you for the explanation. So this is a more accurate bullet. It will take some training for the troops to master for target practice."

"That's why they are being given to the Imperial Guards to try out."

"Thank you, captain."

"So we are in good shape for now gentlemen. Go get some food and rest, tomorrow will be a long day," the emperor said.

"I will inspect the garrison and the walls," General Notaras said. "Colonel Longo, you will have the early morning duty. Get some rest, you need it"

"I will, sir."

As everyone got up to leave, the emperor motioned for George to stay. "I want to go to the hospital and visit our wounded. Mary is feeling much better, she is eating normally and her wound is healing well. She will be able to assist our good doctor in a few days according to her."

"That is good news Constantine, but she will need to stay in bed until Anna gives her the okay. Tell her that is an order as she is still under my command."

"You tell her that, George." Both men started to laugh.

Both men walked out of the palace, boarded the emperor's carriage and were driven to the hospital under Imperial Guard escort. Each guard had a bayonet tipped Mosin Nagant rifle slung over their shoulder, except for the lieutenant in charge of the detail, who was armed with a Makarov pistol. Both George and the emperor also had their side arms with them, not taking any chances since the last assassination attempt, which they blamed on the sultan.

It was late in the evening when they arrived at the hospital; both men got off the carriage and walked inside escorted by two Imperial Guards. The hospital was humming with activity due to the amount of wounded that had been brought in. Nurses and several of the Byzantine physicians and student doctors were making their rounds in the dimly lit wards. They walked into Anna's office and found her passed out on a small wooden cot and a half eaten plate of food on the table. Someone had thrown a blanket over her. She began to stir when she heard them enter. George lit one of the candles in the room for more light and threw some wood into the fire place. Anna opened her eyes, "Oh, hi guys. I must have fallen asleep."

"You look exhausted. Take her home, George"

"No, I can't leave. I have patients that need me. I worked hard putting them back together."

"Anna, you forget that you are also pregnant, so think of the child too."

"I am fine, Constantine."

"You are still in the military, colonel. I am ordering you to go home with me now."

"Listen to the general. I am also giving you an imperial order to go home and get some rest."

"You both know where you can stick your orders! This is my hospital."

Both men began to laugh. "What a feisty one."

"Mary is the same way. She wants to come here and help tomorrow."

That set Anna off. "No she will not. She needs at least a couple of more days rest. She was severely injured and lost lots of blood."

That made both men laugh even harder. "How about you tell her that, right now? Afterwards you can rest with her and you can be taken to see your patients in the morning. All your patients are now resting. You have trained a very competent staff here, doctor. They can survive a few hours without your presence. You are exhausted and subject to making bad decisions from fatigue."

"The emperor is right, Anna. You need to eat some food and get some needed rest, so you can treat your patients being wide awake and not tired."

"Okay guys, you've convinced me. I will go back with you and see Mary, then get some sleep and be back here in the morning."

"How are the wounded doing?" George Asked.

"Three have died but the rest are expected to survive, barring no serious infections or other complications."

"Great job Anna. Now let's go home."

Chapter 11

Constantinopolis
3 November 1452

The sun had come up over the besieged city. The night had been relatively quiet, just a few bombardments by the ottoman guns, with minor damage to the walls that was quickly repaired. The big show was beginning in the Sea of Marmara. The Ottoman fleet was preparing for battle and taking position outside the straights. Twenty large and several smaller enemy galleasses, were about to enter the Bosporus. The naval base had been on alert most of the night, waiting to see what the enemy's move would be. When the sun finally came up, they were alerted to the enemy movements by patrol vessels and the gunner's on the walls.

George had awakened early and taken his wife to the hospital. On the way there, he had been alerted to the enemy movements and after dropping her off, went over to naval base. The activity on the base was very hectic, as ships prepared to sail and fight. He went over to the headquarters building where he found the emperor and General Notaras. "Good morning gentlemen, it seems that today, will in fact be the decisive day for our navy."

"And for our nation," the emperor, added.

"Yes it will be. It seems the enemy will enter the straights and force a naval battle on us," the admiral said.

"I intend to use the galleys as bait and draw them into the golden horn, where our guns will tear them to pieces and where they Niki will finish them off."

"That is if all goes to plan and they take the bait," admiral.

"That is true, your majesty. The galleys will be the bait. I am sending ten of them to the mouth of the straights and hopefully draw the Ottomans in."

"Why don't we sail out and meet them in battle in the Sea of Marmara and use our superior gunnery and destroy them? They have no guns on their ships. We should beat them easily?" George asked.

"First of all General, the Ottomans control the mouth of the straights with a superior number of ships. Any Byzantine ship trying to break out, would run a gauntlet of enemy ships and be overwhelmed by sheer numbers. Also sailing vessels don't have enough maneuvering room in the straights to fight. The corvettes will sail, but some will be anchored here in the Golden Horn and be used as fighting platforms."

"Fighting platforms? You've been reading Green's naval history books, sir. The French fleet tried that in the battle of Aboukir bay in Egypt and lost."

"The French did not have a steamship or shore batteries that will tear the enemy fleet apart."

"That may be true, admiral. We have issued RPGs and mounted the Russian DSHK heavy Machine gun on the Niki. She will be a machine of destruction to the enemy fleet," George said.

A runner dashed into the meeting room. "Admiral the enemy fleet has entered the straits."

The admiral turned to his aid. "Commander, give the word for the fleet to sail. I will join them soon, with the Niki." The officer ran out and several seconds later a bell started clanging. That was the signal for the fleet to sally. Ten galleys that had already taken up their anchors, started heading for the straits. The Niki began building up steam and several of the corvettes began pulling out of their anchorages. Three Americans would sail with her, her commander Lieutenant Green, Staff Sergeant Davis with the RPGs and Captain Jenkins on the heavy machine gun.

"Let's go to the southern walls and watch the battle, your majesty," George said.

"Yes, let's hurry there."

When George and the emperor reached the walls, the leading Byzantine galleys had almost reached the first enemy ships. The Byzantine commander, a commodore, was leading his ships toward the larger enemy warships. He was going to fire on the lead enemy galley, then break off the attack and hopefully the enemy would follow them deeper into the Bosporus and the Golden Horn. Watching through their binoculars, they saw the lead Byzantine galleys slow down and turn to fire, but were shocked when they heard gunfire erupting from the enemy ships! The Ottomans had caught them by surprise, having also mounted guns on their ships. They were in a fight for their survival. Outnumbered two to one, the Byzantine ships finally opened fire. Fortunately, their superior guns and training were paying dividends, but they were starting to suffer loses. First one, then another galley was boarded. Another unexpected surprise was that the enemy soldiers also had fire arms, increasing the pressure on the Byzantines.

"This is not going as planned, your majesty."

Before the emperor could answer, one of the Byzantine ships erupted in a sudden flash of light. The sound of the explosion echoed across the waters, her captain choosing to destroy his ship along with the enemy ship, rather than having it fall to Ottoman hands. The other Byzantine galley was starting to burn having caught fire by an enemy grenade.

"My god we've already lost two ships. This is not going very well."

"So has the enemy your majesty, but they have many more to spare. No one knew they had mounted guns."

The rest of the Byzantine galleys fought a running duel with the Ottoman ships, dishing out much more punishment then they took, leaving one sinking and two heavily damaged. Seeing the Byzantines retreating, the Ottomans followed with their entire fleet, hoping to destroy the few ships the Byzantines had. "They are following our ships your majesty, but there are so many. Our defenses maybe over whelmed."

"If they are able to enter the Golden horn with so many ships and they manage to land troops, we may lose the base and our entire navy. They will also out flank our defenses."

Both men watched as the battle progressed. The Ottoman fleet had entered the Bosporus with over 30 ships, each filled with hundreds of troops determined to eliminate the Byzantine navy and seize control of the straits. The heavy 18 and 24 pounder guns on the walls began firing, as the enemy ships came within range. After a few ranging shots, hits began to register on the enemy ships as they ran the gauntlet, several catching fire after being hit by explosive shells. Of the 30 enemy ships that had entered the straits 20 had survived with various degrees of damage.

"I am heading for the docks, your majesty. Call out the entire Imperial Guard and bring them to the base along with their cannon. We need to stop a possible landing."

The rest of the Byzantine fleet had sailed and several of the corvettes were already in the entrance of the Golden Horn, heading for the Ottoman fleet. The wind was a light breeze out of the northeast, with lack of maneuvering room in the straights, they would only get one pass at the enemy ships before the either had to drop their sails and stand in fight or break out into the sea of Marmara. When the first two corvettes sailed through the golden horn, they were immediately pounced on by five enemy galleys. The nearest enemy ship was immediately reduced to match sticks; another was holed below the water line and sinking. One of the Byzantine corvettes, the Holy Trinity lost a mast from a lucky cannon hit and was dead in the water, the crew trying to cut the mast and rigging away which acted as a giant sea anchor, with axes. The three surviving enemy ships though damaged and taking on water, grappled with her.

George reached the docks just as the Niki began shoving off, to join the fight with the rest of the squadron. Her captain Lieutenant Roger Green glimpsed the running figure and ordered all stop and and reverse. George leaped aboard just as her paddles began pushing her forward again. He headed up to the bridge, where he also found Admiral Laskaris, "Glad to have you on board general."

"I won't miss this action for the world, admiral."

"This is it gentlemen, we have to stop them from reaching the base and landing troops."

"We'll give it our best, sir. We are still outnumbered by them."

"We need to help the fleet, lieutenant, before this turns into a total disaster."

The enemy fleet had been badly hurt, but there were still plenty of ships left afloat, to win the day for the Ottomans. The Byzantines had also been hurt. The Holy Trinity was a wreck and had run aground to prevent her from sinking, by the south side walls, under the protection of its gun batteries. Several galleys had also been severely damaged or sunk. Three of the corvettes had managed to break out of the Bosporus and were fighting it out with the smaller Ottoman galleys that had remained outside the straights. The remainder of the corvettes had anchored in the narrows of the golden horn, a wall of wood and metal, which the enemy would have to pass to enter the base. The Niki pulled into the main channel, as a cannonade started between the anchored ships and the Ottoman warships, while they tried to force their way into the Golden Horn. Several of the enemy galleys immediately made for the docks, while the rest battled it out with the anchored corvettes. The shore batteries added to the crescendo, pounding several of the Ottoman galleys, as they rowed full speed towards the wharf. One of the galleys began to burn, men leaped into the cold waters preferring to drown, then be burned alive. Four of the enemy galleys badly damaged and sinking, managed to ground and disgorge their troops. Over a thousand heavily armed Ottoman sailors and marines, rushed towards the base.

George and Lieutenant Rogers saw the four Ottoman galleys unload their troops on the shore; they had to prevent any more from landing. As the Niki approached the anchored corvettes, they saw that one was burning and the three others were fighting for their survival.

"Sir, those troops need to be stopped. If they reach the ship yard they will burn our steam frigate.""

"The emperor and the Imperial Guards will have to handle them. Head for the anchored ships, Green, they are in trouble, and we can't afford to lose any more ships."

After leaving the southern battlements, the emperor had rushed to the barracks and immediately called out a battalion of Imperial Guards. They quickly harnessed their light 9 pounder field guns to horses and rushed towards the naval base, in hopes of averting a disaster. When they reached the eastern gate, they saw many of the dock yard workers fleeing back into the city in panic and screaming "the Turks are here." They could hear shooting and screams and see dark smoke coming from inside. Constantine thought about the almost completed steam frigate in the yard. They could not lose her. It would take them to the new world. He ordered the guards to close the city gates behind him.

"Hurry inside men and prepare to deploy." The emperor turned to the guards' deputy commander. "Colonel Stefanos, take a company with you and deploy them to the ship yard. Defend it at all costs. You will fight to the last man to protect the new steam ship being built there."

"It will be my honor, sir." The colonel saluted and took off with a company of men to carry out his orders.

The Imperial Guards some armed with Nagants, flintlocks and some with AK47s, rushed into the base and toward the quay, where several buildings were burning. One group of Ottoman marines had over run and silenced most of the gun batteries that had been firing on their fleet. Another large group of enemy troops headed into the base interior. When the Imperial Guards reached the headquarters parade ground, they formed four ranks with 50 men each and deployed the three cannons they had brought with them.

"Load with canister."

"Here they come, sir," said one of the company commanders as the enemy marines came running up from the dock yards and across the parade grounds.

"Steady men. Make every shot count. On my command, take aim, fire!"

Two hundred rifles and four 9 pounder field guns opened fire sending hundreds of bullets and minie balls down range, decimating the first couple of ranks of enemy soldiers. The enemy kept coming, firing guns and crossbows on the run. Several of the guards went down struck by bullets and crossbow bolts. The Byzantines began independent fire, the Nagants and AK47 slowed the enemy down but they kept advancing towards the lines now less than 100 meters away.

"Fix bayonets and prepare to charge." The Guards quickly fixed the bayonets and pointed their guns down range. The emperor drew his pistol. "Charge them men!"

Over two hundred Imperial Guards charged the oncoming enemy ranks. Soon steel met flesh, the enemy fought hard, but was pushed bank. The emperor emptied his pistol holstered it and drew his sword. Soon he was facing a large heavy set Ottoman officer dressed in expensive armor and brandishing a very ornate jewel encrusted sword. The Turk charged him in a fit of rage, swinging the sword, barely missing the emperor's head. Constantine side stepped and prepared for another attack. The enemy officer stopped and stared at the emperor. "You will soon meet your maker, infidel."

"And whom do I owe the pleasure of sending me to heaven, heathen Turk?"

"I am admiral Hamza Bey, Christian dog."

"I am Emperor Constantine Paleologos."

"The Byzantine emperor himself, this is quite an honor. I will receive many gifts for taking your head to the sultan and be promoted to vizier."

"Surrender and stop any more unnecessary bloodshed. Look around you. You are practically defeated and most of your ships are sunk or severely damaged and will soon be sinking."

"Prepare to die, infidel dog."

With that the Turk thrust his sword; the emperor was barely able to parry the thrust. For the next couple of minutes they went back and forth; the enemy commander was very good with a sword, Constantine was a bit out of practice and beginning to tire. He did notice that the Turk was favoring his left side which was wet from blood. A small wooden splinter had wedged in his side, when a cannon ball had struck the enemy ship's bridge. Taking a chance, Constantine body kicked the Turk on his left side, a move that he had seen on one of Mary's movies, she had stored on her IPAD. His opponent screamed in pain and Constantine lunged. His opponent blocked, but lost his sword in the process.

"Surrender or be killed."

Visibly defeated, Admiral Hamza Bey raised his hands, "I surrender to you most holy emperor and I place my life at your mercy. I am at your command."

"Your surrender is accepted and your life will be spared."

"Thank you, your majesty."

By now the battle had progressed to the point where the Imperial Guard had forced the surviving enemy back towards the docks. "Now let's go try to end this and save some lives on both sides."

The emperor had reloaded his Makarov and put the sword back in carrier. The admiral looked puzzled. "Don't try anything or this gun will kill you."

"You have my word. I have surrendered to you I am your slave to do as you please."

"I do not own slaves. I have only free men."

When the two men were seen by the enemy soldiers they too quickly dropped their weapons and surrendered. The Byzantines began cheering, but quickly stopped as the sound of cannonading and thunderous explosions floated across the waters from the bloody naval battle, still going on in the constricted waters of the Golden Horn.

Having built up a full head of steam, the Niki headed into the fray, trying to save the anchored corvettes that had been swarmed by several galleasses. They had barley saved the

Aghia Sophia, which had been mauled by three enemy ships. She had managed to sink one galley and leave another sinking, but the third had managed to grapple. The Niki sailed up and plastered the enemy ship with the DSHK heavy machine gun and concentrated rifle fire. The enemy ship quickly lowered its ensign and surrendered. George peered through his binoculars and saw one of the corvettes from Trebizond in trouble; she was being attacked by four enemy ships and was in danger of being captured.

"Admiral, I have an idea."

"Let's hear it."

"Steer for that cluster of four enemy ships attacking the corvette. We will hit the first with one with an RPG and you rake the second with gunfire."

"Let's do it. Take us there captain."

"Aye, aye, admiral."

"I'll let Leroy know what he has to do."

George ran over to where Sergeant Davis was standing with the RPGs. "Davis, target the first galley; try to hit her at the water line."

"I will do my best, sir."

The Niki was rapidly approaching the enemy galleys at seven knots. Through his binoculars, George could see that all of the Ottoman galleys had sustained various degrees of damage from the corvettes accurate cannon fire. "Get ready Davis, aim for her waterline, fire!"

The RPG round traveled less than 100 meters and hit the ship's hull penetrating effortlessly, and exploded when it hit stone ballast as it went through the keel, ripping the bottom of the ship open, causing it to immediately begin sinking. The crew of the Niki had no time to watch the enemy ship founder, as they fired their starboard broad side on the next enemy galley. George watched the 18 pound cannon balls rip into the enemy hull and packed decks. They could hear the screams, coming from those that had been horribly injured by flying splinters or the balls themselves. To add insult the injury, the enemy ship was raked with the heavy DSHK machine gun, slaughtering dozens of enemy soldiers and tearing several holes below her waterline. The enemy warship replied, with a few shots with her feeble cannons, but missed, as the Niki shot past.

Two enemy warships remained, one of them grappled to the corvette. Lieutenant Green swung the Niki around the other side of the corvette to deal with the remaining two ships. The DSHK opened fire sending 12,7mm (.50 caliber) rounds into the hull of the first galley. The large bullets splintered the wood and opened her up to the sea. For good measure the Niki fired a broadside into her, ensuring she would sink. "Load guns one and two with canister and prepare to board her."

The Niki was nearing the enemy ship that had grappled on to the port side of the Byzantine ship. "Stand by to grapple. Fire guns one and two." The two guns fired clearing the deck of enemy sailors.

"Give me full reverse and stand by to stop engines." The paddle wells started turning in the opposite direction breaking the Niki's momentum.

"All stop! Toss the grappling lines." Several grappling hooks were tossed over and the Niki quickly secured herself to the galley. Meanwhile, the ship's marines on the Niki's rigging were shooting down into the enemy crew. Before the Niki could send over her borders, the enemy captain surrendered his ship, rather than fight a hopeless action against two warships. The Niki had arrived just in time, to save the allied corvette from capture. They were soon joined by one of the smaller galleasses, the Mystra, who would take the prisoners and prize back to the base.

"I think our Trebizond allies have it under control now. Let's head for the straights and break out into the Sea of Marmara and sink anything they got left."

"That's a great idea, admiral."

"Take us through the straights captain."

"Engine room, give me full speed," Green hollered into the engine room brass communication tube.

Within a few minutes the Niki entered the Bosporus belching smoke from her stack, steaming at 8 knots, in full view of the city walls and the enemy. They could hear cheers and see flags being waived by the garrison on the city walls. The Bosporus was littered with wreckage, bodies and sinking ships. Here and there they spotted an occasional heavily damaged enemy ship, trying to make it to the Anatolian shore to beach itself and keep from sinking. The Niki quickly dispatched them with her guns.

When the Niki reached the Sea of Marmara, they saw more wreckage and bodies signifying that a battle had been fought. Several miles to the west, they could see the sails of the surviving corvettes being chased by several smaller galleys.

"Head for them, Green."

"Aye, aye, admiral."

Within thirty minutes the Niki had caught up with the galleys. Thinking the Niki was an easy victim, they tried to storm her but quickly found out that they had made a fatal mistake when cannon shells and 12.7 MM rounds from the DSHK ripped through their hulls, opening them for the sea to pour in. In less than twenty minutes they had left three galleys sinking and another one had surrendered. The few enemy ships that remained quickly fled in various directions. They Niki, was soon joined by the surviving errant corvettes which dipped their flags to salute the flagship.

"Lieutenant Green, I think we've done enough, the battle is over. Signal to all ships, head back to base."

"Aye, Aye, sir."

"You've won a great victory, admiral. The enemy fleet has been heavily defeated. Most of their ships have either been sunk or captured."

"Yes, general but at what cost?"

"We have suffered loses, sir. But the Byzantine navy controls the sea."

"You are right, George. At least we now control the sea lanes, the Ottomans can't blockade us, nor can they reinforce their army, from Anatolia. Thank god, that we had this steamship, it turned the tide and saved the day from becoming a total disaster. We might have still defeated them, but would not have much of a navy left."

"You need to thank Captain Burns, for that invention."

"You are right general. We owe much of this victory to his inventions and to you Commander Green. But I also do believe, you're coming here, was the miracle we had all been praying for."

"Whatever it was that brought us here, also gave us a new purpose in life, to help save the city and bring her glory back."

"Excuse me, admiral. You said commander?"

"Yes, Commander Green, you earned a promotion today. Your ship designs, crew training and their gunnery skills saved us."

"Congratulations, Roger.

"Thank you, sir and thank you admiral. What the general says is true admiral. I have found a purpose here and I believe I speak for all the Americans. We will, get this city's lost glory back. Once the Ottomans are defeated, that will be a big step in achieving that goal.

"Well I am glad to hear that son. We still have a long struggle ahead of us."

"We can now raid their ports and shipping unmolested, admiral."

"Yes, Commander and I plan to do just that. In the next few days, we will raid their main naval base at Gallipoli and begin raiding their supply lines along the coast. I don't want to give them any chance to recover."

"Good idea, sir."

"But before we do any more attacking gentlemen, we need to see just what our losses are."

A half our later, the Niki reentered the Bosporus with the captured enemy ship and the three surviving corvettes. The cannons on the sea walls fired a 21gun salute, in her and the admiral's honor. It had been a long and bloody day, they had won a great victory, but at a price. Just about every ship suffered some damage. Three galleys, the Limnos, Chios and the Samos had been lost to enemy action, with heavy loss of life. The Corvette Holy Trinity had been severely mauled and beached, she would require many weeks of extensive repairs. The Aghia Sofia had also suffered heavy damage and would need at least a month in the ship yards. The cost in lives had also been heavy; over 500 killed and 200 wounded. Fortunately, many had been only lightly wounded and would be back to duty within a few days.

The Ottomans had suffered dearly. After this day, they were no longer a naval power or a threat anymore, to the Byzantine sea lanes. On the contrary, they were now the ones that were threatened by Byzantine naval superiority in the Sea of Marmara and Aegean coast. They had lost over 20 ships either sunk or captured and had suffered over 4000 casualties. Many of the surviving ships were so severely damaged, that several would sink along the way as they tried to make it back to a friendly port.

When the Niki entered the Golden horn, everyone on board noticed that it was littered with hundreds of floating bodies and several half submerged wrecks. As they approached the dockside, they noticed several smoldering buildings and the signs that a fierce battle had taken place there. A bucket brigade of captured POWs was still pouring water into the damaged structures. Another group was digging a ditch to bury the hundreds of bodies that were washing up on shore and those killed during the assault on the base.

The Niki was met at dockside by the emperor and his Imperial Guard. The men were in formation with the emperor in front. The admiral being the senior officer was first off the ship followed by George and Commander Green.

"Formation present arms." Emperor Constantine did an about face and saluted.

The admiral approached the emperor. "Admiral Laskaris, we salute you for your great victory!"

The admiral saluted his commander in chief and spoke out loudly for all to hear. "I thank you your majesty for this honor and I also thank our savior Jesus Christ, who gave us the wisdom to win and who made the miracle possible that brought our American brothers to us, in our time of need. Without them and their knowledge, this would have never been possible. Long live the empire and the emperor!"

The throngs of soldiers and workers at dockyard broke out in cheers and to shouts of long live the emperor. "Admiral, can we discuss the battle and our next moves in your cabin? I want to go on board and congratulate the men. The base is in the good hands of your executive officer. He has already begun repairs and a cleanup, using the substantial number of POWs we've captured."

"Why of course your, majesty. He is a very competent officer and can manage in my absence."

"His actions and that of the marines saved the frigate from damage."

"Thank god, for that. That frigate holds our future and that of the new world. Please sir, join me in my cabin."

While the emperor had been having a conversation on the dock with the admiral, Green had rushed back onboard the Niki and readied the crew for the commander and chief's visit. When the emperor boarded the ship, in the company of both George and the admiral, he was greeted by the entire crew. "Welcome on board the Niki, your majesty."

"Thank you Lieutenant, oh, I mean Commander Green. Today the Niki lived up to her name. Please put the crew at ease. I would like to speak to them."

Commander Green, put the crew at ease. The emperor began to speak. "Men I want to thank you as does the entire Byzantine nation, from Constantinopolis, Trebizond, the Aegean Islands and Mystra. Today you and your brothers at arms won a great victory against a numerically superior foe, just as our ancestors defeated another threat from the east at Salamis, many centuries ago. Had it not been for this technologically superior fighting ship with her new weapons, her steam propulsion and your excellent training and gunnery, we may have lost or even at best, won a pyric victory. Instead most of our navy, though battered, still remains afloat and there is no one to challenge our control of the sea. The cost was not cheap, many, of our friends and brothers in arms, paid the ultimate price. This day will be remembered in history and hopefully, Byzantium will live for another thousand years. By my order, every member of this crew will be promoted one rank. Long live Byzantium and thank you!"

"Long live the emperor!" Cried Commander Green and was also joined with cheers from the crew.

"Thank you, men. You can dismiss the crew commander and join is in the admiral's cabin." The emperor saluted Green, and followed the admiral to his cabin.

The Niki had only two cabins, one large one for the admiral and the other for the next senior officer. When the admiral was not on board, the cabin was usually used by her captain which had in fact been the case. After dismissing the crew, Green joined the three men in the Admiral's cabin, where he pulled out a bottle containing a dark liquid. "What do you have there, commander?" George asked.

"Would you like to try some moonshine, sir? Some of us built a still.

"What is moonshine?"

"It's an alcoholic drink made from grain, sugar and yeast."

Green poured everyone a healthy shot and raised his cup.

"To victory!"

"This is good," the emperor said after taking a sip. "You must make me a couple of bottles of this, commander."

"We made a few barrels. I will send you one."

"Thanks, commander."

"It's not whiskey but it's not too bad," George said.

"You should patent this. I'm sure it will catch on fast."

"Good idea, your majesty. We may just do that,' Green said as he refilled everyone's cup.

The emperor raised his cup. "I salute you admiral and to all of you that made this day possible."

"Thank you, your majesty for the honors, but we paid a heavy price. Casualty figures are still coming in, we lost over 500 men and several ships. The galleys Limnos, Chios and

Samos were also lost, the Holy Trinity is a beached wreck, but probably salvageable, the Aghia Sophia is heavily damaged and will need a few weeks of repairs. The rest of the fleet also suffered various degrees of damage that should be repaired quickly. This is the only ship that is undamaged."

"Compared to the Ottomans, we were relatively unscathed."

"If you compare loses, that is true. They've lost their entire navy and thousands of experienced sailors. We must follow up our victory, with a raid on their main naval base at Gallipoli and let loose sea raiders that can hit their supply lines."

"Yes, we must keep the heat on them. We can't give them a chance to rebuild. They have vast resources."

"We will your majesty. We just need a few days to repair and regroup. We will send a couple of raiders to operate out of Limnos."

"Well give me a complete report once you have all the details on our losses. I want repair crews 24/7 working on repairing our ships. We must keep up the pressure on them."

"The siege in my time line lasted almost two months, but events are happening much, faster in this timeline. With this defeat, the sultan will be desperate for a victory, they will hit us hard on the walls," George said.

"You're probably right, general. We will have to be extra vigilant and prepared for a full blown assault at any time of the day or night. Now go get some rest. It's been a long day for all of us."

Chapter 12

**Ottoman Camp, outside the walls of Constantinopolis
05 November 1452**

Sultan Mehmet had stayed in his tent taking no visitors, since the disaster that had befallen his fleet. It had been almost two days since the great naval battle had been fought. Two days of bad news, as the reports came back of ship loses and casualty figures. In all they had last 23 top of the line warships. Several more had been damaged beyond repair. All that survived of the once great Ottoman fleet were several small galleasses that had also received damage and had been sent back to the Gallipoli naval base for repairs. The cost in naval personnel had been staggering, over 4500 killed and several hundred injured. Ships could eventually be replaced but not trained sailors. His enemies now controlled the sea-lanes and his officers were now scheming behind his back. That he was sure of.

Many of the survivors spoke about a smoking demon ship that sailed without the wind or oars and spat out death and destruction. It had been responsible for much of the losses heaped on his navy. Its heavy guns easily destroyed any ship that opposed it. Had he not seen it with his own eyes sailing out of the Bosporus and wrecking the few ships that stood in its way, Mehmet would not have believed it. He suspected that the Byzantines had somehow, harnessed steam and were using it to propel the hell ship through the water. Armed with heavy naval guns, it had been virtually unstoppable. The Byzantines now may control the sea but he stilled controlled the land.

Mehmet had debated for the last two days to call off the siege, but that would be taken as a sign of weakness, by his many opponents. Instead he would show them. He would continue the bombardment on the walls and launch a grand assault in the next few days. First he would show generosity and give Constantine another opportunity to surrender the city and leave with honor. He would send his brother in-law Ismail Bey, the vassal ruler of Kastamonu and Sinope on an embassy, into the city tomorrow to offer terms. If that arrogant fool Constantine fails to accept his generous terms he would attack with all his forces and put the emperor's head on a spear! In the meantime he would let his troops rest.

"My sultan, the Grand Vizier is here to see you. Shall I send him away?" One of his Janissary body guards asked.

"No, send him in." It was time he took charge again.

"My padishah, thank you for seeing me, visibly relieved the young sultan, had finally come to his senses."

"I am glad you have come. I seek your advice."

"That is why you made me your Grand Vizier my sultan. I am here to give you support and advise you for the good of the empire."

"I was contemplating after our recent naval set back, to lift the siege and have the city pay tribute to us."

"*More a disaster then a setback,*" The Garand Vizier thought to himself but he dared not say anything. "My padishah, that would be viewed as a sign of weakness by your enemies. They could have you replaced or even murdered. We have superiority on land and large guns that can knock down their walls. Furthermore after their naval victory the emperor would refuse to pay any tribute."

"Yes, I thought the same thing. Instead I have a better proposal for the Byzantines. I will send my brother in-law, Ismail Bey tomorrow to the emperor, with an offer. He has friends among the ruling elite and they may make Constantine come to his senses."

"What do you propose to offer him, my sultan?"

"He must leave for the Morea, in southern Greece and hand over the city to us."

"That is a very generous and wise offer, my padishah."

"I am glad you support me on this. In the interval we will keep harassing fire on the walls but the troops will rest. Send for Ismail Bey here at once."

"As you command my, sultan."

Constantinopolis
5 November 1492

George had quickly reached the palace after being summoned there for a very important meeting; according to the message he had been given. For most of the morning, he had been supervising the repairs to the battlements, from the damage done by the Ottoman guns the night before. If they continued firing at this tempo, sooner or later they would bring down a large section of wall and assault in force. If that happened and they managed a foothold then things could get very difficult. He was very surprised to see a troop of Ottoman cavalry there, under the guise of the Imperial Guard. For the Turks to be there, something important was happening.

George went inside and was shown into the imperial quarters. There he observed several senior Ottoman officers standing in a corner conversing with each other. The emperor was chatting with General Notaras, Admiral Laskaris and Colonel Longo. When he noticed George enter the large room, the emperor motioned for him to come over. "General I'm glad you're here. We have visitors as you can see. They have come here with a proposal from the sultan. What it is, I do not know yet. I waited for all my senior staff to arrive."

"Let's hear what they have to say. Maybe they are asking for terms of their surrender"

"That would be really nice, but I don't think the young sultan has that in mind," General Mavrakis."

"Let's not be rude to our guests. The one in the middle is the sultan's brother-in-law Ismail Bey, the vassal ruler of Kastamonu and Sinope."

"You are right General Notaras, we have been negligent hosts. "Gentlemen, we are ready to hear your proposals," the emperor said.

"I am Isfendiyaroglu Ismail Bey, brother in law of the great Sultan Mehmet II. He has an offer for you to stop the bloodshed."

"I know who you are Ismail Bey. Tell us what the offer is from the young sultan. Hopefully something that will stop this madness? Is he ready to leave and ask me for forgiveness?"

Ismail Bey was visibly irritated at the emperor's brash statement. "My sultan offers you, your lives. You must leave immediately for the Morea and give the city to the Ottomans to rule."

"God forbid, I should live as an emperor without an empire. As my city falls I will fall with it. Who so ever wishes to escape, let him save himself if he can, and whom-ever is ready to face death let him follow me!"

"My emperor, we are all with you to a man, General Notaras said.

"You have our answer."

"Your defeat is inevitable. You are being given an opportunity to leave honorably and save many lives. If we must use force to take the city, it will be sacked and its inhabitants enslaved."

"So I must now thank that little boy for making so generous an offer to me and my people? If he thought the city would be so easy to take, he would not have sent you here, would he? He had to stoop to an assassination attempt on the day of my wedding that almost killed my wife. I will kill the little bastard with my own hands if I get the opportunity!"

"How dare you talk about the sultan in this way? He will have your head on a pole, infidel!"

"We've already destroyed your navy, your reinforcements are stuck on the Asian side of the straits and your ships are being sunk or captured. I will destroy your army next. Now get out before I have your head put on a pike or better yet have it shot out of a cannon to your brother-in-law!"

With that the Ottomans were escorted out of the palace by the Imperial Guards. Ismail Bey could not help but to notice the strange fire arms they were carrying or the side arms the senior officers carried. He would have to tell the sultan in his report, when he returned to camp.

"Well gentlemen, we have now made our bed. We will now either win this siege or die in the process," the emperor said after the Turks had been escorted out.

"I'm not ready to die yet," Admiral Laskaris remarked. We need to make the enemy suffer some more. We're ready to raid and destroy their naval base in Gallipoli, your majesty. With your permission, we can have some ships leave today in the afternoon and the rest leave noon tomorrow. The fleet will rendezvous south east of the port of Panidos and sail the last 40 miles together. We will hit them at sunrise just in time for morning prayers."

"How many ships do we have for the attack admiral?"

"We will have two corvettes, the Aghia Sophia, The Aghia Eleni and the two Corvettes from Trebizond, three galleasses and the Niki. The Niki will carry the contingent of marines and some extra sailors in case we find any ships we can cut out. The rest will be burned, along with the port facilities. We will send two supply ships, with the ships leaving today for Heraclea. The town is still holding out, according to radio reports from our underground base."

"Yes, we must help our people there. That will be a great morale boost. How are they holding out at the base?"

"They are doing just fine, your majesty. There are many enemy troops and supply columns in the area. They are lying low, as instructed."

"That's also good news, General Notaras."

"Who will command the raid?"

"Commander Green, your majesty. He is a very capable officer."

"Yes, he is and that is why we can't have anything happen to him."

"He has been ordered to stay on board the ship."

"Okay admiral, you have my permission to launch the raid. Hit them hard and hurt them bad."

"Thank you your majesty. I must now go back base and issue the orders for the ships to sail.

Ottoman Camp
5 Nov 1492

When the sultan's brother in law returned to camp, he went straight to the Mehmet's tent to give his report. There he found him in the company of two scantily dressed, very attractive harem girls, rolling in the plush rugs and pillows. Mehmet was not the type to miss out on earthy pleasures. He motioned to the two girls, "Leave us." The two girls quickly ran out of the tent.

"Ah my brother you are back. I send you on a dangerous mission, while I play with my pets. I must reward you appropriately for your loyalty. You shall have the Serbian blond tonight. So tell me what happened."

"Thank you for your generosity, my padishah."

"We are family, Ismail Bey. We share our treasures and our pleasures. Now what did that fool, Constantine say?"

"He refused my sultan. He said that without an empire, he is no longer an emperor and would rather prefer to die as one."

"Ha! The fool calls one city an empire? That is all he has left. What else did he say Ismail?"

"He called you a little boy. He threatened that he would kill you with his own hands if he had the opportunity, for attempting to have him assassinated on his wedding day, which resulted in serious injury to his wife."

Ismail Bey watched his brother-in-law turn red. He feared for his safety. The young sultan was known for violent and explosive outburst. "Is that all he said, Ismail?"

"No, my padishah. He said that he has already destroyed your navy and that he will do the same to your army. I also saw his soldiers holding strange fire arms and his generals wearing strange looking guns."

Mehmet burst out laughing. "They are still guns and shoot bullets. Yes, I have heard rumors that their guns can shoot many times without reloading, but we have many soldiers. How many of those weapons do they have? We have not seen too many of them."

"Every soldier I saw in the palace had them."

"No matter, Ismail, maybe it was just for your show. He

thinks that he will defeat my army. We will soon see in the next few days, who will lose."

"Yes, my sultan, you will make the infidel dogs pay, for daring to challenge you."

"I can see why he is a bit mad at me for trying to have him killed on his wedding day! Who would service the bride? I could have of course, just added her to my harem." Mehmet was now beginning to laugh even harder at his own joke, now joined in by Ismail Bey, relieved that the sultan did not throw one of his famous tantrums.

"He was so angry at you my sultan. He even threatened to have my head shot out of a cannon."

"Now that would have been a funny sight. This is why I love you, Ismail. You are honest with me and tell me everything."

"I love you too, my brother. I would never betray you."

"I know that Ismail. Just wait and see what will eventually befall Constantine. I will soon show him who the real leader is. I will let my guns pound his walls for a few days, then when the time is right we will strike."

"You are a great leader, a conqueror!"

"Now let's have a feast and enjoy ourselves."

Gallipoli, Eastern Thrace
7 November 1452

The Niki with Commander Green at her helm had departed the golden horn naval base around mid-day, in the company of three galleys. Having a westerly wind on her back, she used her sails and not her engine. Except for spotting a few fishing boats and a Venetian merchantman that was headed for the city, the voyage across the Sea of Marmara had been quiet and uneventful. The news from the Venetian trader had been heartening. The Venetian fleet was also preparing to sail for the

Aegean. Not that they needed their naval assistance at this point, but any assistance would help. Venice would not know about the destruction of the Ottoman fleer for at least another week, until the galley that the emperor had sent to Venice with the news arrived.

A couple of hours before midnight, the Niki had reached her rendezvous point and met up with the four corvettes that had been dispatched earlier. Commander Green immediately called a conference of all the captains onboard the Niki to go over any last minute changes. No one knew anything about the port of Gallipoli, except for Lieutenant Speliotis, who had once sailed into the port while working as a teenager aboard a merchant ship. When everyone was on board the flagship, Green called the meeting to order. Many of the officers there were much older than Green, but they all had a very high respect for the young man who had proved himself several times in battle.

"Good evening gentlemen, I will make this meeting short, since we must get underway immediately to reach our destination by daybreak. The Niki under the guidance of Lieutenant Speliotis, who is somewhat familiar with the port, will enter first to see if there are any ships we can capture and cut out. I will land the company of marines, who will proceed to torch and destroy anything of value. If we are immediately discovered, engage any targets of opportunity and provide cover for the marine landing. If all goes as planned, you will land your marine contingent, along with your extra sailors to secure the beach and take any ships we capture back with us. Does anyone have any questions?"

"Do we know if they have any guns defending their base from the sea?" One of the Trebizond captains asked.

"That is unknown, Captain Grekos. The last time John visited the place there weren't any guns there, but expect anything."

"We'll be ready, sir."

"Master Sergeant Davis will be landing with the marines. He has a communication device and will be able to provide the flagship with updates. This raid should be a complete surprise. They are not expecting us, but in war, anything can happen. Any other questions?"

Green raised a small cup of wine that the Niki's midshipman had provided everyone. "If there are no other questions gentlemen, proceed back to your ships. Good hunting and long live the emperor!" Everyone drank to the toast and quickly went back to their commands and got under way.

After an uneventful night and making excellent time with a favorable westerly wind, the fleet had finally arrived off of the small fishing town of Gallipoli, named after the peninsula that overlooked the entrance to the Dardanelles. This peninsula would one day become the grave yard for over 100,000 men, when the allies during world war one tried to force passage through the straits to take Constantinopolis and knock Turkey out of the war. Instead they found a determined foe and they failed miserably, suffering one of the costliest defeats of the war. This would take place 450 years in the future and it might never happen if they managed to save the city and defeat the Ottomans.

The sun was just starting to come up in the east. Green peered through his binoculars in the early morning twilight and could see no activity in the port area. There were two galleys in the port. "Well you got us here safely Captain Speliotis. Seems our surprise is complete. We'll cut out those two ships."

"I can't believe they are so arrogant, and that they've not posted any guards looking seaward."

"They figure no one has the audacity to do what we're about to do. Their loss will be our gain. All ahead slow."

"Aye, aye captain, all ahead slow," the helmsman shouted in the engine room speaking tube."

"Captain, prepare your men to hit the beach and take those two ships on the docks."

"Yes, sir," replied their commanding officer.

The Niki had slowed down to where she was barely making headway. Fifty yards from shore he commanded all stop. The Niki slowly glided on to the sand and beached. Several marines armed with Russian Mosin Nagant rifles topped with bayonets jumped into the waist high water and ran ashore towards the docks to take out any sentries and to provide security.

"Drop the ladders. Marines, you know what to do." With that, the men quickly started off loading. Fifty men headed for the docks while the others began fanning out. Soon several rifle shots and screams were heard coming from the dockside. The four corvettes dropped anchor with their guns pointed toward the shore. Their crews quickly lowered the boats and sent their marine contingent and extra sailors to secure the beach and help cut out the two captured ships.

After about fifteen minutes, Green saw the two captured galleys staring to pull away from the wharf. He could also see smoke rising from structures that were beginning to burn and could hear heavy firing coming from the interior of the town. He had not heard anything on the radio from Davis in a while.

"Davis, I need a SITREP." (Situation report)

"Sir, we've run into their main encampment. We caught them asleep. Their trying to fight back but our men are slaughtering them."

"Hurry up. I want you to get back here. There could be heavy cavalry units in the area and..." The conversation was interrupted by a large explosion.

"What the hell was that?"

"That was their powder storage area. We just blew it."

"Good work. Get back here quickly, so we can get out of here. That explosion had to be heard for miles. I'm sure someone will be here to see what happened."

"We'll try to get back quickly. Davis out."

"The enemy sailors and marines had been caught in their sleep and many paid for their lack of proper security with their lives, by being bayoneted in their sleep by the Byzantine marines. Soon their screams had awakened the rest of the garrison and they began putting up a resistance, but were gunned down by the marine's Nagants and muskets.

Sergeant Davis found the marine commander and relayed to him Commander Green's instructions. "Captain, we need to pull back, we did our job."

"Okay will start pulling back. Bugler sound retreat,"

The bugler sounded retreat and the marines began an orderly withdrawal down the main road towards the harbor, leaving behind them a scene of utter death and devastation; buildings were burning and woman screaming. Davis watched as several men were carrying a couple chests of gold and silver, which would have been used to pay the Ottoman sailors.

When they reached the vicinity of the harbor, Davis spotted Ottoman heavy cavalry rapidly approaching. The marine captain ordered several wagons overturned to be used as fighting barricades to cover the withdrawal. "Captain, get your men and those chests on board the Niki I'll stay here with a couple of squads and hold them back."

"Okay Sergeant. When were all on board I'll have the Niki fire one of her guns. Good luck."

"The captain ran off with the rest of the men towards the harbor. "Men they'll be here in less than a minute. Let's see how effective, the new grenades are."

Davis took out his lighter and lit a few pieces of wood and passed them around so the men could light the fuses on their grenades. "Okay here they come, light them up."

The heavy Ottoman cavalry thinking that their enemy was running from them, charged headlong towards the barricades. Davis and the rest of the marines lit their grenade fuses and tossed them at the onrushing horseman. A few seconds later, over a dozen grenades exploded, sending shrapnel into both horses and men. Dead and injured horses fell, throwing their riders to the ground, only to be trampled by the ones coming behind them. Some of the marines continued to toss grenades while other opened fire into the packed horsemen. Unable to withstand this kind of punishment, the surviving cavalry retreated several hundred meters to the rear.

In the distance, the heard the boom of a cannon. "That's our signal, let's move it before these guys get reorganized."

Davis and the marines left the barricades and started running towards the harbor. It was a good quarter of a mile of open ground they had to cover, once the left the built up area. It did not take the well-disciplined enemy horsemen, more than five minutes to get reorganized. This time they pulled out their deadly heavy bows and began charging towards the barricades again. When they were less than 100 meters from the barricades, they fired their arrows. Luckily the marines and Davis had left that area, or most of them would by laying there dead, skewered by the heavy arrows that would have dropped on them. Seeing that there was no one there the enemy commander ordered his men towards the harbor.

Commander Green had heard the grenade explosions and rifle fire. The rest of the marines had boarded the Niki. He looked across the fields and spotted Davis and the rear guard through his binoculars. They had finally reached the open fields and were less than two hundred meters from the ship. That's when he also spotted the enemy cavalry unit bearing down on them. They would not make the last hundred yards. He grabbed his M4 and climbed up on the rigging and began shooting at the horsemen. At one hundred meters the horsemen fired a volley of arrows. Green watched in terror as the arrows flew toward the running men. Several went down, including Davis, less than 50 meters from the ship. Several of the marines on the Niki began shooting at the horsemen with their Nagants. The horsemen momentarily hesitated. Commander Green urged his men forward. Green jumped over the side and onto the beach, before he could even run ten yards he heard the sound of cannon fire. One of the galleys had closer inshore and opened fire on the horsemen. Several were smashed to bits after struck by cannon balls, one of them, being the enemy commander. With their officer dead, the rest of the horseman turned and retreated back into the town.

When Green finally reached Davis he could see that his friend was still alive. An arrow had gone through his thigh and pinned him to the beach. Green reached under Davis's leg and broke off the arrow head. "Ouch Roger, that hurts."

"It's sir, to you, sergeant."

"Screw you Green. When I originally enlisted, I never thought I would get shot at by arrows. Even the Taliban never used them and they are a bunch of screwballs."

"Well you just got shot by their ancestors."

They both started laughing. "You'll live Leroy. It's just a nasty flesh wound. You'll have a scar, to show all your tavern wenches, your combat wounds. A couple of these other guys were not so lucky." Soon they were joined by other marines who picked up the bodies of their dead and brought the injured back to the ship.

Fifteen minutes later, the Niki was backing off the beach and headed towards open water with the rest of the fleet and the two ships they had captured. The mission had been an overwhelming success; it had taken a little over an hour to accomplish. They had destroyed a major naval port, along with several warehouses containing supplies for the sultan's army and killed or injured several hundred enemy troops. As a bonus, they also captured two warships and a couple of chests of loot, at the cost of two dead and three wounded.

The returning task force dropped anchor in the Golden Horn a little after noon the next day. They were met at the dockside by most of the imperial staff. When the Niki's gangplank was lowered, the emperor followed by the admiral and General Mavrakis came on board. Green had the crew on deck in their dress whites and the marines in their dress blues. The emperor and the admiral congratulated the men on a job well done and dismissed them. The marines quickly disembarked the Niki, formed up at the dockside and marched to their barracks to rest and clean up. While they were doing that, Green briefed the command staff on what had occurred during the raid.

"I can't believe you went in to their port undetected and landed troops," the admiral said.

"Those two captured galleys are proof we did it, admiral."

"Yes, you did son and those ships are an excellent addition to the Imperial Navy. Makes up for some of the ones we lost."

"And you only had five casualties? Just those two men killed?"

"Yes, your majesty."

George finally noticed that Davis was missing. "Where is Sergeant Davis? Was he one of the casualties?"

"Yes, general. He was wounded by an arrow through the thigh. He is in sickbay."

"Thank god, he is alive."

"He was trying to be a hero again. He was commanding the rear guard, holding off a company of heavy Sipahi Calvary."

"That's Davis for you. We need to transport him to the hospital for the doctor to see him. Speaking of the devil, there he is." George motioned for the medical orderlies that were carrying Davis to bring him there.

"How goes it, Leroy?"

"Hurts a little, but I'll be okay, sir."

"I heard what you did, Sergeant Davis. You are a hero once again."

"I did my duty, your majesty. Those marines that did not make it back are the true heroes. I was lucky."

"You are too modest, Davis. God was protecting you, so you can accomplish more in the future. Now go get well."

"I'll be out in a couple of days, the doc, she'll fix me up."

"Take him to the ambulance," George said to the orderly.

"He is a very brave soldier. He must be rewarded."

"He is your majesty but takes too many risks sometimes. We will promote him to lieutenant soon, he has good leadership capabilities.

"Oh one more thing I forgot, gentlemen?"

"What more surprises have you for us, commander?"

"Admiral, there are two chests full of gold and silver coins secured in my cabin which the marines captured during the raid. There must be at least 10,000 in god and silver there."

"That will be a very welcome addition to the royal treasury each common soldier will receive two gold pieces, NCOs will get five and officers 10 each as a reward for their services."

"That is good for the men's morale your majesty."

"Let's go back to headquarters and discuss our next move gentlemen."

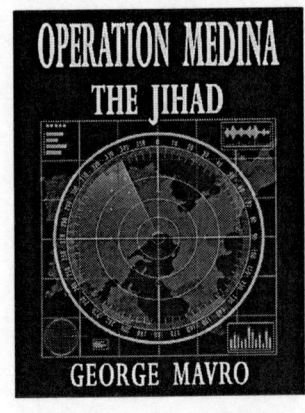

- Title: Operation Medina™: The Jihad
- Author: George Mavro
- Publisher: TotalRecall Publications, Inc.
- Hardcover, ISBN: 978-1-59095-747-9
- Paperback, ISBN: 978-1-59095-748-6
- eBook ISBN: 978-1-59095-749-3
- Number of pages: 320
- Pubdate: 2011

The Balkans and Mideast, a region very much in the news, is the setting for this action novel which takes place in the not too distant future. The secular pro-western government of Turkey has been overthrown in a violent revolution and replaced by an Islamic fundamentalist regime. Her fanatical leader, General Muhammad Kemal, has contrived a devious plan to restore the Ottoman Empire in the Balkans and unite the Islamic world under his evil rule. To accomplish this, Kemal will launch a devastating war with all the tools in his arsenal including Islamic Jihadist terrorists and WMDs. His first targets are US alley Greece and the few remaining American forces stationed in the region.

For his diabolic scheme to be successful, Kemal must eliminate any source of possible outside interference. To accomplish this, he sends a terrorist team to take out the USAF fighters.

A thousand miles to the south, a Palestinian terrorist sails a boat loaded with anti-ship missiles into Greek waters and delivers a devastating attack in the Mediterranean. The next morning, Turkey and her allies launch a devastating surprise attack against Greece.

With the Greeks facing certain defeat, the U.S. President quickly dispatches to Greece, a fighter squadron and a small USAF Security force contingent for airbase ground defense. The USAF expeditionary force is under the command Lieutenant Colonel Jack Logan a veteran fighter pilot. Logan will be faced with the greatest challenge of his career; he must use every bit of his skills to keep his outnumbered command from being annihilated and help stop the enemy onslaught.

- Title: Operation Medina™: The Crusade
- Author: George Mavro
- Publisher: TotalRecall Publications, Inc.
- Hardcover, ISBN: 978-1-59095-663-2
- Paper Back, ISBN: 978-1-59095-664-9
- eBook:, ISBN: 978-1-59095-665-6
- Number of pages: 352
- Pubdate: 2012

The second book of the series Operation Medina, Crusade, opens up with the Greeks retreating on all fronts from the Turkish onslaught. The U.S. has dispatched an expeditionary force consisting of a fighter squadron and a small USAF Security Force to assist the Greeks.

As the Americans join the fight against the Turks, they begin to exact a heavy toll on the enemy. The Greeks manage to stabilize their Albanian and Macedonian fronts, yet are unable to halt the Turks, who continue to push them back. As the tide of battle begins to turn against General Kemal, he plans a final act of madness. A daring plan is formulated involving a simultaneous attack from both air and land to stop the madman from carrying out his deadly scheme. If the plan fails, the Americans will use the only other alternative left to stop him, a B-2 bomber with a nuclear payload which could lead to a nuclear showdown with other Islamic states. With the odds stacked highly against them, the allies must find a way to stop Kemal and avert a nuclear holocaust.

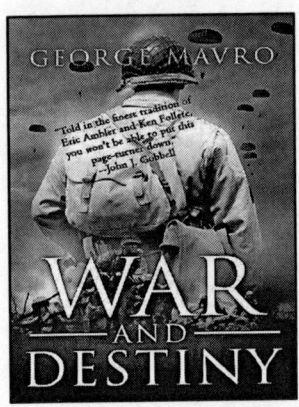

- Title: War and Destiny™
- Author: George Mavro
- Publisher: TotalRecall Publications, Inc.
- Hardcover, ISBN: 9781590955710
- Paper Back, ISBN: 9781590955727
- eBook:, ISBN: 9781590955734
- Number of pages: 352
- Pubdate: 2013

When the young New Yorker Markos Androlakis visited the island of Crete in the summer of 1940 for a sabbatical he unwittingly put himself on a trajectory to test the fates of destiny. War soon engulfs the tiny peaceful nation of Greece and she does her best to hold off the Fascist hordes. Markos soon finds himself on the Greek and allied side and fights for survival and for the liberation of his ancestral homeland. War and destiny is an epic tale of war, adventure, intrigue and love.

On 20 May 1941, Germany launched Operation Merkur (Mercury) the largest airborne invasion in history to capture the strategic island of Crete from the allies. . Markos is tasked by the allied commander to help evacuate the Hellenic King to the island's south coast to be transported by the Royal Navy. Unbeknownst to Markos the German Reichsfuhrer Heinrich Himmler has dispatched a ruthless SS officer Georg Mueller to capture the King and return him to Germany. Markos manages to evacuate the king and journeys to Cairo where he is recruited into the US army and the COI which would soon become the OSS, Office of strategic services under the leadership of "Wild Bill Donovan." Markos returns to America to help organize a cadre of Greek American agents to help the Greek resistance fight the ruthless and bloody Nazi occupation.

- Title: The Resistance™
- Author: George Mavro
- Publisher: TotalRecall Publications, Inc.
- Hardcover, ISBN: 9781590954850
- Paper Back, ISBN: 9781590954867
- eBook:, ISBN: 9781590954874
- Number of pages: 336
- Pubdate: 2017

In the sequel to *War and Destiny* Markos leads his small band of OSS agents into the heart of occupied Greece to strike a decisive blow to the Axis forces occupying his ancestral homeland. His mission to destroy one of the railroad viaducts of the main railroad artery carrying supplies for Rommel's Africa corp. The task almost impossible to do under normal military circumstances will be complicated as he has to get the two major Greek resistance groups, the Royalists and communists to cooperate with each other to carry out this vital mission. Further complicating the mission will be his arch nemesis Standartenführer Georg Muller, a brutal but very efficient Nazi SS officer, who is bent on capturing and killing Markos at any cost. Follow Markos and his team as they try to survive in occupied Europe, during modern history's bloodiest conflict.

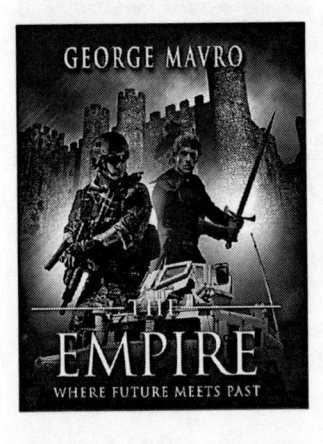

- Title: The Empire™ Constantinoplis Under Siege
- Author: George Mavro
- Publisher: TotalRecall Publications, Inc.
- Hardcover, ISBN: 9781590954898
- Paper Back, ISBN: 9781590954904
- eBook:, ISBN: 9781590954911
- Number of pages: 256
- Pubdate: 2017

While escorting a supply convoy to an off base communications site north of Bagram Airbase Afghanistan, Master Sergeant George Mavrakis and his team are ambushed by the Taliban. Running for their lives with the few survivors of the ambush they manage to flee to an underground mine, but are trapped inside when a Taliban suicide bomber blows himself up in the entrance, sealing them inside. Traveling deeper into the mine they discover an underground base left there by the Soviets. While exploring the base they find a control room filled with computers and equipment which activated after generator power was restored and a countdown is automatically started.

The arrival of George and his troops from the future have drastically altered the timeline. The Ottoman Sultan Mehmet II will soon put the city of Constantinoplis under siege with over 80,000 troops and 60 huge guns that can tear down the city's walls. In the American's past time line, the Ottomans do capture the city and the emperor is killed in battle. It will be race against time to assist the Byzantines in building up their technical and military capabilities with the skills and knowledge, they brought back from the future, to stop the Ottomans. If they are unsuccessful the future is very bleak for George and his team, whom are lost in time.